At last K̲ ̲ ̲ ̲ ̲ ̲ ̲ ̲ ̲ ̲ ̲ ̲ ome
of his ow̲ ̲ ̲ ̲ ̲ ̲ ̲ ̲ ̲ ̲ ̲ ̲ ake,
but finally they began moving down the hillside into the Oahuan encampment.

They found the young Oahuans sprawled
upon their mats in deepest sleep. Kamehameha's men moved in quickly, silently
slitting the throats of the sleeping men.
Not one escaped. Neither the attacked nor
the attacker cried out. Men sleeping next
to their slaughtered comrades slept through
the assault, and never wakened, even as
their turn came to die.

Kamehameha swelled with pride. Standing
there alone, as if separated from the rest of
the universe, the earth, the sky, the bloody
land upon which he stood, he breathed,
feeling the bursting sense of accomplishment, of destiny realized. He stared out into
the limitless space where a comet fired itself across the blackened heavens. He
stirred with a keen awareness of life and
death, certain of his own fate.

ISLAND of KINGS

LYNX BOOKS

New York

ISLAND OF KINGS

ISBN: 1-55802-170-1

First Printing/January 1989

This is a work of fiction. Names, characters, places, and incidents are either the product of the author's imagination or are used fictitiously. Any resemblance to actual events, locales, or persons, living or dead, is entirely coincidental.

This book is published by Lynx Books, a division of Lynx Communications, Inc., 41 Madison Avenue, New York, New York, 10010. The name "Lynx" together with the logotype consisting of a stylized head of a lynx is a trademark of Lynx Communications, Inc.

Printed in the United States of America

0 9 8 7 6 5 4 3 2 1

ISLAND of KINGS

BOOK ONE

Day of Vengeance

Chapter I

He stood and howled out his agony.

His face twisted with hatred and misery, he stared upward toward the cloud-banked heavens. Tears spilled from his black eyes down his cheeks, unchecked. He did not hide his crying from the silent men seated a respectful distance from him. Let them see him weep. Let the gods look down upon his grief. He swiped at his nose with the back of his fist. He kept his head back, staring toward the sky as if seeking the gods in their hiding places.

"You cannot hide," he howled. "Come out. Come out. Face me with your evil, your intolerable evil. Come out. Face me."

His voice choked. "I dare you," he wept. "Show your face. Show your evil face."

He stood at the brink of the great yellow-green ocean. Its waters lapped about his feet, unnoticed.

Hundreds of years before, his ancestors had come in their great outrigger canoes to this island so fair, so beautiful and serene. But now the first touch of evil had struck and nothing in this paradise would ever be the same again. . . .

At his feet lay the body of his brother. The water rolled in and almost playfully touched the body, covering his eyes in a soft, rising and falling rhythm. The sunlight sparkled on the water; on the wide clear sandy beach dozens of outrigger canoes lay grounded and forgotten. Above the beach the bearded sea oats and wild grasses grew profusely, and beyond them rose the date palms, the betel palms, the coconut palms, catching the breezes in their fronds, playing the sweet tunes of the wind, because this was paradise, an Eden of flowers, of birds and trees, a joyful island that had just had its first taste of hell.

"Tell me," he pleaded in agony, "what can I do? What is there to do in my sorrow?"

The men crouched near the beached outriggers stirred restively. They had no answers. They looked to him for answers. It was his wisdom they looked for and trusted, no matter what befell them. They had never before seen him wounded, broken and bitter, helpless. Until this moment they had never suspected his weakness.

His legs were heavy and muscular, as if set upon great springs. When he moved, he strode like a stallion, proud and virile, aware of his virility and arrogant about it. Since he had come down from the mountains, a stranger to his own people, the glory of his ancestors had begun to show in him. There was dignity about him, a dignity handed down to each succeeding Polynesian noble to wear like a purple robe. He appeared taller than six feet six inches. It was in the way he walked, the way he carried himself, the way he looked down at all other men. There was about him a sense of curiosity, innate courage, and a complete absence of fear.

His skin was the color of light mahogany, a warm brown, like the polished woods with oily tints of red in his face. His eyes were spaced wide on each side of his perfect nose. The features were sharp and regular, his nostrils flared with each breath. The large, even teeth were set behind his wide lips. His jaw was square.

The head was that of a pagan prince. Like the rough carvings found on all the islands his people visited, from Samoa to Fiji, a record of gods and great men. He looked capable of defending himself against man or god, of demanding his rights from the world and the deities. Now his throat muscles bulged with the agony of his sobbing, his hands trembled, and he glared about him defiantly, daring even the gods to cross him.

At long last he lowered his head and stared down at the body of his brother. His skull was split open. Blood seeped into the water and the sand. A'Kane lay stilled forever.

"My brother," he whispered. In life they had been much alike, although they had been separated at Kamehameha's birth and had not met until they were grown men, when A'Kane was almost in his twentieth year. They were brothers in talent and worth and often in their very laughter. One might have thought them twins.

"My older brother. My dear brother." Kamehameha gazed down at his slain sibling. Though their acquaintance had been brief, it had been close, as close as blood ties and family warmth could make it, as strong as mutual affection would have it. Their origins were one. They shared the same belief in the origins of land and man and the descent of man. Ancestry was their religion.

They, like all Polynesians, believed that out of chaos were born the sky and the land and from them came the gods and from these gods, came man. So each person was given social rank according to the directness of his descent from the gods.

Kamehameha and A'Kane shared the same parents. At the time of the birth of Kamehameha, A'Kane was a year and a half old, the heir apparent to the rule of their father, Kaumualii, the high chief of Kauai. But at that time in northern Hawaii the gods—through the high priests—predicted that a "superman" would be born, a chief who would kill all rival chiefs.

While Queen Be'ole was pregnant with her second child, she had a vision that this son would be godlike, and, being godlike, invincible. Although he would be only second in line of succession, she feared for its life. The high priests had decreed that all males born in that year be slain. Queen Be'ole gave birth to a boy and in horror and fear arranged secretly for her son to be "kidnapped" and taken by people she trusted to distant mountains of the big island. There Kamehameha was brought up in seclusion.

He grew up without knowing his real mother. The mother he loved was a gentle woman, the wife of a priest, and he was a quiet boy who loved and laughed easily and did not even dream of life in the village where his father was the high chief. Until the moment he was to return to Kauai he knew nothing of his heritage, his destiny, or of his direct ancestry from the gods.

When he heard the truth his head had reeled with excitement, amazed at the reverence suddenly shown him.

He was a grown youth of nineteen when he returned to the village of his people. It was really a small group of huts in the lee of a quiet harbor, but it was the largest settlement he had ever seen. He stared, impressed by the numbers of people, of dogs and pigs. The people stared at him, recognizing the son of the great chief of Kauai, the brother of A'Kane, almost a twin of the young prince. There was no doubt about who he was, who his father was, who his ancestors back to the god Lono were. That night his story was told around the fire.

Kamehameha and A'Kane faced each other for the first time over the fire pit. A'Kane laughed and said it was like looking at his own reflection in a pond. Even though Kamehameha was taller and his bearing was even more majestic, they were much alike. And they were friends from the first moment when they stood together before parents, aunts and uncles, brothers and sisters, as all their cousins were called.

His life in the mountain stronghold had been passed in simple living, accepting the world around him, learning to build outrigger canoes, handling the shell-tipped spear, the shell knife, the olona fiber nets. Though he had been raised by a high priest, he had been told nothing of his past. A'Kane was to be the next king. The high priest saw no reason to fill the young boy's mind with tales of pomp and splendor.

So when Kamehameha came down from the hills and into the bosom of his loving family, he accepted that A'Kane was the next king. A'Kane was a great fisherman, seafarer, fighter, a man of dignity and kingly bearing. There was no reason to think anything but that in time A'Kane would ascend to the throne.

Now Kamehameha sobbed bitterly recalling the short time he had known A'Kane. He remembered the playful fights he soon learned to lose. For the shadow of a lesser person to fall on a noble was a taboo; for a lower being to overcome his liege even in a sham battle was unconscionable. But Kamehameha had loved his brother and had always found ways to lose at the last minute and save his brother's dignity. Looking down at him now, Kamehameha smiled faintly. He doubted that his beloved brother had ever suspected. Such was Kamehameha's love that he would have cut off his own arm rather than diminish the power and glory that set A'Kane apart from his people. A'Kane was an arrogant and stately lord, dignified and domineering, but these were good traits in a king. In many other ways he was modest and affable, a good and loving man, a man one would serve with pride and contentment.

Kamehameha was content with the status quo. No thought of ascension to the throne, through design or accident, occurred to him. But now because of the enmity of the Oahuans, led by Aprilhana, A'Kane lay dead on the beach like a great sea being, dragged upon the shore to rot and smell and draw flies. His laughter was stilled, his goodness and delight gone.

Kamehameha watched four men walk slowly toward him, their faces showing the sadness of their own loss. They were A'Kane's age and had grown up with him, hunting, fishing, boating with him. Their memories of A'Kane were long ones, filled with secret sadnesses and raucous laughter.

The men came and stood quietly before Kamehameha. Their shadows fell across the body of A'Kane. They had each of them arm-wrestled, wrestled, and fought with Kamehameha. All of them but one. Mihuana was a commoner, accepted as a leader because of his prowess, his strength, his beauty, and his quiet bearing.

Kamehameha gazed for a moment at the twisted face of Mihuana, feeling even through his pain the challenge. They had never fought, not even in the friendliest of tusslings. Yet, there was about Mihuana that daring, that strength and defiance that rose between them. Mihuana was as tall as the young chieftain, slender and muscular, but as a commoner he could never lay a hand on one of the noble family.

The other men, Nahalo, Mauro, and Wiari, came from families who traced their ancestry back to the gods. These distinctions were sharp and rigidly set. There were no clans among the Polynesians, but the power of Polynesian kings or high chiefs, and even the high priests, rested on the sacred character of the ruling family.

Kamehameha growled at the men who stood before him.

They stood their ground. Nahalo said, "Shall we not bury A'Kane at sea?"

Kamehameha's wide shoulders slumped. He shook his head. "Not yet."

Mauro spoke in a low, deliberate tone. "It is fitting—all these hours after A'Kane's death—that he be safely buried at sea. His body must not be left to birds of prey—or to those cannibals who find flesh of the human body so sweet."

"I cannot think of such matters at this time," Kamehameha said.

"Then we do not ask that you concern yourself. But we have been gone three days now from our land. We must go home with our sad news. We shall take A'Kane's body far out to sea and return it to the gods."

Kamehameha stared at the four men. Their faces were set. Kamehameha spread his hands. "Take his body, then. We shall remain here until you return from his burial. But note you this: I have not done with Aprilhana and the Oahuans. They shall pay for my brother's death. In the most violent way shall they pay. I swear this to you. I swear it to the gods."

Chapter II

The murder had begun with the festive air of a celebration.

The fleet of outriggers entered the waters of Molokai in the early morning. Each boat was ten feet long and a foot broad, hollowed of the lightest-weight wood. Outriggers on each side prevented their oversetting. Fleet, agile, and beautiful to watch, the boats cut through the water at great speeds.

There were jokes, dares, and challenges among the oarsmen. Only A'Kane kept quiet and watchful, standing proud and tall in the lead proa. It was A'Kane's responsibility as leader of the fishing fleet to sight the first schools of fish. At a signal from him, the boats would converge, gliding across the surface effortlessly, and the "fish drive" would begin. Then the olona fiber nets would be flung and the catch, slapping and leaping, hauled in.

It was a ritual and a privilege older than the memory of the eldest among them. The right to fish these waters had, as far as any of them knew, been theirs since the beginning of time, since the time of the gods Kane and Lono. Their fathers and their fathers' fathers had netted fish in this way in these waters.

This manner of fishing was a hard task. The wet nets grew heavy and strained the shoulders and the thighs. But, hard as it was, Kamehameha enjoyed this work. It seemed like play because all the others loved it too. They worked together, free and all-powerful, flinging their nets on the sunstruck waters. What more could a man ask of the gods than freedom and pleasures such as this? Gradually Kamehameha lost himself in his thoughts.

Like a lovely and beguiling woman, the sea smiled and sparkled and beckoned, luring the seafarers beyond the point of no return, into the face of sudden storm and unsuspected typhoon. Its spell was irresistible and its rages sudden and cruel. Strong men put out upon her breast with childlike faiths and childlike hearts and found the sea to be beautiful, seductive—and deadly.

14

Why did men love the sea so fiercely and seek her so fearlessly?

Kamehameha sighed, hearing his comrades calling across the open spaces. Like every alluring charmer, its mystery lay in its silences and swelled in the hearts of its worshippers. These hearts altered, the men came and went, or died by her vagaries, but were always drawn back to her mystery and her promise.

Gradually, his thoughts wandered back across the past to the years in the hills of the big island. His steady, unbroken muscular motion was now automatic. He sent his paddle cutting into the green heart of the sea, stirring it and filling it with froth.

"Ay." A'Kane's cry brought all faces up, all eyes fixed upon him and his outstretched arm. He had sighted well. Off to the right a large school of fish appeared. The ten boats turned silently as one. As they converged on the boiling cauldron of fish, men stood ready and trembling with their nets. Suddenly the nets fluttered outward, arching in the sunlight, and settling at last upon the water. All paddles were quickly set aside and every man strained, pulling, hauling at the nets. The fish spilled into the canoes.

"A beautiful catch," A'Kane cried. "A few more like that and our boats will be swamped."

Nahalo laughed. "I for one will swim, pushing the boat before me."

"All the way back home?" A'Kane laughed at him.

"All the way," Nahalo said. "Has one ever seen such a catch? Smoked, roasted in leaves, or cooked open over the pit. By the god Lono, my mouth waters."

The sun burned down upon the boat. The serenity spread down from the cloudless sky to the ocean and the men. Their voices carried as they looked at their catch and discussed turning home.

A fleet of outriggers—forty at least—suddenly appeared over the horizon, closing in upon them at great speed. There were no hailing voices, no sounds at all as men put their arms and backs and shoulders into the rapid forward propulsion of their boats. Whatever these newcomers had in mind, it was part of a well-laid, premeditated plan.

"Where did they come from?" Nahalo wondered aloud.

A'Kane had stood steadfastly during the netting, braced against the rise and fall of the sea, at the front of his boat. Now he stood watching the approaching fleet of boats.

"They must have come up as we filled our nets," he said. "Our attention was so fixed on fishing, we didn't see them before."

"Or they lay in wait," Mauro said.

"Lay in wait? For what? Why would they

lay in wait for a few fishing boats?" A'Kane said.

"Who are they?" someone wondered.

A'Kane frowned, shading his eyes with his arm. "Oahuans," he decided. "A long ways from home."

"Yes, Oahuans," Mauro agreed.

"Yes. I have met with them many times before," A'Kane said. "Only never in such numbers as this."

"Or in such silence," Mauro said.

A'Kane smiled and nodded. "Then I will call out to them," he said. He raised his arms, cupping his hands about his mouth, and called a greeting.

Nothing happened. A man stood up in the lead boat, but he made no effort to wave or to reply. The boats bore down swiftly and in moments had completely surrounded the ten outriggers of the Kauaians.

The lead boat bumped the outrigging of A'Kane's boat and snugged it, forcing A'Kane to steady himself. His smile died. He stared at the men standing rigidly in the other boat.

"Don't I know you?" A'Kane said. "Aren't you Aprilhana of Oahu?"

"I am." The other man bowed arrogantly. His face showed no warmth. "What do you in these waters?"

Surprised by this question, A'Kane laughed. "We are taking fish. As we always have. Look you at this fine catch."

"This territory is closed to you," April-hana said.

A'Kane laughed again, this time at the ridiculous idea that the seas could be closed to their fishing. "Is this some kind of trick?" he asked.

Aprilhana seemed to tremble at the suggestion that his action was a joke.

"We have you surrounded," he said. "Does this seem a joke?"

"I hope it is a joke," A'Kane said, still not realizing the deadly seriousness of the Oahuan. Aprilhana was dark-skinned, his brow and lips thick and heavy. Beside A'Kane he seemed small. But it was the size of his fleet that gave Aprilhana his strength and courage and bravado.

Aprilhana took up a paddle, holding it before him threateningly. A'Kane, still puzzled, knelt in his own boat and took up a paddle, holding it across his chest like a weapon.

A'Kane said, "Why have you come upon us like this?"

"Because it is time you learned. The seas around this island are our seas. The seas around all the islands are ours. You will fish in these waters only as we permit—and by payment of half your catch."

A'Kane bit back the laughter of disbelief. "The seas are open. They have been forever open. To our ancestors they were open."

"Yes. Well, they are open no more. We

shall patrol these waters from this day into the future. If we see your boats, we shall attack them."

A'Kane stared at Aprilhana and shook his head. Some of the tribes battled each other, usually out of boredom, but this threat was difficult to take with any kind of seriousness. How could seas no longer be open to the seafarer who had always ridden them?

"Why would you do this? The seas lie broad and filled with fish. More than enough for all. If all of us ate forever, the fish would still fill these waters."

"Do you not hear well? I want half the fish you have caught here today. If we see your boats again, it will not be so easy."

A'Kane glanced around. Perhaps compromise would be wise. His fleet was outnumbered. The Oahuans sat in their canoes, eyes dark and faces set. Was this some fool idea? Or did the Oahuans want to assert their authority over the other kingdoms? For all these years, the tribes had lived at peace with one another.

A'Kane stared at Aprilhana. He could hand over half the catch, but then could he live with himself? He could admit the Oahuans owned the waterways around the islands but stand diminished in his own eyes. He could fight, but ten canoes against forty were poor odds. What would his men decide? But he didn't have time to ask. He faced the crisis, and any decisions were his.

It never occurred to him that his men would not follow his lead, but had he the right to endanger their lives in such an unequal battle?

A'Kane gazed at Aprilhana steadily. He spoke in a low tone. "If you would have our catch, then you'll have to take them."

To A'Kane's surprise, a lusty cheer rose from the throats of every one of his men. He felt a tingling surge of pride. The hackles stood at his neck. His men were badly outnumbered, yet their decision was his. They would fight for their rights.

"If you do not count the fish over to us," Aprilhana said, "we will take them."

A'Kane laughed in his face. "Did you not hear what I said? If you want our catch, take them."

Aprilhana, standing a few feet from A'Kane, lashed out with his paddle. A'Kane saw the stroke coming and parried it. The two boats danced awkwardly on the sunstruck water.

The lesser man gropes his way, waits for his brothers to act. The man of steadfastness does not understand this way of delay and charges ahead, against all odds, filled with contempt for his enemy; his fears and common sense put behind him, he lives by his outrage. He never loses his way. He knows what he must do, and in that split second A'Kane made up his mind. In his mind he was telling his father, the high chief, and the high priests, that the moment demanded action. He saw his own outnumbered men watching him, waiting for him to prove himself.

He even thought, in a passing idea too swift to be called a thought, that he was making his stand for the future here today.

He straightened, parried with his paddle. The fight was to be between himself and Prince Aprilhana. Aprilhana's men sat in their canoes, confident, surrounding the smaller fleet, all eyes fixed upon the two men.

Aprilhana swung his paddle. It was a wild, vicious swipe, and he grunted with effort. A'Kane moved agilely back, swaying on his hips, his legs unmoving. The wild swing missed. As Aprilhana regained his balance, A'Kane swung, his gaze fixed on Aprilhana's chest.

Aprilhana moved quickly for such a heavy man and the paddle slipped harmlessly past him.

Now A'Kane was off balance. He swung out wildly, clutching at one of the bamboo poles of the outrigging to steady himself.

As A'Kane steadied himself, Aprilhana brought up his own paddle high above his head. Without hesitation he brought it downward.

For a stunned instant no one breathed, no one moved. Their gazes were fixed in horror. The paddle blade, swung like an ax, caught A'Kane as he lifted his head.

The sound was that of a splitting melon. For that moment A'Kane continued to try to right himself, then his legs buckled. He staggered. The paddle fell from his hand, struck the outrigging, and fell into the sea. A'Kane toppled to his knees, his hands still clutching the outrigging.

As the men watched, the blood spewed out and they saw in horror that A'Kane's head had been split open. Blood and brains gushed free and spilled into the sea.

Aprilhana stared at his fallen adversary. Then, tossing his paddle aside, he vomited up his insides.

The wails from the boats were of horror and disbelief. Two leapt to grab A'Kane's body and to lower it into the canoe.

Chapter III

That was how it began. How it was to end, one could not foresee. Kamehameha clutched at his belly with both fists. He stared in horror as his brother was slain, but now he was paralyzed with the agony and shock of it. Until this moment he had never seen death up close, certainly not murder, and not the killing of a kinsman.

He stood up in his boat, silently shaking his head. This was an agony too deep for words. The horror of A'Kane's terrible death; the sight of his head split open and the blood spilling into the sea; the terrible suddenness of this evil, unmanned him.

He closed his eyes tightly against the horror of the moment.

The sky remained clear, the sea calm and serene. The outriggers rocked in place upon the small chop of the tides.

Aprilhana, staring at the slain youth, seeing what he had done, shivered with revulsion. At a signal from him, his oarsmen fell to and the boats spun around on the calm surface of the sea, fleeing as swiftly and as suddenly as they had appeared.

"No!" Kamehameha raged, seeing the murderers escaping. "After them. In the name of Lono, let us avenge this death."

The men were galvanized into action. Their paddles dug deeply into the sea; the lightweight proas seemed to skim across the water. The pursuit lasted for an hour, but still the other boats remained far ahead.

At last Mauro signaled his boatmen to stop paddling. The ten canoes settled on the bright surface of the sea.

"We must get them," Kamehameha wailed.

"They move too fast, they started too far ahead of us," Mauro said.

"They must not be allowed to escape." Kamehameha wept. "We must bring them justice."

"Murder will not go unpunished," Wiari said. "But if we overtook them now, they outnumber us. We must be smarter. We know who they are. We know where they are from. Come, let us return home with the terrible news of A'Kane's death. Let us confer with the high priests and the high chief."

"But how can we live with ourselves if this crime be unpunished?" Kamehameha asked.

Mauro gave an order and the boats turned back to land. Kamehameha sank into the deck of his boat, gripping each side with fists showing gray at the knuckles. He stared straight ahead, unseeing. Men spoke to him but he did not hear them. He kept reliving the crime, remembering A'Kane. He kept recalling something he had heard somewhere, he had no idea where he had heard it, only that it seemed to have been spoken for this moment, for this sorrow: He whom the gods love dies young.

His eyes filled with tears. He tried to tell himself there had been pride and a certain glory in the way A'Kane had died. There had been no suggestion of hesitation as he met his death. His slayer threw down the challenge, and A'Kane took it up. He had died a man. Kamehameha swore in that instant that he would live as A'Kane had lived, bravely, and that when the moment came for his death, he would march as courageously to meet it.

He was barely aware of the boats striking the shore and being hauled above the water line.

He went to the boat where A'Kane's body still lay curled on the deck. He knelt beside his brother, took him up, and held him for a long time in his arms. Then, at last, he laid him down at the water's edge and stood weeping above him.

He shuddered with the terrible truth that he recognized within himself. From a calm and gentle youth he felt himself changing into a bloodthirsty man looking for vengeance.

He stood quietly as Nahalo, Mauro, Wiari, and another man bowed to him and took up A'Kane's slain body. The stain of A'Kane's blood remained in the sand, and for a long time Kamehameha stared down at it.

The four men hefted A'Kane's body high above their heads with great tenderness. They plodded slowly to one of the outriggers and laid A'Kane's body out in it.

Kamehameha did not speak as the four men climbed into the death boat and took up the paddles. Mihuana and three others shoved the canoe out past the breakers.

Most of the men onshore walked silently up the beach and into the shade of the palms. Alone, Kamehameha continued to stand silently watching the swift outward progress of the proa. The boat struck sharply across the sea. Long before it seemed possible, it became a blur on the horizon. And then it was gone from sight.

He considered his revenge. In his mind's eye he saw the way it must be: the cold,

cruel, and calculated murder of the Oahuans, to the last man.

"Kamehameha."

The young prince jerked his head up at
the sound of his own name. His eyes fixed
on Mihuana the commoner.

"I am too ill to speak with you," Kamehameha said.

"But it is most urgent," Mihuana insisted
with the strength of will that set him apart
from the other commoners of the tribe.

Kamehameha jerked around, his black
eyes burning. "What is important enough
now, in this moment of the death of my
brother, that it must be discussed?"

Mihuana sighed, his tone conciliatory. "I,
too, have been hurt by the death of a
brother. A'Kane was a good man. He would
have made a good king. But he is dead now.
We must go on living. You will be the king
in his stead."

"Then think well before making an enemy of me," Kamehameha answered.

"If you are my enemy because I approach
you on a subject of greatest urgency, then
so be it," Mihuana said.

Kamehameha caught his breath. "Do you
not recognize my grief?"

"I do. I see it. But I see, too, that life goes
on—"

"Not for me. The world has stopped turning in its orbit. The sun itself stands still

and the gods are impotent until the death of A'Kane is avenged."

"But what I would speak to you is of the life ahead, not the vengeance and murder of evil men. They will be avenged. No crime but that is repaid, no sin that is not atoned."

"You sound sure of yourself."

"It is the order of things, the plan of the gods."

"I will not wait passively for revenge."

"I am sure you won't. And it is into any such battle that I and my men swear to follow you."

"Good. Good." Kamehameha spoke absently, swinging his arm in a downward gesture of dismissal. "Leave me alone now with my grief."

"Grief is what I have come to discuss with you. It is the grief I feel, a grief as terrible as the loss of your brother."

"What are you talking about? What could compare to the loss by murder of my brother—my king?"

"The loss of Misau."

"What?" Kamehameha trembled. "What has my sister to do with this terrible grief?"

"Because I carry the grief with me. The grief of my love for your sister. I realize she is *alii*—nobility—and I of common blood. But we love each other with all our hearts."

Kamehameha stared at Mihuana as if the

man had lost his mind. "I can't discuss it now. I will not. What can my sister have to do with you?"

"We have met and we love. She has pledged her love to me, as I have to her."

"No." The word raged from Kamehameha. "Why do you plague me with such talk at this moment of trial?"

"I have thought of nothing else. I can think of nothing else until this matter is settled between us."

"Then consider it settled. No. What is to come of it? Nothing good."

Mihuana stared at him. "I cannot believe you are so cold. I cannot help but believe that the way you were raised would make you see things differently than A'Kane—"

"Have you discussed this with A'Kane?"

"A'Kane would not discuss it."

"Why do you think that I shall?"

Mihuana's expression was bleak. "Because it came to me in a great flash of light. At the moment A'Kane was so evilly slain, I stood in my boat, my thoughts all of Misau. I saw the paddle kill A'Kane. I felt a flash of pity. I remembered all the good that A'Kane and I had known together. But in that same instant I knew that you had taken his place. You, from the life of a commoner, you from the hills of the big island. You would understand my love. . . . It was all I could think. I love Misau. She loves me. I would not deceive you about

29

our feelings or try to see her without your permission."

Kamehameha stared at Mihuana. He was certain that such talk was taboo. Just as Mihuana's persistence in discussing it when he had been denied the right to speak by a noble was taboo. Yet Mihuana's chilled dignity left him undecided. The only part he felt no hesitation about was the propriety of the match itself. It was wrong. Taboo. "I am pleased you would not deceive me, and I order you never to look upon Misau again. We will speak of it no more."

Mihuana staggered back, looking as if he had been knifed.

Kamehameha turned and walked away, wading into the water. He saw that the death proa was returning. A'Kane was gone, returned to the gods, and he would see him no more. The other men came running down the beach. The council was quick, the decision made to return to Kauai at once, where Kamehameha was determined to gather a war party to call upon the Oahuans.

As he climbed into his boat, he looked back and saw that Mihuana still stood where he had left him, as if all life, all hope of life, had deserted him.

The boats put up sails that bellied out with the wind and moved them swiftly across the sea. They sailed all that afternoon, and by starlight that night, arriving in the early morning at the harbor at Kauai.

Everyone in the village had come down to the water's edge to greet them. The young girls were singing. Their voices carried out across the water to the approaching boats. Their arms and bodies swayed gracefully. They looked like flowers lining the beach, unconscious of their beauty and nudity, wearing only leis of ginger flowers, or hibiscus behind their ears.

A girl's first years were passed with small groups of other girls; little boys were strictly excluded. Her corner of the village was all-important, and boys were traditional enemies. She had one duty, that of baby tending, but as she took the baby with her, her play was seldom hampered. Before puberty, when she had grown strong enough to take on more difficult tasks and old enough to learn the more skilled techniques like basketry and mat weaving, the little girl's play group ceased to exist. She assumed women's ways and contributed to the work of the household. Puberty brought no change at all. Adolescence was passed over without ceremony. After coming of age, she merely began the pleasant years of casual and pleasant love affairs that she would continue as long as possible before entering the period when marriage was considered fitting.

Their lovely voices rose and carried out across the water, pure and innocent, full of expectancy. Unaware of the news the fleet carried. They came running down to the water's edge, the lovely voices and lovely bodies, promising rest for the seafarers. . . .

Chapter IV

The bower, which Misau had built slowly and lovingly, of plaited limbs and palm fronds, was set high above the Na Pali coast. The rains that came so frequently on the edge of the rain forests could not penetrate the thonged roofing. Its flooring was a mat, woven by Misau. It was located high in the forest, even farther than the places frequented by pig hunters, and was concealed by rocky mesas and tall trees. It was an hour's climb up from the settlement, and Misau had found it many years earlier when as a young girl she had had the freedom of this whole island. It seemed a well-hidden retreat, but she knew better. There was no safety here. Danger lurked. If trackers were sent looking, in a few hours the den would be discovered and destroyed.

She stood watching the trail below her. She had seen the returning boats and had raced up here, breathless, her heart pounding in her breast, expectant.

The vista sprawled out below her was breathtaking. Behind the den rose a sheer precipice. Only a few yards away a waterfall tumbled down to a sun-sparkling pool far below. Beyond the trees she could see the beach below, a half-moon of curved white sand, lined with palm trees.

Around her bloomed the candle bush, its bright flowers red and fragrant. A royal poinciana, the flame tree, rose above her. Ferns and hibiscus all lent color and beauty to her retreat.

Even before she saw Mihuana on the trail below, she sensed his nearness. She felt all the hot liquids of her body flowing down suddenly. It was as it had been the first time she saw Mihuana; he was the handsomest man on earth. When he came near her, she went weak. Her eyes searched the forest below for the first sight of him. She loved him with all her being, and he had been away from her for too long.

When she saw Mihuana she cried out a greeting and ran down to meet him.

"Ah, my love," he said with relief, as if by some miracle she had appeared here, as if every step up this mountain had been beset with doubt. She would not come. She had changed her mind. She had returned to the world of kapu. He wanted to believe she would be waiting for him, but as always when she appeared suddenly before him, it was a delightful miracle.

He caught her arms for a moment, holding her so that he could assure himself that it was really she. Her face was framed by the black hair that spilled about her bared shoulders and breasts. Her teeth were white, sparkling, her features sheer perfection. Her breasts were not large, but they were high-standing, and the nipples were touched with pink against the brown of her skin.

"Oh, god Lono," he said. "I was afraid you might not come."

"And why would I not come?"

"Sooner or later, you must learn what your brothers know so well. You are tapu to me."

She laughed. "I am to you as the air is, as the sunlight. I cover you. I kiss your body, I caress you . . ." She laughed again, looking up at him. "I have been here waiting for you since your boats were first sighted. . . . I thought maybe you would want to see me so terribly that you would fly that distance, that you would cover the ground between us by magic."

Mihuana was as pleased, delighted, and excited to see Misau as she was to see him, but his voice was empty with despair. "I don't know if I can ever cover the ground between us at all. . . . I don't believe there is such magic."

She drew him through the fragrant, damp leaves of trees and ferns, to the opening before their hideaway. "You sound so unhappy. Can you be unhappy, seeing me after so long? So many days? How many sunsets has it been since my arms held you like this?"

"I know that I have thought only of you."

"And I of you. I think you kept me awake at night. Deep past half-night, I would lie stirring, thinking of you, wanting you near me."

"As the crew threw nets and circled the fish, my mind wandered back here to you. To this place. To you."

"Then laugh. Smile. You are here. I am here. Nothing can come between us."

"I am afraid that is not true." He sat down on the mat and drew her down beside him. His hungry hands covered her breasts and she laid her head back against his shoulder; her breathing quickened and her hand closed on his thigh.

Holding her, kissing her fragrant hair, nuzzling her breasts and moving his hands over her nude body, he forced himself to tell her about A'Kane's death. She took it calmly. "My brother courted war," she said.

"He dared death. I believed he would die young."

"Before he died," Mihuana said, "I approached him. I told him that I had fallen in love with you, that my thoughts were with you constantly. That I would marry you."

"And what did he say?"

Mihuana shuddered. A shiver ran down his spine. "What did he not say! What evil things he called me. And strangely—the one that hurt was the one I must say to myself: commoner. I am a commoner. I have no right to touch you like this—" He held his breath and drew his hand through the wetness at her thighs, feeling her body quiver at his touch. "It is *tapu*."

"We have talked of this, Mihuana. We are not different. We are one. We are one soul. The gods made us thus. We can see it. The world, too, must see it."

"Your brothers have told me how different I am. A commoner. And you are an *alii*. I knew this when I first saw you, but it did not matter. Nothing mattered except that somehow I get you in my arms."

She laughed, snuggling close to him, feeling his arousal, finding him harder, more heated, more fierce and sweeter than any other man. "I know only of my love for you," she whispered.

He reacted to her hand on him, covering her small dark patch of hair with his own hand and for a long time they pleasured each other. Finally he groaned, "They won't permit it. You know that. Your parents have spoken. The kahunas have spoken. Only the gods can save us now."

She pushed him back upon the mat. He lay, dispirited, yet trembling with need for her. She raised her body above his, lowering herself upon his manhood, slowly swaying, then twisting as he thrust upward. She caught her arms about him, digging her nails into his back, riding him to a sweet forgetfulness.

At last she sagged upon him, lying with her legs widespread, her body pressed close upon him, locking him inside her.

"We will go away," she said.

"How I've thought about that. But where? Where could we go? They would follow us. The gods themselves are against us."

She smiled, kissing his throat. "I think the gods have looked kindly on us. I don't think they even see two of us. I think they see only one, as I do."

When, at last, Mihuana lay asleep in her arms, Misau remained wakeful. She thought of A'Kane and his violent death. She thought of Kamehameha and what this would mean to him—and to all her sisters and brothers, those with the same mother, those of different mothers, the children of the concubines of the chief. Her eyes filled with tears at the thought of her lovely sister, Waialua, the unhappy wife of A'Kane, now an unhappy widow destined to a life among the priests. Unless, of course, Kamehameha decided to take Waialua as one of his wives. He could have as many wives as he wanted, now that he was to become ruler of his people.

The mountainous island was silent, its greenery stretching from the shoreline to the farthest hill. The clearing was cleanly defined, ringed by royal poincianas, by tall, stately palms, by large tree ferns, broken and speckled by bright red anthurium blooms. Brilliantly plumed parrots and sleek mynah birds hid in the thick foliage of jasminum, glory bushes, plumeria, the dwarf poinciana, and orchids, lovely and odorless.

Kaumualii listened silently as the returning men told of the death of A'Kane and the treachery of the Oahuans. He sat on a throne in the clearing before the royal hut. Beside him, on each side, were arrayed the kahunas.

The returning men sat, heads bowed before the chief. Kamehameha stood aside, watching silently. The entire tribe ringed this open space. Many wept at the news of A'Kane's death. But it was the chief that Kamehameha watched with interest.

The chief was old. Perhaps he was no

more than forty, but his hair was white, his teeth black stubs. He sat on his flower-draped throne, a cape of dwarf poincianas and ginger flowers flowing across his shoulders and spilling down between his legs. There was a great sadness about his eyes; lines ran down from his nose around his mouth and to his still-firm chin. His shoulders were round with age, and he had the habit of breathing deeply and spasmodically.

When the story was told by the young kahuna—a priest—who had accompanied the fishermen, Kaumualii began to sway back and forth on the throne. As the people watched, his head dropped back, he dragged in a deep breath and emitted a howl of agony. He beat his breast. Then he sobbed aloud, the tears streaming down from his black eyes across the leathery skin of his face. "My son," he moaned, "oh, my son."

No one moved or spoke. Their own grief was forgotten in the agony of their king. Queen Be'ole sat near the throne, at the end of the lines of kahunas. Her head was bowed, her body racked with silent tears.

Finally the chief sat as if he had turned to stone. He looked at no one, his gaze fixed on some middle distance. The kahunas and the people watched, waiting for him to speak.

Kamehameha waited. He did not know what to expect. Perhaps that the king would order shiploads of men on a journey of vengeance against the Oahuans. Perhaps he would speak of his son. And at last, when Kamehameha thought the silence would never end, Kaumualii stirred.

He straightened on the throne and looked about oddly, as if he were disoriented. He licked at his lips, then he shifted the heavy cape up on his shoulders and glared out at the assemblage. "Why are you all here? What do you want? What do you want of me?"

Kamehameha knew little of protocol, of kapu and taboo; but he knew what he wanted of this king. He wanted to hear him order the men out on an orgy of vengeance. Nothing else would satisfy the bloodlust that had been building within him.

He stepped forward and bowed. "I request permission to lead the army of vengeance against the Oahuans, my father," he said.

A gasp arose from the crowd around Kamehameha. He had no idea what taboo he had violated, only that it must be a great one indeed.

The king ignored him. The kahunas stood up suddenly and moved like a human phalanx between the old king and his grieving people. The kahunas, or priests, were darkly tattooed, wore flowered capes and flowered hats, and were almost as powerful as the *alii*, the elite from whom sprang the king. They descended in a straight line from the gods, just as the king did. It was their job to interpret omens. Only the kahunas could communicate with the gods. They had a repertory of rituals to determine the will of the gods.

One of the kahunas, a stout man with tattoos along his arms and on his cheeks, spoke to Kamehameha. "One must wait," the kahuna said in a low tone of sadness and yet firm resolve. "One must give the chief time to communicate with the gods."

"The gods must be consulted," said another kahuna. "Lono, Ku, and Kane must give us the benefit of their great wisdom."

Kamehameha stepped forward. His face was gray, his jaw set in a taut line. He could not see the king behind the phalanx of the kahunas. He raked his gaze along the faces of the kahunas. They were all set firmly against him. But he did not care.

He said, his voice thundering with the outrage that boiled up inside him, "And in the meantime what of Aprilhana and the Oahuans?"

"What of them?" the tattooed kahuna inquired.

"While we talk here, while we consult with the gods, the Oahuans get away."

"The gods must be consulted."

"I didn't come here to consult with the gods. I came to report to my father on the death of my brother. To gather troops. We were badly outnumbered. All I want is more men, and I will return to find the evil April-hana."

The kahuna smiled at him in an almost kindly fashion. He shook his flower-capped head. "We will tell you what action you are to take—after the gods have been consulted."

Kamehameha stood, sick at heart. He moved to the left and to the right, trying to see beyond the line of kahunas to the king. But the king was carefully concealed.

Kamehameha stared at the line of kahunas, and suddenly knew that they were not going to do anything. How long would it take to consult with the gods? Time would be lost, punishment delayed. He sagged, helpless against the kahunas, then he turned on his heel and strode out of the council ring.

Chapter V

The sky burned a fiery red. The setting sun was an orange fireball, and its fingers flared outward in shades of red, coloring the clouds, thick and heavy overhead. The reddish cast spread over the island. The ohea trees, the palms, the ferns, stood in dark relief against the brilliant sky.

The kahunas had recalled the nobles, the sons of the chief, the *alii*, and, unwillingly Kamehameha had returned to the council. Kamehameha sat to one side, aloof and alone, scornful, taking little interest in the proceedings. His memory of its morning session was too vivid.

Kaumualii seemed to have recovered

from the agony of his morning seizure. He sat, very straight, very still.

Kamehameha stared at his father, really seeing him for the first time since he'd arrived from the big island. He had accepted this man as his father, as the supreme ruler of Kauai, and had seen him as a distinguished-looking man, rather distant and remote. But, looking at him now, he found Kaumualii to be a caricature of that noble, distinguished man who ruled this island.

The easy living in this paradise had made him into a weak man, a man of goodwill. Kamehameha's mouth twisted at this idea. A man of goodwill—even toward a murderer, the slayer of his own son.

He saw his father as a very human, very ordinary old man with bad teeth and bad eyes, who smiled at everything. This then was the ruler of this jewel of the islands, with its rain forests, its swamplands, lush green grottoes, spectacular white sand beaches, and majestic shield volcanoes and sheer cliffs. This land called for a man of decision, of power, of strength, and of courage. Suddenly Kamehameha understood why the Oahuans had dared challenge them at sea. The weakness of Kaumualii was known—and likely joked about—among the other kingdoms.

Kamehameha sat filled with his impatience, frustration, and contempt. The meeting began with songs and dancing. The dancers were lovely, but he did not see them, their swaying bodies, or hear their enchanting music swelling in the evening light.

He did hear the kahunas speaking of their consultations with the gods, of the omens and portents, good and evil facing the kingdom as an outcome of this tragedy. The tattooed kahuna was especially long-winded. He swung his arms and rolled his eyes as he spoke of the ancestry of the islanders, the story that had been passed down over the centuries.

"We are a warlike people. We are born warlike. Our fathers came in outriggers from Otahiete. They must have gathered their belongings and their people after some devastating battle. The land was not right for them anymore. Or they fought battles and lost. The loser was banished with all his followers from his homeland. They came with all they could carry in their double-hulled boats and in their arms. But they brought with them the belief in human sacrifices. The kapus. The taboos. After many months of travel, following the trail of the small gold-speckled bird that buried its eggs in land to the north, we came upon paradise. It is not natural to hate in a paradise such as this, where the breezes themselves are calming and quieting. We found a haven of peace. We have tried for all these generations to live peacefully one with another. Our taboos now may be expiated by ritual rather than by sacrifice. We do not eat the flesh of our brothers. We sacrifice only to the goddess Pele now—and our sacrifice is the least among us, or one taken in hostage in some rare battle forced upon us. We have beseeched the gods for a sign, for an omen, but we have received none. We have suffered a grievous loss. We have suffered the death of our brother, our future king. I do not have to tell you how lovely he was, how much stronger than the force of the volcano, how kindly, how regal. He was loved by all of us, by the greatest and by the least. But without that omen, that sign from the gods, we do not feel it is the will of the gods that we go to war because of his death."

At last, the old chief Kaumualii stood up. "I have listened well to the counsel of my priests," he said. His voice sounded old, and beaten, especially to Kamehameha. "We have been grievously wounded by this act of the Oahuans. But if we go to them demanding in return the life of their prince, we should instigate a war greater than any we have known in our long and honorable history. No. We must stand firm. We shall stand firm. But we must not go out seeking vengeance. We occasionally fight—over territory, over prisoners taken in battle. But never anything so fearful, so terrible as we would unleash by going to war against the

48

Oahuans at this time. We shall stand firm.
We shall continue to fish in waters around
these islands, waters given to us by the very
gods themselves. We shall continue to
travel, to trade with the other kingdoms. If
we are confronted, we shall fight. But the
gods have spoken; there must not be the
willful slaughter such a war of vengeance
would bring down upon us."

Kamehameha sat for a long time, listening to the empty words and fine phrases of
the priests and of the king. They added up
to surrender. The next time a fleet of outriggers from Kauai set sail to the fishing
grounds, they would be set upon by Oahuans grown brave by this initial surrender. The king would not ask for the life of
a prince in exchange for the life of a prince.
He did not want trouble. He was willing to
see his own son's death go unavenged.

Kamehameha stood up. His face was pale,
his eyes bleak. "If this is the only reply to
this act of murder, then I say, the gods help
us." His voice quavered. He heard the restive stirrings around him. Taboos were being violated, but he could not care. He
shouted, "I say the gods help us, and yet, I
know that the gods won't help us, because
we must help ourselves if we are to please
the gods. We must pray to the gods, but we
must carry our knives unsheathed."

The priests fell silent before him. Some
of the elders came to him and caught his

arm, but he shook free of them. He waited, meeting the eyes of each of the kahunas. Their gazes wilted and fell under his.

Kaumualii put out his arms. "My son. Make your way our way. See the evil of warfare, the terror of wholesale slaughter, the murder for murder which you are asking."

"I'm asking only that my brother's death be avenged."

"He is my son. The son of my heart. Do you not know how my heart hurts at his death?"

"Yet you do nothing. You mouth words. All of you. You should call together an army. An army of strong men. Let me lead them. I shall avenge the death of my brother, of your son, of the next king of this land. It is an act we cannot allow to go unpunished or forever we will be laughed at. Our grandchildren will be scorned. But that does not matter. Nothing matters except the need to punish this terrible wrong, to take the life of the one who took A'Kane's life."

"He is the son of the king of the Oahuans," Kaumualii said, shoulders sagging.

Kamehameha stared at the old man, then turned and walked away. The tribesmen, troubled, whispered among themselves. They were helpless against the kahunas.

Kamehameha walked down to the shoreline. He stood for a long time, staring up at the twin peaks of Kawaikini and Waialeale, the great spires that rose up in the middle of the island. Far to the north rose the An-ahola mountain range and to the south reared the rugged Hoary Heads.

Rimming the shoreline were bright red poinsettias, pink bougainvillea, orange trumpet vines, night-blooming cereus, poinciana, maile, olapa, kuki, and the purpled-flowered jacaranda. It was all so breathtakingly lovely. As lovely as the old timid King Kaumualii said. It was a land of enchantment, a place where the spell of complacency was cast over everything and everybody. He had himself felt this complacency, but suddenly everything had changed. A bloodlust drove him. He found himself obsessed with death and with slaying. All this loveliness that had meant so much to him before the death of A'Kane was now as nothing. He stared unseeingly at the beauties around him. He cared nothing for beauty. He thought only of killing, of massacre, of vengeance.

Suddenly he broke into a run. People glanced up to stare at him.

Before the grass hut of Nahalo, he stood, breathless. The older man watched him narrowly. They did not need to speak what was in their minds. Nahalo sighed heavily, waiting for the youth to speak.

"I return to Molokai," Kamehameha said at last.

Nahalo nodded. The boy's mind had been

made up since the first; it was only a matter of *when* he would disobey the kapus of the kahunas.

"I would have your boats with me," Kamehameha said.

"Why would you want my boats? My men fish well. It is not known that they fight as well."

"They are brave men. When they see the true reason for bravery, they will fight. I have no fear of this."

Nahalo shrugged. "Still, one does not assure that one's boat may go on such a mission as you plan."

"And why not? The Oahuans killed our prince. Our next king. They denied us rights to fish the waters."

"Still, a matter of vengeance."

"Can you stomach a surrender to the Oahuans? Can you say to them that it is all right that they have slain our brother?"

"It is not that simple." Nahalo sat upon his mat and crossed his arms over his keg-like chest. "The attack would be wrong. The chief and the kahunas have forbidden it."

"But they did not witness his death, see the arrogance of his slayers. Were you not there? Did you not see our brother slain? Who is to be next? You? Me? My father, who does not even believe the Oahuans are warlike? Are we then to sit here and wait for them to slay us as they come ashore and we bow before them?"

Nahalo sighed again and nodded. "It is as you say. If you find others, I will go with you. You may count on me and you may count on my boats."

Kamehameha knelt before the older man, caught his shoulders, and embraced him. "I will remember this moment," he promised. "I shall treasure it in my heart forever."

Nahalo smiled. "You have a long way to go yet, my young friend."

Kamehameha walked among the sparsely spaced grass huts to the hut of Moro, a man he trusted and whose violent spirit was well known. He was a small man with a large head and bushy hair. His brow was short, his nose was wide, and his nostrils large. Moro nodded to him without smiling. Kamehameha saw that his mission preceded him. It seemed everyone knew his plans.

Moro remained seated on his mat and shook his head even as Kamehameha began to talk. No matter what argument Kamehameha presented, Moro remained adamant against it.

At last Moro spoke. "It is not that I do not regret the death of A'Kane. For I do. He was a beloved prince, a man to be respected and loved at once. But he is dead. We cannot bring him back from the dead. Can we? No matter what we do, he lies dead. And the kahunas and the chief have spoken. They have forbidden this reckless adventure. And I obey them and their kapus. I have always done this and I have lived well. Why do we have the *alii*, the priests, and the chief to make the laws if we are not to obey them?"

Kamehameha cursed him. "Stay here, then. Stay safely within your hut. Stay with the women, the old, and the sickly. Do you not understand? The kahunas are old. The chief is old. And you—as young as you are— you are old before your time."

Moro merely stared straight ahead. "I wish you well, and aloha, on your mission. Surely you know this."

Kamehameha stared at him hopelessly. He needed every man he could enlist. At last he turned on his heel and walked out.

On the wide beach, he met Wiari and Mauro. They smiled at him. "We hear the whispers that you disobey the kapus of the kahunas, that you seek vengeance on those who struck down our brother."

Kamehameha nodded. Moro's rejection still rankled. It was incredible to him that a man would want to live under the heel of the Oahuans.

"Are you then planning to betray me?" he demanded, standing tall and reserved, remote and dangerous.

The two men peered at him. They looked at each other and laughed. "Now, where would you get an idea like that?"

"It is not so amusing to one Moro back there," Kamehameha answered.

Wiari smiled. "Moro is known as a deeply religious man. If you had realized this, you would not have been surprised that he plans to obey the kapus of the kahunas."

"And you?" Kamehameha relaxed slightly, watching the two younger men.

"Our boats are your boats," Wiari said. "We cannot live among these islands if we are looked down upon by our neighbors."

Chapter VI

Kamehameha found Mihuana sprawled facedown and fast asleep, alone in his hut. His exhaustion was profound. He lay, totally vulnerable, his long, bronzed arms spread above his head, his legs apart, his privates unprotected. His breathing was deep. It was early evening, the sun still rode the sky, and all around people stirred, calling and talking to one another. Mihuana was dead to it all.

Kamehameha stood over him. Mihuana the commoner. The rare, uncommon commoner, more regal-looking than most royalty. Perhaps a reckless young noble had come into his mother's past. At least this would explain Mihuana's height, his arro-

gance, and his self-confidence. It was easy
to see why he had been accepted as a leader
by the mass of the tribes. He led his own
band, but he could never be more than he
was. A *makaainana*. His handsome face was
relaxed in his repose. His chest rose and
fell with his deep and regular breathing.
Kamehameha kicked the youth roughly in
the side.

Mihuana's eyes flew open, at once wide
awake and on guard. He pushed his hands
through the wild black hair that reached almost to his shoulders. A handsome devil,
Kamehameha admitted. Too bad he was
shackled to a commoner status for life.

Mihuana clutched at the pain in his side.
With his other hand he reached for his coral
knife. He rose to his knees before he recognized his caller.

Recognizing the young prince, Mihuana
sighed out his pain and sank back on his
haunches, yawning and massaging his painful flesh.

"What do you want?" Mihuana spoke before the realization crashed in upon him
that Kamehameha had learned of his tryst
with Misau. There were many spies in the
village, many who hoped to gain favor at the
expense of others. The caste system was
strong. The nobility took what they wanted;
the commoners toiled, fished, harvested,
and paid taxes to the nobility, and one way

to curry favor with the all-powerful nobles was by spying and betrayal.

Mihuana drew a deep breath. Perhaps the king's son, apprised of the truth about him and Misau, had come to kill him. He sighed heavily. So be it. If he died for loving Misau, he died happily, with a life fuller than all those who lived beyond him.

He straightened slightly. He thought about Misau and wanted to live for her, not to die for her. He wanted to hold her forever as he had held her today. He knew one thing: Old men and fools sought for other meanings of life, but he had discovered true bliss in the arms of his beloved.

It was kapu worthy of death for a commoner to strike one of the nobility, but he was damned if he would die quietly to satisfy an ancient tribal law he scorned. This time he spoke more slowly, watching the young prince's face. "What do you want of me?"

Kamehameha smiled to himself. Too bad that a wrestling match between him and this commoner was kapu. What a fight there could be between them. Better than the old battle royals he had had with A'Kane, and he would not have to lose. Losing would be the responsibility of the commoner. He felt conflict charging the atmosphere between them, although he could not say why.

"I am preparing a fleet. To return to Molokai. I mean to find Aprilhana, and when I find him, I mean to kill him."

Mihuana shrugged. "The omens are all against it. I am sure you heard the kahunas say this."

"The kahunas are old men. They have coconut milk in their veins. Omens be damned. The omens are ideas for old men with old heads, old minds, old hearts . . . and old bodies."

"Still, they are the law." Mihuana remained on his knees; a commoner must prostrate himself before royalty. "To go against the kahunas is to break the law."

"Does this mean you will not come with me?"

Mihuana sighed. This was so much better than he had hoped since waking and finding Kamehameha standing over him. Still, if the prince had learned the truth about him and Misau, he may well have slain him as he slept upon his mat. It was tabu to touch the body of a noble. And to take her body! Again and again, as he had, greedily, avidly, adoringly. The gods had no words to express the evil of such a thing.

He flexed the muscles in his shoulders, for the moment pleased and relieved that Kamehameha did not yet know.

He shrugged. "I have no wish for war. People like me do not gain much from a war."

Kamehameha winced. His voice hardened. "Do you not understand what it means to allow the Oahuans to defeat us, to slay one of our own people and not to answer back?"

Mihuana shrugged, watching Kamehameha narrowly. Kamehameha suddenly laughed. "You want something in return for your boats and your men? Is that it? This is not the first time I have been met by this answer."

Mihuana shrugged again.

"I'll admit it," Kamehameha said, "I need your boats. Your men. Name your price. You want land? Is that it? You know as well as I that it is forbidden for commoners to own land." He laughed, shaking his head. "But you are an uncommon commoner, eh?"

When Mihuana shrugged Kamehameha grew impatient and demanded coldly, "Out with it. What do you demand of me in exchange for your boats and your men?"

At this moment, he and the young prince seemed as equal as they would ever be. He had something the noble wanted. "I see that you have already forgotten that we spoke, on the island, at the time of the death of A'Kane."

Kamehameha frowned. He had been so wrapped up in his misery and his rages and his plans he had forgotten entirely. "Ah. So you persist in thinking of my sister Misau as . . . as suitable for you? Is that it?"

"It is." Mihuana found it difficult to continue kneeling. This was a subject that demanded that they speak face-to-face and tabu be damned. He spoke coldly. "Either Misau is—suitable for me—or I and my men and my boats are too common to join you in what may prove to be a battle profitable only to the royalty."

Kamehameha shook his head. "By the gods, I've already warned you you have no chance with her. Aren't you smart enough to see? Don't you know that the kahunas, the chief, the *alii* families would never permit such a union?"

"If the son of Kaumualii pronounced such a union good, if he found some way to elevate a man above the place to which he was born . . ."

"Gods! The dreams you dare to dream. The insult. . . ."

"It would be no insult if the prince declared it valid. Then it would be good and acceptable in the eyes of all."

"I can see you have planned it carefully."

"I've thought of nothing else. It is the way out for us. For Misau who loves me as I love her. For all of us."

"Only I can never do it."

The silence stretched. It was so quiet they could hear the wind in the palm fronds, the distant laughter of children, the playful barking of small dogs.

At last, Mihuana spread his hands. "Then we have nothing to say to each other, my friend. My men and my boats will be busy. They will comply with the laws of the priests. We plan to poison fish in the next few days. The catch promises to be huge. I wish you aloha in your undertaking."

Kamehameha's hand touched at the hasp of his sheathed knife. He had never heard such contempt in the voice of a commoner. Not even royalty spoke to their peers with such venom. That a commoner would dare to refuse his request so boldly and scornfully shocked and amazed him.

"You are refusing my request that your boats accompany me?"

"I have made a request of your holiness. Your royal sister loves me. I know this to be true. I would not dare speak these words, knowing you could behead me for even speaking them, but I trust in the goodness of your heart, in your great compassion, in your understanding."

"You take a great risk to cross me like this."

"It is the risk that makes my life worthwhile."

"You could die for this. Simply by looking at Misau you have put your life in jeopardy. To speak this way of royalty is a crime. Yet you persist."

"Because without her I have no life. There is no reason for me to go on, living safely and securely, the life of a *makaainana* on this island. I have tried to be honest with you. I hoped this might weigh well in the matter."

"Say no more. I warn you. Put her from

63

your mind. You will be happier for it. When you recognize the truth, when you learn to live with it, you will be happier."

"No. I will never learn to live without her. That is why I beg of you to consider the match of your sister, who loves me with all her heart and I who love her with all I am, all I can ever be. I don't even ask that you make a decision now. Only that you consider it. Discuss it with Misau. If you would speak with her, I am sure you would find a love too great to be bound by taboo, too honest to be denied."

"I know only what taboo says. There must be some reason for it if taboo has been set against it. The mixing of blood. Something. I know only it was taboo on the big island. It is taboo here."

Mihuana sighed. His wide shoulders slumped. He looked gray. Looking beyond the young prince out into the dying daylight, he saw life along the beach, going on as usual. How strange that life could be so uncaring as his world toppled.

He looked up at last. "Then I wish you aloha on your errand and we have nothing more to say one to the other."

Kamehameha clenched his fists. He longed to sink his dagger into Mihuana's flesh. But Mihuana's men were brave. Without them, he would be much weakened. Mihuana knew this as well as he did. They had reached an impasse in their unequal talk.

Kamehameha turned away to the door of

the hut. He could feel Mihuana's eyes on his back. Mihuana knew how badly he needed his boats and his men.

Kamehameha drew a deep breath. In that moment he made the first of his regal decisions. Guile and deceit had never been part of his makeup, but now expediency and nothing else mattered. He tempered honesty with reality. He thought about his lovely sister Misau. He could never condemn her to a life as the consort of a *makaainana*. And yet at this moment he had a desperate need for the services of this uncommon man.

He tightened his jaw. What did it matter what he promised Mihuana on the eve of a savage battle? As long as he got what he wanted. Mihuana may well be slain in the heat of the battle. Kamehameha vowed to send Mihuana and his men into the hottest fighting. If he never came back ... Suddenly he found himself praying that the man would not return alive.

Kamehameha smiled faintly, his face twisting with a fraudulent smile of goodwill. If Mihuana did survive the fighting and returned here alive, what strength would a promise made at this moment have? What could Mihuana do to force him to act upon his promise?

The important thing, the only important thing, was that the fighter Mihuana join him in this crusade, willingly, anxiously, and fullheartedly. He sighed heavily and turned to

65

face Mihuana, who sat unmoving on the grass mat. Kamehameha felt that this was a historic moment, the first time when he, in a regal manner, said one thing and meant quite another. Lying for a royal cause was not lying.

"All right," Kamehameha said. "You have my word. I shall consider the means and ways that one of the royal family could possibly overcome the ancient kapu against such a union and marry a commoner. It is all I can promise."

It was enough. Mihuana sprang to his feet. He dropped the knife and extended his arms. Before Kamehameha could repel him, Mihuana had thrown his arms about him and hugged him tightly.

Another taboo broken. The shadow of a commoner had fallen upon a royal person. A commoner had touched the person of a noble. Kamehameha realized for the first time what the ancient kapus meant to him and decided that his kingdom would be ruled by kapus. There was good reason for them. But it didn't matter here and now. No one had seen the kapu shattered. All that mattered was that he had what he wanted—a fighting force.

Chapter VII

Mihuana waited only until Kamehameha had disappeared out of sight along the beach. His heart battered furiously against his ribs. His legs felt weak. Now that he had the word of the noble, he felt as if his heart might fail, as if fate might play some desperate trick on him. He had never in his wildest imagining dreamed that his love of Misau might meet with regal approval. He had lied to Misau about his hopes because he had known this was what she wanted to hear: that there was some way in this uncaring world for them to love, to live together as one, as the gods must have intended. He had been cruelly repulsed by A'Kane, threatened with beheading if he ever broached the subject again. A'Kane had warned him never to look upon Misau's face again. He had never told Misau, afraid to break her heart. Then, when A'Kane was killed, he had prayed to the gods Ku, Kane, Longo, and Kanaloa, that Kamehameha, born and reared among commoners on the Big Island, might feel warmth, compassion, in his heart.

He was filled with love for all humanity. The news was too good to keep.

He stood for a long time outside his hut before setting out. The sun boiled near the horizon, but a land breeze moved gently in the palms, making them loud in the late-afternoon silences.

He came to a large grass hut, with a hanging door of pandamus leaves. The big house was silent, yet he knew much went on inside. The sisters and daughters of kings lived here. It was taboo for one like himself to enter. He walked back and forth.

At last Misau pushed aside the screen of the doorway. Her face betrayed a secret smile. At the sight of her, his heart leapt. She was so lovely. Her bronzed skin shone fresh, clear, unblemished. Her dark hair hung loosely in curly waves between her slender shoulders. Her dark eyes were wide and deep and serene. She was the loveliest girl he'd ever seen. Her breasts stood firm and lovely and she moved with unselfconscious ease, as if to music playing in the background.

Walking like a dancer, Misau stepped out from the doorway of the hut. She did not even glance at Mihuana. Except for the faint smile of her limpid eyes, he might have thought her totally unaware of him. But he understood.

There was much going on around them. Men worked on the double-hulled boats, preparing them for some journey. They moved between the huts and the boats, their arms heavy with supplies, their minds preoccupied. Only Mihuana seemed passive and unemployed.

Mihuana walked casually toward Misau and prostrated himself. He was, after all, a commoner and she was the daughter of the king. For a *makaainana* to do less might be cause for a public whipping.

He sank to his knees before her and then lowered his head until he touched the sand with his forehead. He whispered tensely, barely moving his lips. Anyone watching had to be very alert to notice that he had spoken. "I must see you. At once."

He lifted his head enough so that the lovely vision was clear before him. He saw her nod her head almost imperceptibly. Then she moved toward the forest. He nodded, remaining on his knees in the sand until she turned and walked with that lithe step of the dancer, past the cottages that lined the beach. He stayed where he was, watching her walk away among the poinciana and the palms and disappearing from sight in the dense undergrowth. He remained there, holding his breath, looking both ways. No one was paying attention to him. They were all preparing for Kamehameha's crusade and were too busy to be curious.

The men and women were occupied with loading their boats. Kamehameha meant to depart tonight, under cover of darkness, pretending that the kahunas and the chief did not know that he was defying the royal ruling.

Mihuana sighed. He would have a great deal to do to gather his men and provisions by nightfall, but now he did not care. He walked, with elaborate casualness, along the beach. Taking a circuitous path, past a half-dozen grass huts, he turned suddenly, striding into the undergrowth.

He found his love awaiting him beside a stream. She heard him coming and leapt up, running into his arms, her breasts quivering as she moved. He caught his breath, entranced as always by her loveliness.

"What is the matter?" she said. She stared into his face, troubled. "Were we followed to our secret place today?"

He drew her close to him, comforting her, reassuring her. He felt the pounding of his heart, the sense of weakness that always at-

70

tacked him at the first moment of their meeting.

"No. No," he whispered, reassuring her. "No. I have good news. Such news that could not wait."

"I saw you walk before our house." Misau laughed. "I am sure that everyone saw you."

"I could not care, the news is that great."

"I knew that something must have happened or you would not be so bold."

"It could not be helped. I knew of no other way to get to you." He held her against his body.

She reached up and smoothed his face with her slender fingers. "You are so beautiful. Like a volcano erupting, you are beautiful."

"I dream only of you. I had to see you."

"I am here now," she said gently. "What is it? What has happened?"

He took a deep breath and released her slightly, then stood back and peered down into her dark, wide eyes. "I have spoken to Kamehameha."

"About us?" She winced, fearing for him.

"About us." He nodded emphatically. He smiled, pleased with himself, and with his news. He explained quickly how Kamehameha's urgent need for his men and his boats made the timing right.

She clung to his arms, her face twisted with worry. "Don't you know the risk, speaking to him of us?"

71

"You know I do. I found out from A'Kane. I spoke to him of my love for you and he threatened to behead me if I ever spoke your name again. I was forbidden to look at you. I was charged with removing myself at once from any place where you might walk. But I could not stay away, even knowing the danger. But now A'Kane is dead. Kamehameha was born among commoners and he grew up among them. I prayed that Kamehameha would show compassion toward me and my love for you, and my prayers were answered."

Misau felt a sickness that was almost physical run down through her body. She clung to Mihuana, seeing him in his gentleness and honesty, his trusting nature.

She spoke slowly. "You must be careful. One learns the rights and privileges of royalty, the demands of kapu, as one associates with the nobles and the priests. Kamehameha has not been among them very long. He may turn upon you and all you have said to him may well be used against you."

But Mihuana laughed and held her close. "No, he has promised. He has given me his solemn word. In exchange for my fighting with him in the attack on the Oahuans, he will consider warmly our love."

She was afraid to believe him, afraid to trust this strange turn of events. "Even if he feels kindly toward us now, he will be subject to many pressures from the priests when he broaches the subject to them, and in order to change an ancient rite the priests must be consulted. . . . I am afraid."

"Don't be afraid."

She sighed heavily. "You don't know what they can do to us."

"But I have his promise. Don't you understand? He promises to look with favor upon us."

"Did he say that?" She kissed him gently. Despite her doubts, she, too, wanted to believe with Mihuana.

"No. But what else could he mean?" He smiled at the memory. "We . . . we embraced."

"Embraced?"

Her face showed her fear. He laughed, remembering the spontaneity of the moment. "Oh, you mean the kapu against touching the person of a noble?"

"Yes."

"I could not help it. When I thought how I had loved you, had held you in my arms . . . to touch the exalted body of a prince seemed not too important."

"And he did nothing to stop you?"

"He seemed pleased. He is willing now to accept me."

"As an equal?" She stared up into his face.

"I do not know. I did not think that far ahead. I thought only that at last our lovemaking could be open before the world. Do you not feel the wonder and excitement of this?"

"Oh, yes. I see that the whole world has changed. All that has been all these years is overturned. All that has gone before is as nothing. My brother accepts you as an equal; he promises to look with favor upon us. Oh, my poor Mihuana, don't you *feel* something is wrong?"

"No. For the first time, I feel life is good. The world is suddenly a beautiful place. If only you could have been there."

"Yes, I wish that I had been there. I wish I could accept with you that this world and the way we know it is suddenly to be changed, that my brother is going to accept us."

She saw nothing like that.

She had seen some kapus that were instigated by chiefs, priests, or influential royalty on a whim, under the name of religion, or to oppress or to destroy a person for whom the noble had taken a dislike. Even as a child she had seen the children of the *makaainana* and of the untouchable outcasts called the *kauwa* put to death if in their playing they forgot to prostrate themselves before nobility, or if in their excitement they touched the person of the young princess.

She had lost friends. They were there one day; the next they were gone. When one asked for them, the answer was a shrug. She had wept alone at night, but it was the law, and she had seen these laws at work all her life, until finally she had come to accept their cruelty.

Women in her class were proscribed by law from many activities. The foods they might eat, with whom they could eat, what they might wear, was controlled by law. The taboos were passed rigorously from generation to generation.

Now the idea of the laws suddenly changing troubled her deeply. She understood that Kamehameha was new to royalty, new to the ways of the kapus. But she was afraid to believe that the old traditions had changed as easily as Mihuana believed. He believed because he wanted with all his heart to believe. There was no place in his heart for doubt.

She told herself there was a chance that she and Mihuana might be allowed to meet, to socialize, to speak openly.

She even smiled slightly thinking of all they had done secretly on the high tor, the passion and ardor of their lovemaking. The gods themselves must tremble at their glory and excitement. She quivered with the delight of the memory. Surely, the gods themselves were pleased by the beauty and strength and goodness of Mihuana. His mother may well be a commoner, but his father must have been a god, or a demigod, at the least! They had the memory of their lovemaking to sustain them no matter what happened.

"You doubt, but you will see," Mihuana said, smiling. "I can see you are afraid to believe so much good could befall us. Well, believe it. It is true."

Still, the doubt persisted in Misau's mind. She urged Mihuana to tell her in detail what Kamehameha had said to him. The tone of the young prince's voice, the very inflection of his tone. All of it was so terribly important.

But Mihuana was convinced that her brother was sincere. Kamehameha had promised that they would be permitted to speak, to walk together, to be seen together before all the people. Against her better judgment she allowed Mihuana to convince her. She began to hope. He was so certain that she began to share his confidence. Her heart quickened. In her mind, she began to see how life might be changed if she and Mihuana were permitted to behave openly as lovers.

It still didn't make sense to her, but at last she was convinced by his certitude. She pressed close in his arms, stilling her trembling and forcing herself to smile with him.

Chapter VIII

"Pray to Laamaomao," Kamehameha said.

The stout sails were sprung, and the god of the winds appeared to be answering their prayers. The fifteen outriggers Kamehameha had been able to assemble were fragile, light, blunt-bowed craft. The men sat silent in their narrow prows as the night breezes incited the sails to fierce activity. The bouncing canoes seemed charming, gay, and happy, almost as if they were on some mission of pleasure and knew nothing of the wicked sea and the dangers of storms and battles of vengeance.

The boats plowed through the warm night on their mission of death. The excitement grew as the miles swished past on the wind. The sense of waiting, of desperate anxiety, increased. Men touched the knives sheathed at their sides, tentatively felt the razor-sharp heads of their long lances.

With daybreak, landfall was sighted. Kamehameha had skirted the harbor from which the Oahuans had come, bringing his boats around the island to a secret cove.

It was broad daylight when the boats lowered their sails and were paddled into the cove and carried onto the white sands. The men spilled from the crafts to find their legs weak and wobbly.

They wandered about the cove, disoriented and fatigued after the long night's journey. Kamehameha ordered them into the shade of palms above the shoreline for a long rest and a hearty meal. While the main party ate and slept, he sent Mihuana and a group of scouts to reconnoiter the island.

Later that afternoon the men returned, swollen with pride and excitement. Mihuana reported to Kamehameha at once, who set his face in a blank expression he hoped would hide the eagerness that drove him.

"We ventured to the very edge of the Oahuan encampment across the island," Mihuana reported with pride. "The forty boats remain in the big harbor. They are presently going out to fish. But they return, because they left the greater number of boats onshore."

Greatly cheered by the report, Kamehameha found himself looking with favor again upon Mihuana. Few nobles could be entrusted with tasks which this commoner accomplished with ease. But he quickly put aside this feeling. He would send Mihuana into the most savage places of battle until the news came that he had fallen.

For the first time he spoke of his battle plans. A hush fell across the young men and boys assembled before him on the beach. They looked at him with renewed respect. He had planned well. War was part of his nature. The men realized this and knew they would follow him into battle because he was a warrior above all other warriors.

"We shall await the night." Kamehameha spoke quietly, but clearly. "We shall rest here. Tonight, when the campfires burn low in the camp of the enemy, we shall with great stealth cross the island."

"We had better start in the daylight," Mihuana said. "The way across the mountains is rough. They may place guards of their own, though I think not. We saw no signs of guards. The Oahuans seem at ease on this island, as if they had made peace of some sort with the king of Molokai."

"Still, we won't take chances," Kamehameha decided. He looked about at the faces of his leaders, Nahalo, Mairo, Wiari, all young nobles, all good men.

His gaze stopped at Mihuana for a moment, then he looked past him, as if his mind were not already made up. Finally he brought his gaze back to the commoner's handsome face. "We will send a small force ahead. Men who will move silently and swiftly and remain alert at all times for lookouts."

He moved his gaze across the faces of the leaders, the nobles, always returning to Mihuana. He spoke, smiling. "I think Mihuana. He will take men amounting to the fingers of both hands"—he held his splayed fingers aloft—"and go ahead to watch for lookouts, to report whatever goes on in the camp of the Oahuans."

Mihuana nodded silently. He was desperately tired from his earlier mission, but he said nothing. He knew the task was dangerous, but there were no easy chores ahead for any of Kamehameha's army. He counted out ten men, sent two lookouts on ahead, and then started across the island again.

Mihuana's men were heavily armed with lances, spears, and knives, but their minds were the most important of their weapons. Their job was to watch the enemy while staying hidden and to send back reports to Kamehameha's men, who were approaching under the cover of darkness.

Mihuana found a secure lookout, high

and well concealed. From this post he could watch the entire encampment of Oahuans. The people down there were casually going about their ordinary activities. They had no thought of approaching disaster. The boats that had gone out in the morning had returned. The entire settlement trooped down to the shoreline to greet the returning fishermen and to clean the catch.

By sundown a large fire had been built in a pit and fish were being wrapped in leaves and buried in the hot sand. Young men sat around the fire, some silent, some laughing, many drinking.

Mihuana kept runners coming and going throughout the day, down the mountain trail, across the island to their main forces. These returning men brought news of Kamehameha's army. Three hundred men armed to the teeth, moving silently and inexorably forward across the island.

In the deepest night, Kamehameha came to the hidden place where Mihuana had set up his watch. Kamehameha stood silently, watching the Oahuans drinking and eating and shouting with laughter on the wide beach below as their boats lay in wait above the waterline.

Time passed slowly. Kamehameha's manner was cold and deadly. Gradually, the party on the beach broke up and the men wandered off to their mats to sleep.

At last the final straggler tottered away

from the firepit and toppled onto his mat.
The dying fire gleamed on the sleeping bodies. Kamehameha warned his men to set
well in their minds where the men slept, because surprise was to be their advantage.
They were badly outnumbered, but this was
not important, Kamehameha impressed
upon his men, if each Kauaian moved
quickly and stealthily upon his deadly mission.

The waiting men grew restive, and still
Kamehameha ordered them to wait. No one
replenished the wood in the firepit. The fire
sputtered and quavered; the embers died,
and the camp grew silent.

At last Kamehameha gave the signal.
Some of his own men had to be shaken
awake, but finally they began moving
stealthily down the hillside into the Oahuan
encampment.

They found the young Oahuans sprawled
upon their mats in deepest sleep. Kamehameha's men moved in silently, slitting the
throats of the sleeping men quickly.

Not one man escaped. Neither the attacked nor the attacker cried out. Men
sleeping next to their slaughtered comrades
slept through the assault, and never wakened, even as their turn came to die.

Kamehameha swelled with pride. He ran
with his men, his own knife drawn. Spotting a sleeping man, he killed him with a
quick but steady motion. His blood spurted

out, and Kamehameha's hands were soon slick with blood.

Standing there alone, as if separated from the rest of the universe, the earth, the sky, the bloody land upon which he stood, he breathed, feeling the bursting sense of accomplishment of destiny realized. He stared out into the limitless spaces where a comet fired itself across the blackened heavens, with a sudden keen awareness of life and death and certain of his own fate.

He stood a moment, looking around, fixing in his mind the place where, earlier, he had watched Aprilhana bed down. Aprilhana of evil memory, Aprilhana of nightmares in which his prince was slain cruelly a thousand times.

Then he ran ahead of his fighting forces. He saw the log by which Aprilhana had lain down earlier to sleep. Standing over the sleeping prince, he was helpless against a great wave of emotion—exultance, pride, and righteous rage. In his mind he saw the oar descending, splitting A'Kane's skull, and changing his own life forever. He looked down at the sleeping form, that hated body. The desire for vengeance swept him along. This was the moment he had lived for.

"Aprilhana."

It was the first word spoken during the entire bloody night. Speaking the hated name overwhelmed Kamehameha and he forgot all else.

"Aprilhana."

He watched the Oahuan prince come slowly and unwillingly awake. Aprilhana tried to sit up, but Kamehameha thrust his huge legs across the noble's chest, pinning him to earth. Over the beach a night mist hid the carnage, the stars were pale, and a silvery-gray tint crept across the face of the heavens. The night winds seemed to have ceased. There was not a breath of air, not even a rustling of palm fronds. Ocean, beach, and sky were all wrapped in a deep sleep from which there could be no waking.

Aprilhana's eyes flew open as he realized he couldn't breathe. "Who?" he asked, staring at the murderous face bent above his own.

This was what Kamehameha wanted. He had lived this moment in a hundred savage dreams. Aprilhana must be conscious, awake, and aware. To kill the man in his sleep was not enough. Aprilhana must live long enough to know who his attacker was, to understand that retribution had come.

"Aprilhana, it is I. Kamehameha. Brother of A'Kane. You should have killed me that day on the boats. You may have gotten away with your heinous crime if you had slain me too."

Aprilhana's cobwebbed mind cleared swiftly. Terror replaced surprise.

Aprilhana reached for the knife at his side. Kamahameha let the prince's fingers almost touch his weapon. Then he knocked it away in the sand.

"You won't need it," Kamehameha said. "Your days of killing innocent men are over."

Chapter IX

Aprilhana opened his mouth to scream. But Kamehameha was too swift. His left hand covered Aprilhana's mouth, and with his index finger and thumb, he closed the prince's nostrils. Struggling violently, Aprilhana gasped for breath but was unable to cry out a warning to his men.

With one sure stroke Kamehameha plunged his knife into the prince's chest. His blood spurted upward. But his death was not enough for Kamehameha. He drew his knife across Aprilhana's throat.

Clutching the prince's hair in his fist, Kamehameha began to hack with his knife until the muscles and bone had been severed.

Then Kamehameha sat for a long time, holding his prize.

Suddenly it seemed that the skies were filled with light. Though the beach remained in darkness, though all around him his men continued the killing, he sat in a blaze of light. The stars zoomed out of the heavens in balls of fire. Night clouds were illuminated and the thickening night mists, stirred by a gentle sea breeze, wheeled around and broke into bright drifts. Vengeance was accomplished.

Kamehameha was the first to walk down to the firepit. In his fist he carried the severed head of the prince. He threw logs on the wavering embers and stood as they sparked and flared and caught, flaming. The others gathered slowly.

Daylight came at last to the scene of carnage. Along the beach as far as the eye could see lay the bodies of the Oahuans. A hum of voices, the occasional wail of a child, the rapid and abruptly terminated roll of a drum, together with some distant hailing in the first dawn light by returning fishermen, reached Kamehameha where he stood.

"Not one Oahuan remains alive" was the report of the investigating men. "We lost no man. The worst casualty is one of the man who was bitten as he held his man down to cut his throat."

Kamehameha nodded, pleased. No dead.

No wounded. There could be no calls for reprisals among the nobles back at Kauai.

"Can I believe what you tell me?" Kamehameha's voice sounded doubtful, but there was a strange smile about his eyes. It was a look that both puzzled and frightened his men. Sitting cross-legged on an abandoned mat near the firepit, Kamehameha looked fixedly at whoever spoke.

"The villagers have heard of the massacre, your highness, and in their terror have taken to the forests. The village lies open and deserted. Not even a pig or a dog has been left behind."

These last words had a most profound effect on Kamehameha. His plans until this moment, had been uncertain. Suddenly the fire shot upward against the black curtain of the forest. His exultance knew no bounds, his heart pounded, his pulses raced. He felt he might fall forward. The feeling was within him; the final mystery had been unfolded. His life now lay before him clearly and hauntingly real. His way was lighted as it had never been before in his life.

His eyes burned with the newfound zeal that drove and obsessed him, but he spoke quietly. "That is good. The village is too big a prize to surrender. And why should we surrender it? By harboring the evil Aprilhana, these people approved his actions. Aprilhana came here and impressed his will upon these people. Aprilhana is dead now. And we live. And those people who supported him against us live. But they shall pay for their part in this murder of A'Kane. Our lives have just begun, lives of victory, of conquest, of taking whatever there is before us to be taken, by strength of arms, by the right of the god Lono."

He nodded at this and sat for some moments in silence. The gods were with him. Nothing could harm him.

"Wiara, I charge you: Take this bloodied head of Aprilhana. Choose a few men. Bright men who can speak well of our victories here. Go back to Kauai with the news of the assault. Of the victory. Show them this trophy, this head of Aprilhana." He held the severed head aloft accompanied by the guttural cries of the men.

Wiara stood up. He was trembling with his anxiety to be off. "I go," he said. He stood tall, his arms crossed over his chest.

"But wait," Kamehameha ordered. "There is this that I further order of you. I order that you tell the nobles and priests and the chief himself. Tell them that my small band has slain all the Oahuans. That the village lies desolated, its people hiding in terror from us. That we are going to attack the villagers, we are going to seek them out. We shall await reinforcements. But mark this well, if additional men are not forthcoming, we shall press on—alone. We mean to take the island of Molokai."

Wiara and four men set sail at once for Kauai. The head of Aprilhana, still bloodied and wildly staring through its wide open eyes, began the legend of Kamehameha.

Wiara's boat skimmed the seas, the sails bellied out, hastened by the gods themselves. They reached Kauai quickly, riding the crests of waves into the shore, where crowds gathered in deadly silence.

Cries and sobs crossed the water to greet the returning men.

The dismay rising from the shore told Wiara what the people expected. A single boat had returned. A single boat and five men. Alarm ran through the village, on the fleet wings of rumor, before Wiara could draw his craft up above the waterline.

The priests and the chief gathered. The saddened people crowded close to hear of the battle, of the losses. Most families had lost at least one man.

Wiara spoke. "We set sail and arrived at the island. We found the Oahuans were still there, still swaggering in their conquest, still celebrating the death of A'Kane. Kamehameha's leadership was flawless. He held up fast across the island from the Oahuans, who never even suspected we were in their waters. He sent men to spy on the enemy. Slowly, we crossed the island and came to the place where we could look down on the Oahuan encampment. When finally the Oahuans went to their mats to sleep, we struck. Most died without even waking. Not a man of the Kauaians was lost or harmed." A cry of relief rose from the crowd. "Not one Oahuan escaped our knives, our lances, our spears."

From a bag that he carried at his side Wiara drew the head of Aprilhana, holding it by a clump of hair, and thrust it high. The head twisted slowly, the eyes wide in death, blood and gore still hanging down from the crudely severed neck. Wiara swung the head up so that all could see.

People gasped, shocked and stunned and mesmerized by this ghastly specter of death. They pressed forward and then fell back, repelled. The head swung before them, sightless eyes fixed on them.

"The head of the evil Aprilhana!" Wiara shouted. "Kamehameha sent it back as a symbol of his success. As I speak, he prepares to attack the island village. These people have aided Aprilhana and must be punished. Most of them cower in fear in the forests, but the army of King Keoua will come out to meet our forces. Kamehameha has sent me back here for additional men.

But he also sent this word. If the men are not forthcoming, his party will press on alone, and though terribly outnumbered by the soldiers of Keoua, they will fight bravely and to the last man."

Wiara's challenge was emphatic. The people spoke to each other in low tones, nodding, their gazes fixed on the priests and magistrates.

The priests were enraged at Wiara's tone. They went at once into consultation. Formerly, they would have retired to meditate, to question the stars, the gods, the ancestors. But Wiara's tone, and Kamehameha's ultimatum, delivered as it was in the hearing of the people, allowed them no such luxury of time. The risks were great and there was no precedent for what was being demanded.

The tattooed priest spoke to the king. For some time he rambled on about the impropriety of the request, the offensive tone, the need for meditation, the threat of improvident action taken hastily and without due consultation. "However, if we do not reinforce Kamehameha's men, we may well assure their destruction at the hands of a larger force."

Another priest agreed. "If we lose the men and boats with Kamehameha, we deprive our people of much of our fishing fleet."

King Kaumualii listened to the arguments of his advisers. In the blaze and heat of sunlight he sat sweating and deeply troubled. He felt that destiny was passing him by, that age had overtaken him. There seemed no place for him in this new world of violence and disorder and quickly made decisions. So he acceded to Wiara's request. There was nothing else he could do. The people were talking louder and louder. Not that he gave a damn about the people, but this business with Kamehameha was giving the people something to talk about, something to think about: a savage and bloodthirsty young noble, arising and taking stands on issues, while he, the king, sat and pondered and did not act. He gave his order loudly and with an enthusiasm he wished he felt. As the day rushed past and the village swarmed about him, outfitting an armada, he withdrew with his wine, finding it hard to believe that his boats were sailing, fully armed and supplied, while he stood by in his old age and watched them go.

With Wiara in the lead boat, almost a hundred craft sailed from the silent, sleeping coast. The outriggers made a formidable scene, heading toward the island, their sails set, skimming across the sea. The villagers and the nobles and priests left behind stood on the high ground watching long after the fleet had disappeared from sight.

When word came to Kamehameha that an armada was arriving to reinforce him, he began to see his recklessly heroic aspirations as reality. With every passing moment he was penetrating deeper into that dream world of achievement and conquest. His destiny was being realized. He felt drunk with the sure knowledge that it was foreordained. It was as if the very pace of his existence speeded up. His heart felt as if it might fail with the first sight of his arriving armada. His boats and his men to order at his will. A strange look of exultance spread over his face, his eyes hardened and glowed as if a torch burned inside them.

Kamehameha was as certain of his destiny as he was of the hundreds of Kauaian boats that sailed into the cove. The excited, armed men rushed forward and pledged themselves to him. Regally he stood with arms crossed as the new arrivals joined with his regular forces and knelt before him along the shoreline.

He spoke to them patiently, explaining that the people of King Keoua had taken to the hills in terror. "What we shall do," he said, "is to send hunting parties into the forests, seeking all those in hiding. We shall accept their surrender. And the total surrender of the island. There shall be no deaths if the terms of this agreement are met at once. But death shall be the fate for any who oppose us."

A cheer went up from the hundreds of armed men. He began to feel a little angry. Most of these men had sat waiting at Kauai until news of his staggering victory reached them. Now they came rushing to partake of the spoils of victory.

Chapter X

Sometimes Kamehameha felt that he had gone mad, that nothing happening around him had any reality or substance. He had to adapt himself to the new and inexplicable facts of his life.

He spent the next hour dividing the men into troops. Each troop was given its orders. They would await the return of the first sally into the forests, then they would strike, as one man, anything and everything that moved.

To head his point point unit, Kamehameha named Mihuana. If there was to be resistance, it would strike the point and this man surely would fall in battle.

With two dozen heavily armed men, Mihuana was sent into the village. His men found the place deserted. Mihuana surveyed the empty shore and wondered why it looked as empty as he felt. He found objects lying where they had been abandoned in haste by people fleeing from the massacre. At last he shook his head, set his lance before him, and with slow, watchful steps entered into the forest.

His men moved stealthily forward through fern and underbrush. They had gone for an hour into this silent wilderness, when Mihuana spied a group of people huddled together in terror.

He signaled his men and they surrounded the wretched group. He sent a runner back with news of his find to Kamehameha. "Tell him that we find no sign of arms, and no resistance. Tell him that we shall question these people as to the whereabouts of the others, the armed forces of the king. By the time Kamehameha arrives here we should know the hiding place of King Keoua." The runner nodded and disappeared into the forest.

By the time Kamehameha arrived, the prisoners were seated quietly, convinced by the soft and reasonable tones of Mihuana that they would be permitted to live if they surrendered and pledged allegiance to the Kauaians. A few had even eaten a little, the first meal of which they had partaken since the massacre began.

Reassured, the people spoke openly, revealing the hiding places of other villagers and of King Keoua. Some of the Oahuans even smiled, bowing to Kamehameha and promising eternal fidelity if only they were allowed to live. Kamehameha stared in disbelief.

He was forced to commend Mihuana. "You appear to be a man of destiny. I know you are a commoner. Yet, few nobles could accomplish what you achieve with ease. No matter what task I assign to you, you carry it out well—and quickly."

Mihuana smiled and tilted his head back, pleased. The image of the beloved Misau flashed into his mind. There was happiness to come for them. The happiness that he earned in battle, performing every mission assigned to him to the best of his ability. He had been certain the young prince would have to notice. He smiled warmly. As Kamehameha suggested, Mihuana did feel a certain oneness with destiny, a belief that time and love would prove themselves for him and for Misau.

Kamehameha marched the captives ahead of his army. They found the second hiding place, exactly as described by the frightened prisoners. These survivors were also quickly pacified. It was not the reception Kamehameha had anticipated, and he realized he had to credit Mihuana.

At last they found the hiding place of King Keoua, a building deep in a sylvan glen beside a waterfall. And here Kamehameha encountered the first resistance. Men carrying wooden shields suddenly appeared, shouting and growling, brandishing lances, clubs, knives, and spears.

One warrior flourished a bloody flag while another beat a savage rhythm on a drum, trying to rally the king's forces and encourage the captives to run for freedom. But the prisoners had seen the savagery of Kamehameha. They sat passively in the midst of the battle, shielding their own bodies and their loved ones as best they could.

The king's army came out in full battle array. But their hearts were not in the fighting. Rumors and threats had taken the heart out of the men who remained loyal to King Keoua of Molokai."

Kamehameha's army was too large, too terrifying. As more and more armed soldiers appeared out of the forest, the drum stopped abruptly, the bloody flag was lowered, and the soldiers slowed their pace to a walk. Then they dropped their weapons, threw away their shields, and sank to their knees before the conquerors in swift, unexpected surrender.

After the soldiers had been disarmed, Kamehameha sent his men into the houses. Led by Mihuana, the troops found the king hiding under robes woven of leaves.

"Your army has laid down its weaponry. They have surrendered. You will be spared, you will be accorded courtesies, but you will be required to pledge your fealty to our prince," Mihuana announced.

The king, a middle-aged man, looked forlornly at his people kneeling in the clearing. He saw the man whom he supposed to be his conqueror, standing, oiled hair, wild of eye, his mouth twisted, massive arms folded across his chest. He was a prince unknown to Keoua, but he realized that the man was a noble. The king said, almost as an afterthought, "The king of Oahu has pledged mutual aid and assistance to our island in time of war."

"I shall certainly inform our prince of this matter," Mihuana said with a faint smile.

He lined up the king and his priests and nobles and marched them out into the sunlight, where Kamehameha waited. He stood aside and let the royalty stand before the young prince. Mihuana spoke in a low, flat tone. "The king has the pledge of the Oahuans to aid and assist in the case of a battle."

"Has he?" Kamehameha's face darkened. He compressed his lips, showing his displeasure. It was as if a pebble had been dropped in a quiet pool, sending out its ripples. The fight had begun because an Oahuan prince slew A'Kane. Now the prince was dead, his men massacred, and the island taken as well. Suddenly Kamehameha saw that Oahu would have to be dealt with. "Has he indeed?"

The tone of Kamehameha's voice made the king wish that he had never made that foolish statement. He clearly read the hatred Kamehameha felt for him. King Keoua put both his hands over his face.

Kamehameha stood for a long time, his arms folded across his chest while King Keoua sagged, staring down at the earth at his bared feet.

At last Kamehameha spoke directly to the king. "Does this mean, then, that you are not surrendering this island and all its people to me?"

King Keoua sank to one knee, his pale face abject. He was afraid he was going to be ill. Hot bile swelled up into his throat, and he swallowed hard. He shook his head vigorously.

"I most humbly and deeply apologize to your highness for the stupidity of my remark. I regret having said it at all, my master. From this day forward, this island shall know but one ruler, one king, one monarchy. You alone now rule this island."

Kamehameha nodded his head. At first he made no answer. He let the king stew in his own terror. "You have done a very smart thing, your highness. You have spared your own neck as well as the lives of your priests and nobles. I shall leave an army of occupation here on this island. You will remain in your main house. Your first act will be a message conveyed at once to the king of Oahu, informing him of the death of his son, Aprilhana, and of your ending your alliance with the king and the land of Oahu. Is that clear?"

"Perfectly. It shall be done. At once. Your kindness and goodness shall be recognized."

"I want it understood, you shall not be permitted an army of any kind. A small group of bodyguards shall be furnished you from my own forces."

King Keoua nodded. "It is clear. It is most kind."

Kamehameha could not satisfactorily explain, even to himself, the suspicions he felt about King Keoua. The king was his first conquest. There was every reason to feel a sense of exultance, and yet instead he felt unease.

It leapt to the forefront of his mind that he should put Keoua to death. Some inner sense assured him that he would sleep better if Keoua were dead. He could foresee months and even years of secret plotting to retake this island. Perhaps even at this moment the king was hatching such a plan. So long as Keoua remained alive, Kamehameha's head would lie uneasy on its pillow.

* * *

In Waimea Bay, a mob poured out from the shore, running waist-deep into the water to meet the returning fleet. Kamehameha sat forward in the lead boat, wearing a flowered robe befitting a king. The robe was King Keoua's. He would have taken it, but the king, noticing his interest, insisted that the robe be a gift. He sat regally before his adoring people.

His life, from the moment when A'Kane was slain, seemed to him laid out clearly. It had all come to pass so perfectly. He was now King of Molokai and he accepted as his privileged right the homage paid to him and to his returning troops.

He was not even surprised when his father, Kaumualii, came down to the beach to welcome him home. Kaumualii arrived with great dignity, with robes and fan bearers, priests and royal dignitaries.

Kamehameha rose from his kneeling position in the lead boat. He leapt from the craft in four feet of water, landing erect, his flowered cape spreading out around him atop the water. He waded ahead of the other boats, strode up on shore, and knelt before his father.

"The word we have is good," Kaumualii said. "Your advance men told of your great victory. Of the total surrender of King Keoua to my troops."

Kamehameha winced slightly at his father's careful wording. The troops did indeed belong to his father, but he had led them into war.

He remained on his knees. He was the son of Kaumualii and a patriot. Unless his father demanded lands or booty outright, he would say nothing.

His father touched his wide shoulders with the staff he carried, and Kamehameha arose and stood, a giant beside his aging father. His large face, framed with oiled and stiffened hair, betrayed nothing to the onlookers. He stared at the nobles and priests, looking each of them directly in the eyes.

Watching his eyes, Kaumualii said, "The islanders so captured shall be brought under the rule of our kingdom."

This was the moment Kamehameha had feared. The moment of confrontation. He had slain Aprilhana, he had killed all the Oahuans, he had taken the island.

Kamehameha met his father's gaze. He found himself thinking back to his days on the big island. Raised as a commoner, he had memories of shaking down avocados and coconuts, of taking stones out of fields, of working tirelessly and fiercely without clothes. Then he recalled the sounds of the battle and the way King Keoua's men rushed out to fight and quickly folded before the terrible forces of his own men. But most of all, through his mind raced the memory of the nobles and priests refusing his request for an army. He knew why the royalty had suddenly changed its mind. Aprilhana's severed head testified to his victory. They had agreed to supply troops because there was no other way.

Chapter XI

Kamehameha drew a deep breath and met his father's gaze levelly. "I am afraid, my revered father, that these people have named me their king. They have sworn allegiance to me. I have no wish to disturb the tranquility of Kauai, or to push myself here upon you. But I have been proclaimed king of Molokai. And I won this title with honor and dignity and with courage. And I believe it must remain so."

He spoke softly, almost apologetically, and yet the hardness was apparent in every word.

His father retreated a step. The words had been heard by all the priests and the nobles. They stood silently, shocked and stunned. They stared, collectively holding their breath as they awaited the next event.

Kaumualii's face seemed to have sagged, grayed, and grown ten years older. He folded his arms on his breast and dropped his head. Sadness and insecurity were sentiments to which he was a stranger. He was a king in paradise, leading a life which left little time for introspection. He had never known a direct challenge to his power.

"I wonder what the omen for me will be?" he thought, and concluded contentedly that for him there would be no augury, that he would die in his bed. The king retreated a few steps, back into the crowd of his advisers, into the old warm safety that had been his as long as he could remember. These sages closed ranks about him and spoke in low, despondent tones.

It became clear to Kamehameha that the men now hauling the outriggers onto the beach held the key to the outcome of this first confrontation with his father. What would they do if Kaumualii called on them, fresh from the campaign at Molokai, the smell of blood and victory still hot in their nostrils? Would they take Kamehameha prisoner if so ordered by the sages and priests? Or would they in the excitement and joy of the moment support him, as they had supported him in battle?

The priests and nobles whispered together, gazing at the horde of men now standing in their wet loincloths all along the beach. The king could not predict where the loyalties of his fighting men lay. And this was hardly the moment to demand a decision. This was a victory party, a celebration, the return of a conquering prince. A very popular prince, the priests noted. A battler. A fighter. One who slew royalty with impunity. Hot memories of the battles still infected the minds of the men. Never had they entertained a disloyal thought toward their king. But never before had they been faced with a choice.

They studied Kamehameha. He stood, taller than any of the men around him, regal despite the oiled hair and the rawness of youth.

They lowered their voices and counseled caution and patience. The time to discuss the merits of Kamehameha's claim to Molokai was later, in a small meeting of nobles and priests.

They spoke earnestly, warning Kaumualii of the consequences of precipitate action. They felt neither love nor resentment toward the prince. In the old days, returning soldiers would have spread the booty before the king, acclaimed the new land in his name, but all this was changed. This son was a stranger.

At last Kaumualii turned back to his son. He smiled and nodded his head. "So be it," he said.

The celebration of victory began. Singing and dancing continued long into the night. New legends about Kamehameha appeared and were repeated in song and dance.

Later the priests summoned Kamehameha to the council chambers.

They smiled unctuously upon him and invited him to be seated among them, to speak freely of his plans for the future. Did he plan to accept the kingdom of Kauai upon the death of his father, or was it his plan to separate himself and form a new kingdom?

"You are the second son," a priest said. "This is not the same as being the first-born. You understand this?"

Kamehameha frowned and stared at the priest. The priest smiled. "As a second son you have only the rights and privileges of all the other sons of the king. Sons who may be named in your stead to replace A'Kane."

"This would be a most serious mistake," Kamehameha said. "I am now the eldest son."

"Death of the eldest son does not necessarily confer his rights and privileges to the second son. This is the judgment of the priests and nobles. That is an action of the entire council."

"But now A'Kane is dead," Kamehameha said. "He is dead and I am the eldest son in his stead."

The high priest looked up at him oddly. "We regret the death of your brother. But it remains that the death of the elder does not confer rights upon the second son. You are a noble. But so are we all. So are your brothers."

Kamehameha stared at the priest. "I felt the death strongly of my brother. I would have done nothing to interfere with his right to rule. But now my dearest brother is dead."

"Your sadness at the loss of your older brother was plain for all to see. Your wish for vengeance seemed a natural thing, not a wish to succeed your brother. Now suddenly the tears are wiped away, and you see yourself in your brother's stead."

"Yes, the weeping has ended. Strength is born in the deep silences of affliction."

"What are you saying?"

"That A'Kane is dead. That A'Kane was my own brother. He was the eldest son of my father. I have tasted the bitterness of his death. But we must not overlook the hand and heart of the gods in our afflictions. Was A'Kane's death mere accident or was it part of some immortal plan? If we view his death so, it becomes absolute and positive evil which admits of no remedy or relief. . . . If we view our troubles and trials aside from the divine designs and agencies in them, we can find no comfort. And I can tell you, I have in the night felt the spirit of my brother A'Kane come to me and tell me that I am his chosen successor. There is great comfort for me in this thought."

"And you find comfort in A'Kane's death?"

"I find only sorrow in his passing. But he is dead. I find the plan and the divine design of the gods in his death. I have accepted my sorrow. I have found peace in it. The soul that suffers finds strength. And I have found strength. No matter what you say, no matter the rules of past laws, I am now the eldest son of my father."

"The line of succession does not work in this fashion."

"It should. I stand the rightful heir to all the worldly goods of my father. I stand before you, the accepted king of Molokai. If there is some law that alters this, I warn you now, I shall oppose it with all the strength at my command."

The high priest stared at him, too stunned to speak. Kamehameha got to his feet.

"It came to me in the night," he said. "It was as if spoken by the gods for my ears alone. They spoke to me of ambitions. Of my great ambitions. That ambition from which nobility grows. I have found purpose in A'Kane's death. And I believe that purpose to be the uniting of all the kingdoms of the seven islands. Think well before opposing my intentions. If I am denied an army here on this island, I shall recruit an

army on my own land. But I shall not be
stayed."

It was the celebration of Lono.

As the celebration intensified, the setting
sun inflamed the overcast sky. To the north,
storm clouds rose. People gathered by the
hundreds at Kealakekua to celebrate the
makahiki festival, that annual joyful trib-
ute to the god Lono-i-ka-mahiki. All else was
forgotten in this paean to the greatest god
in the trio of gods.

The king sat on a raised dais, his nobles
and priests gathered about him. The king
was deeply troubled by Kamehameha. The
idea of warfare among the seven islands
was unheard of. Except for minor skir-
mishes, they had lived in peace for hundreds of years. The priests spoke in low,
solemn tones. It was almost as if the gods
had conferred some special power upon
Kamehameha. The people viewed him suspiciously and few were willing to confront
him.

There was much talk, secret and quiet, of
the possible death of the young prince, who
was now swollen and driven by ambition.
He would not be the first to be so dealt with.
There were many ways to poison a man—a
drop of a certain powder in his drink, the
poisoning of his food—all for the good of
the state. These special people were seldom
good for the state in the long run. Ambi-

tions obsessed him. He saw his true destiny in the stars. The priests could hardly see how this boded well for King Kaumualii.

Still, the king hesitated. He would entertain no such talk during the festival. "Let us leave it with the gods," Kaumualii declared. "Let us enjoy the food, the music, the dancing, the stories. Perhaps by sunrise the truth will become clear to the confused, perhaps by then the threat will have played itself out. This is not the time for secret plotting but for celebrating the god Lono."

None of the priests agreed. The young prince was plainly a man possessed. He should be dealt with at once.

Queen Be'ole lay sprawled upon a mat in her royal hut. Bitterness ate at her, evil memories flooded her mind. The augurs of the long-dead priests stirred. They had been right in their reading of the stars twenty years earlier. They had foreseen the coming of one determined to rule, to decimate his enemies, to take power. The sight of the severed head of Aprilhana had convinced her and brought it all swirling back to haunt her.

"The priests were right," she said, rolling her head back and forth on a bower of flowers. "They foretold the coming of the bloody one." She shuddered, recalling her own betrayal of the omen.

She recalled her horror when Wiari arrived on the island, bearing the severed head of Aprilhana. Such a sense of cold, of death's chill, flooded through her that she could barely stand. Even before she heard that Kamehameha had severed the head with his own hands, she had known.

And now that Kamehameha was back on the island with his flowered robes, his oiled hair, his fierce looks, she was physically ill. There seemed little connection between this warlike creature and the youth who had sailed away on that fishing expedition.

"The omens were right," she moaned. "And I in my selfishness, I stood against them. I betrayed them. How the gods must grieve. How they must stand laughing at me and my foolish error. I have set him loose upon the world. This poor son of mine is lost to bloodlust."

Mihuana wasted no time in seeking Misau. He came openly to her cottage, asking for her by name, standing tall and smiling, with all taboos forgotten. But she heard the whispers, saw the heads pressed together, knew what was being said about the daring young commoner.

She walked with him before the villagers. She felt their gazes like the pricklings of daggers fixed upon her. This flaunting of an ancient taboo was a matter of life and death.

"Your brother has promised," Mihuana

spoke loudly, his head held high. He was blind to the looks of noble and commoner. "He has pledged to me his word."

"No one is safe from treachery," Misau said after a moment's silence.

"But he made me a vow. Before we went out," Mihuana said, smiling and attempting to reassure her. "I told you then what he promised. He has said nothing to change it. We have gone through much since we left here."

She caught his arm. "I am sure of it. And before the gods, I hope you're right."

The celebration raged on, ebbing and flowing around Kamehameha. He sat, separated from the king and his nobles. It was not his place to force himself upon them. Still, he was a king now. As much a king as Kaumualii. He felt sadness. This might be his last festival on this island as the princeling son of Kaumualii. There was already a difference in the way the others spoke to him, when they bothered to speak at all.

He sat apart, troubled, but at the same time bursting with a sense of anticipation. He began to plan how he would approach the soldiers who had fought with him against the Oahuans at Molokai. If they would agree to accompany him, he would pledge them wealth and land, something they did not have at Kauai and would never have. If these soldiers came with him, he would have the nucleus of the army he needed to make his dreams come true. He thought about Mauro, Wiari, and then his thoughts turned to the finest of them all—Mihuana.

He felt a strange tightness in his chest. His gaze moved across the feasting people, the dancers, the singers, all caught up in the spirit of the festival. He sought Mihuana. He remembered the young commoner's uncommon bravery, the cunning in dealing with captives, his cleverness as he had become a leader through sheer will and strength and intelligence.

His gaze found Mihuana seated with a group of nobles. His eyes widened. Mihuana was not alone. Close at his side sat Misau. Through Kamehameha's mind raced the promise he had made Mihuana. If he survived the battles, if he returned to Kauai . . .

He clenched his fists under his flowered robe. He had forgotten until now this alliance between his sister and the commoner. It was a terrible violation of tapus, and it was now being played out for all the world to see.

Sick at his stomach, he watched Mihuana bend over Misau, saw the way the girl smiled up at Mihuana and touched him.

A rage built up inside Kamehameha against the brazenness of the commoner. He quickly forgot Mihuana's bravery on the battlefield. He deplored the promise he had made the commoner. He had never intended for it to go this far. By all rights the man should be dead.

And yet, there he sat, with all the ease of a noble, his arm about the princess Misau.

Kamehameha felt a strange sense of terror surge through him. The veil of clouds had thickened over his head as the afternoon waned. He fought back the impulse to leap to his feet. But, he reminded himself, he needed self-control. He had given the commoner his word. As the music swelled about him, the feeling of terrible wrong increased and he sat sweating, dizzy, swearing to put an end to this evil alliance for once and for all.

BOOK TWO

Night Storm

Chapter XII

The main deck was lighted forward, the aft lay in heavy darkness, but halfway through the open hatches flashes of lamplight cut through the blackness. The decks had been swept down, the windlass oiled and painted as it must be daily in the tropics. Two ropes lay in long bights on the main decks. From where he stood amidship, he could see in the distance the brightly lighted *Discovery* traveling in the wake of the *Resolution*. Cutter Murphy cursed the ships, his own fate, the endless seas, the five or six knots these crafts traveled at their best speeds.

Around him, men pushed against one another. They talked desultorily. All they had to say had long been said. After months to-gether aboard ship, talk runs dry, and men begin to repeat themselves or to grow surly and silent. Hell, Cutter thought, days and nights begin to repeat themselves out here. How could he ever have thought to find his fortune wandering the dark and empty seas of this earth? Where was the excitement? The forgetfulness? The compensation? When he had been trapped in the bright, worldly parts of the globe, he had longed for the adventure, new experiences, the ex-citement of exotic places. But, it was all de-lusion. There was only boredom aboard ship; the waves are all alike, dreams be-come repetitious, and old longings take over again.

Damn! What was wrong with him? Why must every good thing be always just be-yond the next horizon, over a hill some-where, across a fence, a river, a world? Why, when he found a woman, must he tire so quickly of her? Each time, he believed, was real, forever. And each time he looked across her shoulder to see another pretty wench, with brighter hair, a wider smile, a deeper promise in her eyes. Would he waste his life yearning after the unobtainable? No. Somewhere he would find his dream. If only he knew for sure what it was!

Why did he feel that if he were forced to remain aboard this ship another hour, an-other day, he would go stark raving mad?

Thousands of men would gladly trade places with him, to be aboard the *Discovery*, or the *Resolution*, in the company of the great sea master Cook, exploring the unknown world. After these months of boredom, they could have it. It was a madman's mission with a captain who saw no farther than the end of his own nose. He smiled to himself. He was rather a self-centered, vainglorious soul himself.

He glanced at his reflection in the lighted window and grinned, shaking his head. He admitted he looked an ass in the uniform of Her Majesty's Navy. Every man jack did. Perhaps this was part of the plan for controlling the masses. Make the men look like asses, they will be less apt to rise against rotten food, stale water, injustice, and an officious, arbitrary power.

But despite the ludicrous cut of the uniform, he was still quite presentable. He had the dash, the élan, that the rest of this shabby crew lacked. Handsome men did have an easier time than ordinary souls. His height stared out at him from the weathered depths of the glass. The shoulders, so broad that they filled the entire glass, stretched the broadcloth of his jacket. The trousers fit him like his skin, and the linen waistcoat lay smooth and taut over his flat stomach. The silk stock was slightly askew, and he straightened it and then ran his fingers over his jawline. The sooty outlines of a beard were plainly visible on his olive skin, but the dark outlines would not be shaved away. As his fingers explored his jawline, he studied himself, quite satisfied with his own reflection if not with the uniform. His straight nose was a perfect line between jutting chin and high forehead. The gray eyes contrasted to the darkly olive skin; above them arched questioning brows. The navy had cut his hair and now it was slowly growing out. He was a savage, horny bastard, but women seemed to like him that way.

He watched the rise and fall of the ship, the jiggling of lanterns, heard the distant hum of voices, and shivered. Large lamps with huge reflectors that shed an intense hard glare were arranged on the deck. Watching, Cutter Murphy felt his heart sink. Gradually, the men gathered, all of them in their dress uniform of the day, all looking like asses.

Three wretched men in leg irons and arm shackles were brought up on deck. From where he stood, apart and detached from the main body of the men, Cutter studied the prisoners. Young Billy Hutch was lean and long-necked. His face showed his cold terror and something else that Cutter could interpret only as shame and anxiety. He was a street boy, his face precocious, knowing, and clever.

Charley Young was chained to Hutch.

Charley boasted he had sailed since the age of thirteen, with no more than a few months on land in the past fifteen years. He knew nothing of the life ashore; he cared even less. He stood, staring straight ahead, unmoved by the pomp that accompanied the arrival of the ship's officers.

The third felon, bound and shackled, was altogether different. Hugh Rice was a thin-necked, scrawny seaman who looked ill-dressed even in his best uniform. He kept his head lowered and stared down at the deck.

A drumroll announced the arrival of the captain. A small table had been set on the deck, covered with a cloth and furnished with a carafe of water and a large glass. The captain strode out to the table, followed by three senior officers who stood at attention while he settled himself in the pillowed chair.

Cutter sighed. He watched the great man seat himself, remove a kerchief from his cuff, and touch it to his nostrils, breathing deeply of the aromatic spirits secreted there. He guessed that to be treated like a god did spoil a man.

Captain James Cook was a man of medium height. He wore his brown hair long and caught in a tail at his collar. There was a quizzical look about his eyes. His mouth was full-lipped. His body was hard, even in the somewhat effeminate cut of his uniform. His voice was modulated, with a feigned Oxford accent that he never forgot even in moments of stress.

He'd been born in Marton-in-Cleveland, Yorkshire, October 27, 1728. At twenty-seven he had entered the navy, and from 1759 to 1767 was engaged in surveying the St. Lawrence River and the coast of Labrador and Newfoundland. The accuracy of the charts and the observations Cook made of this region brought him to the attention of the Royal Society of London, and it was there in London, it was whispered by his detractors, that his modulated tones and Oxford accent were born and flourished. In 1768 he was put in command of the *Endeavour Bark* and truly came into his own as a man of magnificence, power, and consequence. He was a popular as well as renowned hero of the realm. He was sought after by the reporters of the daily papers as well as by kings and princes. All of this had, perhaps understandably, gone to his head, and by the time he took over the *Resolution* and the *Discovery*, he was an arrogant, domineering, martinet as unyielding as his Oxford accent.

The captain waved his manicured hand in a tired, foppish gesture and the captain's mast began. A junior officer read from a paper. "Able Seaman Hugh Rice is charged with petty theft. It is alleged that Seaman Rice stole a sum of money, two pounds to be precise, from the ditty bag of Able Seaman Claude Hakim. The theft was witnessed by a third seaman who lay asleep in a nearby bunk during the commission of the crime. He awoke to find Able Seaman Rice rifling the belongings of Seaman Hakim. Rice stared at the third seaman, who pretended to be asleep. Seaman Rice then secreted the money and left the area. As soon as was safe, the witness reported to Seaman Hakim. Seaman Hakim then checked his belongings and, finding the two pounds missing, reported the theft to the officer of the day."

The captain cleared his throat and stared at Seaman Rice. "And what says the defendant? How do you plead?"

Rice's voice shook badly. "Not guilty, your lordship. Not guilty at all."

"And of the witness? What say you of him?"

Rice grimaced. "He says he were asleep, your lordship. That's the only thing I can figure what must have happened. He was asleep and he dreamed he saw me."

"And of Seaman Hakim's finding two pounds missing from his belongings?" the captain asked.

"I cannot understand it, sir. Perhaps he lost it. At cards. And then he forgot. All I know, sir, is that I am as innocent as a baby."

The captain peered at the accused sailor.

Sweat beaded his forehead and ran down along his cheeks. He stared straight ahead, his face ghastly white and pallid.

The captain smiled to himself and glanced across his shoulder at the senior officers and the scientists who accompanied them on this trip of exploration. He saw that they smiled, too, knowingly, waiting for him to dispense justice.

"I am sorry, Seaman—uh, Rice? Yes, Rice. Well, Seaman Rice, I am sorry to say that I simply do not believe your story. A story must have the ring of truth, eh? And there is no ring of truth to the tale you tell. I am convinced that the witness did indeed catch you in the act of theft."

"Oh, no, your lordship. I am innocent. I swear I am innocent."

"Well, we have the word of witnesses and the victim. We have no word on where you were during the commission of the crime. I regret, I must find you guilty and sentence you to two lashes of the cat-o'-nine-tails."

Hugh Rice opened his mouth to protest but was hauled away by two burly seamen. The junior officer waited until Charley Young was positioned before the table, then he began to read. "As of yesterday noon, after an exercise employing the heavy guns of the boat, it is charged that Seaman Charles Young did not lash down one of the cannons. Soon thereafter, a storm arose, with wind and high waves, causing the cannon to loose itself from its lashings and causing much damage aboard the ship in its area before it was recovered and its lashings secured. It must be reported that Seaman Young worked very hard recovering the loose gun. But it was proved beyond a shadow of doubt that the seaman also had forgotten to secure the cannon after the gunnery exercises."

Captain Cook gazed at Charley Young. "How could a seaman forget to lash down heavy artillery?"

There was the clatter of metal as Charley Young tried to spread his shackled hands.

"We was rushed, your lordship. We was moved from the exercise with the guns to a disaster drill. In the rush to get to the drill, I must have forgotten the lashings. That is all I can say. I must have forgot."

"Well, it is refreshing at least to hear a man admit his crime." The captain nodded, looking pleased. "And it is to your credit also that you worked very hard in recovering the loose cannon."

"I did, sir. Very hard. The winds was high and the waves mighty. The gun was loose and dangerous, but I knowed what must be done and I did it."

"Very commendable," Captain Cook said. "I am sure your heroics match your negligence. However, you will agree, it is negligence that we are confronted with here."

"Aye, sir." Charley Young lowered his head.

"I sentence you to two lashes with the cat-o'-nine-tails," the captain said. "At the same time, I order a senior officer of your deck to write you a commendation to be placed in your jacket for your heroism in recovering the loose weapon."

Charley Young's eyes filled with tears. He nodded his head. "I thank you most deeply, sir."

The captain waved his hand and Charley Young was led away. Into his place was brought the fourteen-year-old Billy Hutch. Billy looked ill as the officer began to read the charges against him. "This is cabin boy Billy Hutch. He was caught amidships, hiding, and in the act of masturbation."

The captain looked along his nose at the cabin boy. His mouth twisted with distaste and disdain. He wiped his hand across his mouth and smelled once more the scented kerchief at his cuff.

At long last the captain spoke. "There is one way to undermine the very spirit and morale of a ship," he said, gazing along his nose at the miserable boy. "That is in the act of hidden, forbidden sexual acts. The lowest of these, I declare to be the act of masturbation. Nothing else so turns the soul inward, dirties the mind, and soils the body of the perpetrator. Nothing else is surer to weaken the mind and sap the strength of the poor wretch who succumbs to the ugly temptation. It is the one act, the crime against nature, if you will, which I refuse to tolerate aboard the ships of my command. I find the practice filthy, deplorable, unsavory, offensive, and disgusting. I command the perpetrator be punished by five lashes of the cat-o'-nine-tails. Take him away. I do not wish to hear him speak in my presence."

Cutter stared at the captain. This confirmed what he had believed for months and made him more eager than ever to escape this floating hotbed of hypocrisy and pretense.

The boy Billy Hutch was borne away by seamen and put in the brig, still in chains. His sobbing and howling could be heard far into the night.

Chapter XIII

Cutter Murphy had never been a man to endure boredom or hypocrisy. Face life and accept it, warts and all, this was his philosophy. Orphaned at an early age, he had escaped this life as quickly as possible. He had realized early that as an illiterate street child he would be doomed to misery. So he had learned to read and write. He read every book, including the Bible, that he could get his hands on. Reading had opened up the world for him, set him apart from those around him. Then he began to steal for food and shelter and for the thrill of it. It was as a cutpurse that he had won the name Cutter.

It was rough, a dangerous way of life, and

he stayed just ahead of the law. But he began to eat well. His reading opened up the world of the upper classes to him. And he began to open up his operations. He needed more money. A man who wanted a nice hat, a soft shirt, and a clean jacket needed extra money. He looked around and found it. Dressed well, he presented a totally false picture. A young man on his way up. A new class of people spoke to him, accepted him, and suffered for it.

He was an enigma to those he met in the strictly stratified English society. He learned to speak properly. The "bow bells" accent receded and was replaced by what one young girl called the "international." He was kind to her. When he left her, he took only the money in her purse, money hard won on the streets of the Strand, St. Paul's, and Oxford Street.

He had let the city swallow him up more than once.

One day he'd met an elegant lady obviously drunk and in trouble. He had bowed to her and offered his services. Beyond belief, she had accepted. He hailed a cab and was soon in her home. By morning she had declared her eternal devotion to him, and before the week was out she was clinging to him, begging him never to leave her and promising to settle half her estate upon him. But she was usually under the influence of alcohol. By day—by night—on every public occasion, she wore a necklace of matching pearls. He became mesmerized by the beauty and perfection of that necklace. At last, overcome with greed, Cutter removed the necklace one night when she passed out in his arms, and then walked out of her life, disappearing into the city.

Sometimes he missed Kitty. She was a voracious lover, a generous and at times elegant lady. But he lived well for over a year on the proceeds from her necklace and even finally stopped looking over his shoulder for her.

So free once more, he searched for that ideal place he sought so fiercely.

Now, on the eve of his twenty-second birthday, he paced his small rented room, watched the drizzle outside, and knew there had to be more to life. Nothing he had yet done pleased him; no woman he had yet met held any lasting charm for him. Somewhere things had to be better. There was talk of the possibilities open to a young and ambitious man in the new world. But the colonies offered no lure at all for him. He saw the insurrection against the king in America as a battle perpetrated by men who meant to gather unto themselves the immense profits and untold wealth of the new world. Why share these riches with the mother country? Why not rise up and take control, give it all the name of a war for freedom? Freedom from what? Three thousand miles from England, the colonists enjoyed all the blessings of freedom known to man, except the gratification of greed. This greed was something that Cutter Murphy understood. It was just the hypocrisy behind it all that angered him.

In the past year he had gravitated to the theater. In the Strand he mingled with actors, got to know them, to speak their own peculiar language. Before too long, thanks to admiring men and succulent ladies, he was playing small roles on the stage. His good looks attracted the audiences, who hardly seemed to notice that as an actor he was barely adequate.

He remained in the theater because it offered an opportunity to meet rich women. As long as the looks held out and he kept his natural charm and élan, there would always be women eager to make his acquaintance and to pay for his favors. Bags under the eyes, a second chin, a paunch, and it would all be over.

His latest conquest was Lady Mary Wexford. She was a svelte and lovely woman with a penchant for handsome young men. She met Cutter at a theater party and she opened an entirely new world for him.

Cutter used his acquaintance with Lady Mary as a key to the locks of a dozen upper-crust boudoirs. He stayed three steps ahead of the law, two steps ahead of jealous husbands, and always one step ahead of violent death.

He began to blackmail the wives of nobles. He cheated and defrauded people who were so taken by him they had difficulty in accepting that he was the culprit.

At a party hostessed by Lady Wexford, he met a small, stiffly formal man introduced as the Earl of Sandwich. Cutter was impressed by his rank and the earl, being deeply and at once intrigued by Cutter's male beauty, proved easy to know. The group around the earl was full of charm and excitement, and Cutter decided that theirs was a life that might in the long run prove satisfying to him.

Then, to complicate matters, Cutter met Lady Esther Sanford, and for weeks he lived under the delusion that at last he had fallen truly and faithfully in love. The seduction had proved to be deceptively simple. One might even look back and decide she had determined all the moves in advance.

With Esther, it was as simple as going to the apartment in the drafty Sandwich castle where she resided and knocking on the door. She answered herself, almost as if she had been awaiting him, though they had never exchanged a word. She wore a long velvet robe, and as far as he could see, nothing under it except her underclothing. She was perfectly at ease.

There followed, of course, his carefully rehearsed speech about how he had dreamed of nothing but her delicate beauty since the first moment he saw her. Her cheeks colored delicately, but she said nothing. His carefully rehearsed speech at an end, he was forced to improvise. The unhappiest man of all, he told her, is he who loves and is loved not in return. All this time he was moving nearer to her, finally laying one trembling hand upon her shoulder, lightly, so that his intent be not misinterpreted. She allowed his hand to remain on her shoulder, her eyes held his, but still she said nothing. He sought for something new and fresh—and even honest—to say, because suddenly he truly wanted her as he had never wanted any other woman.

She came toward him slowly and tantalizingly, and his hand slid up her neck into the rich texture of her hair. Gently he pulled her head over until her cheek rested upon his shoulder. Her violet eyes remained open and she watched him solemnly in a manner that unnerved but did not stop him. He was truly roused by her nearness, her beauty, and the enticing way her robe fell open at the waist. His hands moved to the soft, warm skin beneath.

When his hand covered her full, high-standing breast, she pulled away slightly, catching her breath. He had never encountered a lovelier bosom in all of London. She shuddered slightly and sank against him, her arms at her sides, her eyes closed at last. His other hand reached down and covered hers in her lap, drawing one of them to him. Her fingers, led by his own, started to explore beneath the loosened buttons of his breeches. It was as if some fantasy had been unleashed and she found what she sought. With each stroke she made it harder. Finally she sank upon him, sobbing out her delight. At first Cutter tried to hold her back, but finally gave over as her lips caught at his. The conquest was complete. She nuzzled her body closer to his as he removed first her robe and then her underthings.

He swung her up in his arms and started toward the bedroom. But then something caught his eye and he stopped, standing tall, with her naked body in his arms, staring toward the door he had entered and closed behind him only a short time before.

It stood open. He gazed at it, his mouth wide, his heart sinking into his boots. She followed the direction of his gaze and caught her breath.

"My God," he said. "Didn't you lock your door?"

"I never thought of it," she whispered. "I thought you had."

"Who could have opened it?" he asked. "Perhaps a servant. No? Wouldn't anyone else have knocked?"

She shivered in his arms. "Perhaps whoever it was did knock," she said. "I would
not have heard them at all. Would you?"

Feeling ill, he had to admit he had heard
nothing but the rush of blood to his temples. Who in God's name had caught them?

Chapter XIV

Cutter rearranged his clothing and returned to his own quarters. He found the corridors strangely silent and empty. The very atmosphere had changed. Someone had seen them, and had silently withdrawn. Who? And what was to happen now?

He stayed in his room the rest of the afternoon, having no wish to meet anyone. He began to be angry. Dammit, anyone who walked into a closed room without knocking—or even upon knocking when that knocking went unanswered—deserved what he got. If he saw something scandalous, so be it. It should end there. But he knew better.

When a servant knocked discreetly upon

his door and announced that dinner was served, Cutter realized he was ravenously hungry. He shaved quickly, donned a fresh shirt and stock, and walked out into the large main dining room where all the guests were gathered around the table.

He saw Lady Esther far down the table from him. Her face was wan and pallid, she kept her purple eyes lowered, but she had dressed carefully and rather daringly. He was certain that whoever had seen them had not yet confronted her ladyship. He sighed. Perhaps they would not.

Dinner ended at last. The guests moved to the main hall for games, dancing, and music. Lady Esther retired early, claiming a headache, and soon after, Cutter left too.

When he returned to his room Cutter found his servant missing. In his place were two imposing six-foot-tall men looking ludicrous in servants' livery. One had a smashed nose, part of his right eyebrow was missing, and one eye was half closed. The other was dark, his cheek scarred, his shoulders massive in the ill-fitting uniform. Surprisingly, they were polite and solicitous, and seemed to know about the art of the valet. They did the best they could to make Cutter comfortable. But they made one thing clear: He was a prisoner in the earl's castle.

The next morning the servants were cordial and helped Cutter dress. He found the

Earl of Sandwich at breakfast with a large entourage. The earl was most friendly and courteous, introducing Cutter around among the scientists and seamen gathered at table. One of the names Cutter heard was that of Captain Cook.

The earl was occupied with the seamen and scientists most of the day. Something of great moment was being hatched, Cutter realized.

That afternoon he found in his room an envelope addressed to him. At first his heart leapt when he thought it might be Lady Esther writing to him. The note was brief and to the point. He was asked to call in the apartment of Lord Sanford at two. He glanced at the clock across the room and found it already ten past that hour.

He crushed the letter in his fist, tossed it upon the floor, and hurried along the corridor to Lord Sanford's apartment. He paused outside the door before knocking. He had no idea what Lord Sanford would say. The tone and terseness of the letter assured him that the meeting would be less than cordial. Still, he was free and twenty-two, and if he wanted to enter a lady's apartment and she welcomed him in, it seemed no one's business but their own.

He looked down at his varnished boots on the dull carpeting of the hallway. From far along it he heard the sounds of music and of someone's seductive laughter. When he rapped on the door he could hear movement inside the room, and despite all he had told himself, he regretted that he had involved Lady Esther in a scandalous situation.

The door opened slowly, enough to disclose a very tall, very gray, and very rigid man, his aging face topped by thick gray hair, his eyes a steely blue, his mouth lined and obdurate. The figure bowed slightly. It was on Cutter's tongue to apologize for the fact that he was a quarter of an hour late, but he said nothing. He stepped into the room. It was strange to find any man, an aging man at that, towering above him as Lord Sanford did.

"Mr. Murphy, I believe?" The lord's voice was deep, modulated, and strong.

"Yes. I am Cutter Murphy, sir. And you?"

"I am Lord Sanford," said the deep, cold voice.

Cutter Murphy walked into the well-furnished room; a fire blazed at a distant hearth. Cutter saw a small, indeterminate-looking man seated in a chair near the fire. This individual looked to belong to the class of society that claimed Cutter Murphy, and Cutter smiled faintly in recognition. Both of them were out of place in this sumptuous setting. The little man did not meet his glance, but, looking at him, Cutter felt a chill of foreboding in the warm room.

"Why don't you sit down over here, Mr.

Murphy?" Lord Sanford swung his arm, indicating one of the chairs placed near the fireplace.

Cutter shrugged and walked ahead of the soldierly old man to one of the wing chairs. He sat down and waited until the other man seated himself, stretching his long legs toward the fire. The firelight glowed and crackled. Cutter sat silently, awaiting the older man's pleasure.

At last Lord Sanford seemed to become aware of the third man in the room. He shifted his gaze to him, obviously finding what he saw little more to his taste than looking at Cutter Murphy.

Cutter shifted his own gaze to the man in the cheap clothing. His eyes were like a spaniel's, unhappy, darting around the room and settling nowhere.

"This is Mr. Emlyn Astor," Lord Sanford said, his mouth pulling just slightly when he spoke the man's name. "He investigates things for me."

"Mr. Astor is a private inspector," Lord Sanford said.

Cutter felt his heart slip its moorings. He drew a deep breath and shrugged again. Whatever Astor had to say, it could hardly come as a surprise to Cutter.

"Would you care to begin?" Lord Sanford inquired in that mild, cold tone.

"Yes, sir." Emlyn Astor glanced up at Cutter for a long moment with a look almost of apology in his spaniel eyes. He adjusted his glasses and glanced at a piece of paper in his lap.

As he began to read, Cutter felt his face flush, his hands sweat. He named the street in which Cutter Murphy first saw light of day, told of the years as an orphan, the bitterly hungry teen years and his first crimes, the stealing of food and clothing, the fight for a warm place to sleep at night.

Then the report became more interesting. It revealed secret, long-forgotten crimes that Cutter had believed were known only to God and himself. When he came to the sale of Kitty Frothingham's pearl necklace, Cutter sighed heavily. This ugly little man had penetrated every cranny of his life, coming up with details that, spread over the years, seemed not too sordid, but that, enumerated like a laundry list, provided a damning document.

At last Mr. Astor stopped reading. It grew very quiet in the room. The ticking of the great clock, the rattling of logs on the fire, were the loudest sounds. Finally, Lord Sanford stood up to his full height. He stared down, unforgiving, upon Cutter Murphy. "Thank you, Mr. Astor. I am sure your report is quite full and final. I am also sure there are as many crimes unreported there as made your listing."

"I done me work very carefully," Astor said in his own defense.

"Oh, I'm sure you did, and I am also certain that you worked diligently. For that I thank you, and you certainly shall be fittingly rewarded."

Lord Sanford drew a deep breath and addressed Cutter Murphy again. "And now, sir, if I may, I would like to inquire about your intentions toward my daughter, Lady Esther. What were your plans with this innocent girl, eh? Blackmail? Blackmail has certainly been part of your style in the past. Or perhaps robbery? Whatever it is, I want you to know I am onto your villainy. And I shall not endure a moment longer of your presence."

"I don't suppose it would help to say I regret deeply that I have hurt her ladyship. This was my last intention on this earth."

"Well, that's a nice speech, but I'm afraid it doesn't mean much when one thinks of all your crimes. I could have you arrested, dragged in disgrace from this place, and if you attempt even to see my daughter one more time, I shall do that. Is that clear?"

Dismally, Cutter Murphy walked down the corridor to his own room. The two stalwart servants greeted him there. He looked at them and shrugged. "If you will be kind enough to pack my things," he said. "I am leaving."

One of the servants merely smiled. "I am sorry, sir. We will have to check with the earl before we can help you leave."

One of the servants returned. "The earl wants to see you, Mr. Murphy. Now. If you please."

Both servants accompanied Cutter to the library. As soon as the door closed behind him, Cutter saw that he and the earl were not alone. His heart sank. Lord Sanford stood smoking a pipe and staring at Cutter coolly.

It was some moments before what the earl was saying was clear to Cutter. Captain James Cook was making an expedition, seeking a northern passage to America in the Pacific Ocean. Cutter wondered what this had to do with him, but he listened in pained silence.

"There has been some unpleasantness," the earl said. "But I myself have always found you to be a good person, handsome and personable. What your background is is of little interest to me. I congratulate you for what you have made of yourself. I regret deeply that you have deflowered a young woman of the upper class. I am afraid you have forever stigmatized her. Her father would denounce you to my guests, and, if possible, cause your arrest for past crimes. But your culpability as far as I see it lies only in your misbehavior behind an unlocked door. And as I have suggested to Lord Sanford, it takes two to fraternize. This wounds my old friend deeply, and I am sorry to have to say it. I am convinced that Lady Esther welcomed you into her chamber, and your greatest crime was forgetting to lock a door."

"Unspeakable," Lord Sanford said. "I find his conduct unspeakable."

"I am sure you do, your lordship," the earl said. "That is why my solution seems the ideal one. It quiets the scandal. And if the word gets out, there will even be talk that the tryst was merely a sweet farewell. Surely this will satisfy all your claims, Lord Sanford?"

His lordship managed to nod his head stiffly, agreeing but with bad humor. The earl smiled. "Good. It is settled, then. Young Murphy will leave today to join the Cook expeditions, which I am sponsoring. I have arranged a commission as midshipman. I wish you well, and I hope the time at sea will straighten you out and that you will return a stronger person."

Another era in Cutter Murphy's life had come to an abrupt close.

Cutter Murphy decided the excitement and delight he looked for in life would come to him aboard ship, at sea. But this proved another dead-end dream.

Cutter's devil-may-care attitude was foreign to everything in this run-by-the-numbers ship. He was forever running athwart the rules and regulations. He slept too late, falling to sleep late, lulled by the pound of waves against the plankings of the hull. He had collected more than his share of despised demerits.

The ships moved slowly upon an unchanging sea; life was cramped and stifling aboard ship. He was as far as ever from his dream. He began to doubt it even existed. Perhaps there was no place on earth for him. One thing was certain. It was not here in the Pacific, aboard Captain Cook's ship.

Chapter XV

A wondrous stillness spread across the ocean; moonlight glistened on the water like tiny alluring diamonds. The moon rose high above the evening star on the dark horizon. The Pacific rolled easily. The wind snapped in the sails as though they'd become part of this strange, eerie night. The *Discovery* plowed through gray swells, leaving a white wake in its path.

Cutter, remaining on the bridge after the prisoners had been hauled away to await their punishment, was struck by the unknown into which they sailed. Few white men had preceded them. The only maps were Spanish, poorly drawn and uncertain. It was this aspect of the voyage that held him in thrall. He paced, staring at that unreachable horizon, sighed, and moved with the stream of the ship's officers toward the captain's quarters.

Cutter was the last to arrive, the most junior officer aboard, the most reluctant guest. Captain Cook never tired of these "parties," as he called them.

Night after night the martinet gathered together his captive audience, his officers, scientists, and even Malu, the Malayan interpreter, around his table. His orderlies served tea and scones, and the captain continued the saga about his favorite subject—himself. He praised himself to the skies in Oxonian accents, as if he were speaking of some absent third person.

Cutter had heard all the stories of the voyages and discoveries of Captain Cook at least a half-dozen times before and scarcely listened anymore. He had learned to nod in his canvas-back chair at the far end of the table, sinking into an open-eyed sleep, allowing the captain's voice to become a meaningless drone. He kept a smile of admiring wonder pasted on his face. It was this look the captain wanted to see, especially on the face of the London *Times* reporter who sat near him, pad in hand, glowing with anticipation.

If ever one of the famous scientists accompanying the captain were permitted to speak, to tell of *his* accomplishments, Cutter might have looked with greater favor upon these nightly affairs. But it was as if only Cook had experienced the wondrous, the marvelous, and the unknown. The captain kept repeating the same stories, adding and embellishing them as he went.

Cutter looked about at the other faces and found none as bored as his own. No one appeared to share his boredom at another retelling of the exploits of the famous Captain Cook.

Captain Cook sat at the head of the table in a comfortable chair with a high back. He leaned forward, filled with excitement, flushed with the need to speak of his exploits, to watch them being transcribed. He instructed a yeoman to transcribe his monologues so that nothing of his great accomplishments be lost. One day, he knew, it would be a story to thrill the world, as the telling thrilled him. He spoke solemnly and slowly, giving the yeoman plenty of time to transcribe what he said, making the telling interminable.

Cutter was rudely awakened by the applause that arose at the most appropriate times in Cook's soliloquy. It had all become as formalized as an opera at West End. Cook reached a certain point in his narrative and, from old habit, paused for applause. Cutter sweated. Oh, God, deliver him.

But there was no delivery. The captain's

voice began again, sonorously retelling of his Australian discoveries.

Finally Cook sat back and smiled. The men all spoke admiringly of his adventures and got up to take their leave, it being well past ten o'clock.

Cutter Murphy managed to leap up with the rest, yawning and shaking himself. He realized he had been fast asleep and snoring quietly in his chair.

Chapter XVI

Next morning, at daybreak, the bugler sounded reveille and Cutter got up unwillingly from his hammock in the small cabin he shared with Lieutenant j. g. Calder Dawkins.

It was beyond his comprehension why a day had to begin so damned early. Where was anyone going? What was there to do? By the time he had attended to his toilet, dressed, and come up on deck, the sun was truly up, but lost in thick clouds along the horizon.

There was a strange and unnatural silence that settled over water and ship. Cutter strode along the deck, aware of the silences. Nobody talked but everyone was aware of the eerie cast of the sky.

Cutter had no particular duties. He had long ago learned that all he had to do was to look busy, to stay out of the way and yet to be available when someone needed him. He watched the seamen for a while, struggling with the ropes, swabbing down the deck, clambering up the rigging.

The sun soon took on a brassy cast. As far as the eye could see, the sea lay stunned with bright sunlight. But the stillness was an ominous kind. Men who knew the sea said it looked like the beginnings of a storm. And yet the sea lay as calm as a pond, and as silvery bright as a polished floor.

The three prisoners were brought amidships, still shackled. Cutter moved forward to watch the barbaric rite. Captain Cook, his guests, and senior officers gathered on the bridge to stare down at the solemn and formalized ceremony.

Two drummers stood to one side. At a signal from the captain they began a solemn tattoo. The first of the three miscreants was led forward to a tripod with ropes dangling from its apex. Hugh Rice, the thief, was the first to be lashed. He was secured by the ropes, and he hung there, resigned and silent.

The sailor wielding the lash was a big man with rippling muscles. His head was round and bearded. He, like his victim, was bare to the belt. The cat-o'-nine-tails looked almost small and inoffensive in his large hands.

The thief was asked if he had anything to say. He merely shook his head and repeated his innocence. The captain waved his hand like a decadent Roman emperor, to signal the beginning of the games.

The whipper drew back his arm and brought the nine knotted cords across the bared back of Hugh Rice. The man cried out, but the second one came so quickly that it was over before the poor devil could scream again.

Hugh Rice was lowered and half carried to where a doctor awaited with soothing ointment and water.

Charley Young was stoic. Across his bared back were the faint scars of previous beatings. He had been at sea since his thirteenth summer. The whipper lashed his glistening back and it was quickly over.

Cutter winced, watching the cabin boy being strung up to the tripod. His bare back was very white, as if he never allowed the sun on his bare skin. His head hung loosely between his shoulders; he stared at the deck. His wrists were secured and he hung, scarcely breathing. He wore cut-off trousers, and deck shoes. Otherwise he was nude.

A shadow raced across the ship. The sun was lost behind a gathering of storm clouds.

In the sudden chill of the moment, with the breeze rising and the sun gone, Cutter shivered.

The cat-o'-nine-tails cracked across the boy's back. It seemed to Cutter that the man was using excessive strength.

The boy was spun around by the force of the blow. As Cutter watched he saw a flush of excitement in the boy's face as the whip landed. An erection became clearly visible in his cut-off trousers.

Sick at heart, Cutter watched the second blow. The boy staggered but did not cry out. Cutter looked around to see if anyone else noticed the boy's obvious arousal. The ship's company, the senior officers, and the guests all watched, transfixed.

The lash fell the third time. The boy's back was already deeply cut and bleeding. He had accepted the first two lashes silently, but with the third lashing he became a howling madman, involuntarily bucking at the hips.

The fourth lash fell. The blood spurted. The boy continued to writhe and work his hips. His mouth was wide open and he was making mewling, unintelligible sounds, but the look on his face had nothing to do with physical pain.

The fifth lash either caused his ejaculation or coincided with it. The boy swung there on the tripod, blood flowing down his back and semen staining his pants. The watching seamen began to howl with laughter, slapping at each other. Some of the guests on the upper deck had turned away. Only Captain Cook remained immobile, staring down as the boy was untied and removed.

Cutter stood and stared up at the face of the ship's captain.

What a strange and hypocritical world. One would have thought this was a ship of saints, not a craft bearing a complement of men diseased with syphilis and gonorrhea, with minds trapped forever in the gutters.

He walked over to where the cabin boy's savagely cut back was being treated. The cuts were deep; there would be weals when this beating healed. The boy sat, red-faced, confused, and eager to escape the ministrations of the young ship's doctor. The doctor was kindly enough. He spoke in soft tones to the boy, but Billy Hutch answered in monosyllables, keeping his face averted.

He muttered something about "a drink of water," and was given a cup. He gulped the water down quickly, looking at nobody.

Finally, the boy was released and he slipped away quickly and quietly. Cutter stood for a long time looking up at the captain, who still stared down at the tripod.

"I wonder if he doesn't wish now he had ordered ten lashes of the whip?" Cutter said to himself.

But the young doctor overheard him. He

smiled in a sympathetic manner and said, "I think five is the maximum for that particular crime. It was a good show, though. A good brutal show."

"I suppose that is all that matters." Cutter turned and walked away.

He went below decks, down into the dark bowels of the ship. The smells of humanity, unwashed and unrepentant, hung in the humid air, and Cutter began to long for a breath of fresh air. Smells of oily food cooking, of soiled underwear, of unwashed bodies—the odors were too strong ever to dissipate.

He was not surprised to find himself standing beside Billy Hutch's hammock. The other hammocks had been stowed for the day; the chests were all closed. Except for the overpowering smell, the place was bearable. Billy Hutch lay sprawled on his hammock, his bare back turned to catch any breezes from the portholes, but there was no relief from heat and stink.

Cutter had no idea what he might say to the boy. What was there to say? Yet, the boy was so alone, so forlorn.

He spoke softly. "How are you, son?" He knew it was a stupid question, but it was as good as anything.

The boy lifted his head. "Oh, it's you, sir. You've always been most kind." He looked away again. "I'm all right," he said finally. "Though it will be hard to face the others."

"Why? What happened to you was not that terrible." Cutter forced himself to laugh. "Listen to me. If they flogged every grown man who reached that moment of unbearable desire and who pounded his meat secretly, most of the men aboard this ship would look worse than you."

The boy turned slowly. "But I am disgraced. I even got hard when they whipped me. Do you think there was a man in the ship's company who did not see? Oh, my God ... I—ejaculated when they whipped me. Every man aboard knows about me now. And plenty of them will be after me. Men who treated me decently before will be trying to get me alone."

"My God. That's just your imagination. At least I hope it is. If you will report to me any man who makes overtures to you, I'll put him on report."

"Then my life would be worth less than a farthing."

Cutter sighed. "Well, there must be something you can do. A man's body is his own to give or keep at his own will."

The cabin boy shook his head. "Not aboard this ship, it ain't, sir. . . . But that don't matter as much as the fact that I am a terrible sinner. I dream of nothing but sex. I am alone for a few minutes and these images flood into my mind and my rod comes up."

"There's nothing wrong with that, either," Cutter said. "A lot more men than will admit to it spend their daydreams on erotic images. I might have been as bad off as you if I were in this unnatural world. Luckily, I could always find a woman when I felt horns rising."

The boy could not be comforted. "But I am a sinner. My minister warned me about this sinfulness," Billy whispered, his face white and drawn. He shivered, clenching his fists at his sides. "I have let myself be mastered by the devil, by passions unworthy of a self-respecting man."

"You are just a human being. Unlike the animals, you have been blessed with an imagination, and that is your undoing." Cutter smiled. "You must put all that has happened behind you," Cutter advised.

The boy hung his head. "Do you think that will be easy, aboard this ship, with the men knowing what they know about me?"

Cutter shrugged. "Perhaps not. But remember, you are as much a man as any of them. Maybe even more."

The boy shook his head. His despair was so profound he believed suicide the only way out. He shrank from the act, but at the thought of the days ahead aboard a ship where everybody knew his shameful secret . . .

"I hate this ship," he whispered. "Do you have any idea how much I hate it?"

Cutter smiled. "As much as I do?"

"More. It has become a waking hell for me. I wake up in the middle of the night with this horrible urge rousing me and afraid some of the other men in the other hammocks may be light sleepers. They might catch me—and I'd be beaten again. I can't stand that again. My back is afire, my mind is burning, and yet I remain the same sinner as before, with the same wicked thoughts."

"Jesus," Cutter said. "Just be careful."

"How easy is it to be careful when you are as God made you? Does anybody consider that? I am God's creation. If he made me like this, what in hell can I do about it?"

"Not much, I'm afraid. Just be careful not to be caught."

"And then there's them that don't want me beat. They would like to use me, like a woman. . . ." He took a deep breath, staring up into Cutter's face for some moments, seeking a faith, a trust. "There is one man, a mate, who would ride me night and day if he got the chance. It was him who got me when I first come aboard. He grabbed me and I didn't even know what he wanted of me.

"He sodomized me that first day. It was up there amidships, in a dark corner. I resisted, but it was no good. He was so much bigger, so much stronger, and he knew what he wanted. He boogered me. It was the first time I'd ever heard of such a thing. It was like lightning had struck me. I cried out. I screamed for help, but no one came, no one seemed to hear. Then, when I slipped back up into this same safe spot, where no one overheard or bothered to come near when I screamed, I was caught with my pecker in my fist, whipping it—and I was whipped and laughed at. I can't stand this . . . I can't stand it anymore."

Cutter sighed. "I am sorry," he said. There seemed to be more he should say and yet nothing seemed appropriate. He walked away, empty and sick at heart, longing once more for some way out of this hell in which he found himself.

Chapter XVII

Two days later Cutter Murphy strolled the decks with a growing sense of unease. It was a cloudy day, overcast, with the darker depths of the ocean flecked with whitecaps and a rising wind that snapped the sails. The waves began to roll. Cutter heard the older seamen talking. One had been in a monsoon in the Indian Ocean that had sneaked up exactly like this, a terrible looming quiet before a crackling storm. "You can bet on it," the seaman said, nodding his head. "I'se seen it too many times to be fooled. We're in for a washer, I can guarantee."

Cutter watched the storm approach. Suddenly the ship came alive as men from every watch were pressed into service, preparing for the worst. Everything was battened down and the orders given to furl the sails. Cutter donned his oilskin jacket and stood in the protection of the poop deck, watching the wild activity fore and aft.

The sun, which had ridden all day under a heavy blanket of cloud cover, now disappeared completely, and, the world darkened, the horizon was suddenly cut off from view. An immense ripple quivered over the sea, as if the waters themselves trembled under the sudden plummeting of the barometer.

When the sun failed, the icy south wind rose. Black oilskin coats appeared everywhere as the watches all turned out to secure the ship against what was being called "the coming typhoon." The cold struck the men through their jackets; their teeth chattered as they cursed between blue lips. The men's hands were soon numb. They crawled like insects across the deck against the raging wind.

The *Resolution* ran from the oncoming typhoon, but the first battering showers soon overtook the men.

Hatches were closed and secured. Washboards were fit to cabin doors. Anxious eyes watched the approaching black clouds enveloping them as they bore down. The ship dipped into the swells, and the sky above disappeared from sight. The *Resolution* drove forward, trying valiantly to fight her way through the growing waves and steadily losing ground. Suddenly she listed at a dangerous angle, and while every man jack grabbed at something secure, slowly righted herself in the deepening trough of waves. She shuddered as if in pain, and wallowed helplessly from side to side in the growing seas. Rain beat down mercilessly, blinding the men on deck.

The *Discovery* was soon lost in the darkness and the first rocket was fired. The men watched the flare, weak against the driving rain, and waited for an answer. Eyes and spyglasses were turned in every direction. Finally, the sister ship answered from a vast distance away across an impassable, churning sea.

The wind screamed in from the gray and empty void. The men on deck watch crouched in corners, clinging to the ship against the fury of the sea. The officers grasped the weather railing grimly, bent forward in their long coats. Waves pounded and shook the hull, like some monstrous animal. The wind rose until its howl was deafening, driving the stinging rain.

The seamen went swinging from brace to brace along the decks. The decks were already partly submerged by waves washing across them. The men were driven to their knees. Fountains of gray spume roared over their heads. They felt the ropes strain and they hung on, reaching forward to grab at a cleat or a stanchion.

When the ship swung upward, clearing the tip of the wave for a moment, the wind caught the men cleanly and tossed them around like pieces of flotsam. The slow backwash of the waves seethed around their feet. They moved on, forgetting where they were going or what they were doing, except that they were hanging on, gray-knuckled, for dear life. A lurch of the ship could send them overboard. They clutched at railings, feeling the hull quiver under them.

They cursed and had little hope that the ship was strong enough to ride out the typhoon. They made things fast and saw them ripped out and spun away, never to be seen again. It was as if the sea were in a rage to tear the vessel apart.

The seamen raced across the decks as the ship leapt and swerved. They hung on to the rails, clambered over anchor chains, embraced the forecapstan. They waved their arms helplessly, knelt against the force of the gale, and then sprawled flat, facedown as waves washed over them and threatened to carry them overboard.

Finally the sails were furled and a shout of joy went up. It was a superhuman accomplishment against wind and rain. The masts stood like giant poles reaching toward the sky. The wind whipped the dangling lines. At an order from the captain bellowed by a mate on the middecks, the men tied ropes about their waists and, thus secured to the ship, they fought the rising waves.

The hauling and tightening went on interminably. There was always one more chore to accomplish, one job undone by the raging of the storm. In the wild scramble the men hauled on ropes and fought against the pull of waves, by now breaking five feet over their heads. Occasionally a man would pause, sometimes on his knees, marvel at the fury of the storm, and pray, too, that the ship would weather it.

The *Resolution* rode unsteadily, as tired and dispirited as the men aboard her. The waves were higher than hills, the little ship smaller than ever against this terrible fury. They were surrounded by walls of water, rising, breaking across the decks, and pounding at the hull. The men swore another wave like that and it was all over for the *Resolution*.

"She was never built for a run like this," a seaman declared. "She was built in the yards of England, in a civilized world, where nothing like this is even imagined."

The captain stood on the bridge in his long coat, the faint light of a lantern swinging beside him, feeble against the storm. He was now secured with ropes to keep him upright in the yawing and pitching of the ship. Once again he ordered a flare sent up to alert the *Discovery* as to their position.

All hands watched the rocket rise, burst open, and die in the wind. They waited with bated breath for the answering flare that would mean the *Discovery* was still afloat. It took forever coming, and when it rocketed up into the pelting rain it shone far to the starboard, far off course, its distant glow disheartening.

Flares were sent up every hour during the night, though there was nothing the sister ship could do except answer as it drifted farther away.

"We must keep in touch," the captain insisted as the ship trembled upward on a massive wave, lurched head-on into it, then side-slipped and fell back in an avalanche of pounding water. She came around with a sudden violent jerk to windward, as if breaking loose from the terrible hold of the storm. There were loud wrenching sounds as if the ship were breaking up. Water thundered against the iron portholes like an uncontrollable waterfall. She tossed violently, quivered, and slowly righted in time to be taken over again on her side. Lifted by a towering wave, the ship rode its crest for what seemed an eternity, teetering and then falling, slipping into a dark and bottomless trough.

The men still on forward deck were beaten and pummeled by the raging waves, but it was too dangerous to loose themselves from the ropes and make a run for a closed hatch. One man attempted to make the break, though his mates screamed out to warn him. He was caught and washed hard against the railing, where he hung helplessly, screaming for assistance.

Cursing him for being every kind of stupid ass, two other men inched toward him as the ship climbed another incredible wave. They made it just as the water began to spill across the deck and grasped him by the wrists and legs, clinging together as the wave washed over them. The poor man was secured in his line again and thoroughly cursed and berated. He knelt against the bulkhead, clinging to the forecapstan, sobbing.

The helmsman clung to the wheel and tried to guide the ship through the turmoil. But the *Resolution* rose on the waves, defying any puny attempts of men to steer her. Like a leaf in a hurricane, the ship was carried miles and miles off course into uncharted waters where white men had never been before.

Toward morning the captain ordered another flare shot off. The entire crew waited and the more devout began to pray openly, but there was no answer.

"Dammit to hell," a drenched seaman raged. "The storm has taken her and every man jack aboard. I feel it in me bones."

No one slept onboard the *Resolution* that night. Nothing remained for the tired seamen but a world of darkness, of water, of being cold and numb through to the bone. Men lucky enough to reach that sanctuary lay booted in their hammocks and wary, their eyes open and staring. No one spoke and everyone listened. It was never said in words, but they were waiting for the moment when the ship's hull broke and water rushed in. Some of the men believed the worst of the storm had passed because "it can't possibly blow no harder than this." But there was always another fierce squall to drive the ship's bow downward and to rattle its boards.

Somehow the night passed. But the storm did not let up in its intensity with the coming of daylight.

But something happened on the bridge that the tired captain passed off at first as nightmare, induced by long sleepless hours. Off to his left there appeared a land mass. The storm quickly obscured it, but the image remained; others had seen it too. Maps were spread out under the lantern. No land was shown in this part of the ocean, far north of Otaheite. The captain reckoned their position at a thousand miles north of the Tahitian islands, and the maps were clear: There was no land in this part of the ocean.

In any case, the ship was helpless to turn. It was being carried along like a top.

"My God, we'll come back this way if this storm ever lets up," the captain said. His excitement rose. He was certain that the storm had carried them far west of the known sea-lanes. Though the Spanish claimed to have explored all this area, nothing was shown on the maps. "My name of God, what a discovery if it proves to be true."

By ten o'clock the storm appeared to have abated slightly. The men trapped on the deck were able to go below and to towel off their drenched bodies and get into fresh clothing. A renewed sense of courage took over. Men who had during the eternal night forsaken any hope of riding out this terrible typhoon began to plan their lives at least a few days ahead.

The captain forgot to be sleepy. He stood watching the ocean through a spyglass. Another big foaming land mass appeared far to the starboard, and the captain was beside himself with anticipation.

Hours passed. Captain Cook chafed as the storm blew itself out, blowing them ever north. The sky was clearing. A tentative rainbow appeared over the sea. The gale was ending in a clear blow. There was nothing to do but wait, and finally, when a loathsome cloud broke and the sun shone through for a moment, land appeared dead ahead. Rather than lose it, the captain ordered every man jack on deck to raise the sails, at least enough so they could control their path through the seas and enter the harbor that loomed ahead. Captain Cook had made the discovery of the age.

BOOK THREE

Death in Paradise

Chapter XVIII

This morning the sun, as if suddenly reappearing from the shield of storm clouds, emerged with a brilliant burst of light, pouring the concentrated fire of her luster on the smashed deck of the *Resolution*. Nature seemed to have no memory of the storm. Lightness pervaded the breezes as the ship sailed serenely, licking its wounds and checking its hurts.

Cutter Murphy was assigned along with carpenters and damage crews to inspect the ship. A close inspection showed the damage was not extensive. But to Cutter, the wonder was not that the repairs would be minor, but that the ship had withstood the fury of the storm. The others might soon forget it, accept it as part of sailing, but he could not. The nightmare would haunt him.

By midday, lookouts in the crow's nest shouted, "The *Discovery* is in sight." The captain declared his prayers answered. The two ships came close enough together to exchange messages. The *Discovery* had sustained serious damage and would need extensive repairs.

Captain Cook relayed the news of the land masses they had been blown past during the storm. The *Discovery* crew had no record of such sightings, but they hoped it was true because they needed a friendly port and time to make repairs.

A call of "Land ho!" brought the captain running. The man in the crow's nest pointed dead ahead to the north and the captain fixed his spyglass on the green shore looming before them. The signal was passed along to the sister ship, and the *Resolution*, coming up from the south, hit the treacherous waters outside Waimea Bay at an ebb tide and rode in smoothly. The *Discovery* followed, and the entire crews of both ships stood on the deck staring at the heavenly sight of lush green lands.

The captain ordered his mapmakers to take sightings. He was beside himself with excitement. This was a major discovery. "Perhaps the greatest discovery of my voyages," the captain proclaimed to anyone in hearing.

Driven north by the storms, the ships had come upon the northernmost of the islands. Secrets of a million years were about to be divulged, and the captain was certain that he had been divinely chosen to discover this new land. He couldn't stand still. He paced the deck and studied the land through his spyglass.

The coast was rugged and unyielding, jutting perilously into the ocean. Mountains rose in the mists above the lush green foliage of jungle and white sands of the beaches. Miles of pristine beaches stretched as far as the captain's spyglass could discern. Towering above them were great emerald cliffs with razor-edge ridges. Giant waterfalls flowed down them. The captain's overwhelming first impression was one of green, in every shade imaginable.

The captain spoke as quickly as he could, describing his visions and feelings and reactions to a yeoman, standing beside him, pen and paper in hand. He knew this to be a historic moment, and he meant to capture it all. "On the morning of January 18, 1778, Captain Cook anchored his boats HMS *Resolution* and HMS *Discovery* in the deep water harbor on the southern most shores of what appears to be a large island, perhaps one in a chain of islands, which I name in honor of my sponsor and dearest friend, the Earl of Sandwich. I hereby declare to have discovered the Sandwich Islands and claim them in the name of George Third of England."

The ship maneuvered in the bay cautiously. At the first warning of shallows, the captain ordered the anchors lowered.

The ships' companies were busy, securing the ships and preparing to go ashore, when suddenly hundreds of people appeared on the beach. They seemed to be in the midst of some celebration. They stood along the shoreline, or waded into the water, open-mouthed at the great "floating island." Although they were nude, or only partially clothed, they appeared entirely unselfconscious.

Captain Cook realized he had come upon a totally innocent and natural people. They were so plainly stunned at the sight of the huge boat, it was probably the first ship any of them had ever seen.

He stood, enthralled. One of the mates declared the bay as a most convenient harbor for the wounded *Discovery*. Cook answered vaguely, unable to take his gaze from the natives standing silent and awestruck along the shore. He muttered to his yeoman, "How shall we account for these people hidden for so long far over this vast ocean?"

As he watched, the people on the beach came to life. Many ran into the water, swimming out to the ship effortlessly, like young fish in schools.

Then the canoes and double-prowed dugout outriggers appeared as if by magic, and people by the hundreds bore down on the two ships. Since the *Discovery* had ventured closer to land, it was quickly surrounded by people. They all converged at once upon the wounded ship, crowding to the starboard side, and began to scramble up the sides, screaming and talking at once. A thousand people, all fighting their way up the side of the ship. The vessel began to heel over. Still, the frantic people clambered aboard.

At first fearful seamen attempted to stop the natives from boarding. But the sailors were too few and unable to resist the terrible numbers. Under the weight of the curious natives the big craft lay on its side.

Apprehensive that the *Discovery* might be damaged, the second in command, Lieutenant James King, ordered one of the cannon fired. Two gunmen ran with tender and lighter to a small cannon aft. They stuffed in powder and let it off. The explosion was the loudest noise any of these people had ever heard. They retreated, backing off the boat, leaping into the water in panic, staring up in awe and terror at the gun that had belched fire.

They retreated some distance from the boat, but then, overcome with curiosity, they approached again. Lieutenant King shouted for Malu, the Polynesian interpreter. But Malu was occupied aboard the

Resolution, talking with a man who was evidently a king or a noble of these people.

"I cannot make out exactly what they are saying," Malu said to Captain Cook. "From their words, I believe their language was once that of the Polynesians, but it was many hundreds of years ago. They have changed it and altered it over the years, so it is only a strange dialect to me."

By speaking slowly and using much sign language, Malu was able to determine that the king of the island was named Kaumualii, but that he had remained ashore. "You are welcomed to join him there," Malu explained to Captain Cook. "These people are in the midst of a celebration of some kind, the feast of *makahiki*, a festival honoring the god Lono. This makes me certain these people were originally Polynesian, because Lono is a Tahitian god, considered a god of thunder, of the clouds, winds, the sea, agriculture, and fertility. His personage can assume as many as fifty forms. Likely, this is the same god as the Tahitians call Rongo. He is a most benevolent god. He is never appealed to with human sacrifices."

"Human sacrifices?" Cook said. "Are these people cannibals?"

Malu smiled. "I think it would be less than wise to ask that question of them at this time."

Captain Cook shrugged. "I am very interested. I want to know if we have come upon a nation of flesh eaters."

"Perhaps I can learn that later on," Malu said.

"They are most impressed with the explosion of the cannon from the *Discovery*," Malu explained later. "Thunder from the floating island, they call it. The chief, his name appears to be Pareea, is most insistent that you come ashore to meet the king."

Captain Cook ordered a cutter lowered over the side. Ladders were lowered, and Captain Cook chose his company to make the initial run into the shore, where the people now stirred restlessly. Cutter Murphy was chosen as one of the first to go ashore. As the junior officer he was surprised at the honor. Lieutenant James King, the second in command, the scientist, Dr. Robert Lord, and Malu the interpreter completed the company. With two seamen to handle the oars, the cutter set out, surrounded by dugouts and by outriggers and suddenly by the sleekly swimming natives who caught the sides of the boat, peering in at the Englishmen who were attempting to maintain their dignity and at the same time trying not to fall overboard when the cutter was almost overturned by dozens of swimmers clinging to its side.

At least fifty outriggers and canoes accompanied the cutter to shore. As the boat neared the land, people ran out to meet it, grasping the sides and propelling it forward. It rode in on a wave and was beached.

The natives' curiosity was divided between the strangely garbed men and their craft. After Cook and company stepped out of the boat, it remained the center of attention for hundreds of the natives. They touched its sail, its mast, its rounded bottom, the seats. They spoke to one another in wonderment, going back again and again to check it over yet again. Nothing the ship's company produced on that day or the next held half the interest of the cutter for these people.

Pareea introduced Captain Cook formally to the king and to the kahunas and to the princes of the land. Malu had difficulty with the language, and used sign language a great deal. Captain Cook was clearly impressed with the youthful Kamehameha, who towered above even the tallest of the British seamen, his shoulders broad and chest thick. Malu said that Kamehameha was a king, and this was enough for Cook. He deferred to Kamehameha, addressed him when he spoke, and waited while Malu painfully translated what he said.

Kamehameha was most interested in the cannon. Malu explained patiently that the gun spoke death to anything in its path, that it used gunpowder and cannon balls and was fired by a lighter. "I would like one of these," Kamehameha said to Malu.

Malu translated the young king's request, and Cook smiled in a kindly way. "Tell the young king that we have other guns, smaller and easier to handle, which also belch fire and death. I will make him a present of one of these guns."

But Kamehameha remained adamant. He wanted a cannon.

King Kaumualii asked the white men to join them at a table laden with every good food known to the islanders. Cook and his men went to the table and helped themselves to roast pig and chicken and fruits of every kind.

Before too long Malu was able to understand the Kauaians. He listened closely, asked questions, and learned that the first Tahitians, following the trace of the bird, had come here over seven hundred years ago.

"Seven hundred years of living untouched by anything or anyone from outside," he told Captain Cook. "They altered the language as it suited them. There is no written language. They have worshipped the same gods all these years and lived mostly in peace with their neighbors."

"How many of these islands are in this chain?" Cook asked.

He was told there were one hundred and thirty-two, from volcanos and barren tips of mountains to large, fully populated islands. Some had eroded into ragged reef-banks and desolate atolls. Others had been battered or simply sunk back into the sea. Seven of the islands were inhabited. Captain Cook scribbled all this down quickly, and the people marveled at the scratches he made on paper with his pen. Everything the man did impressed the natives. There was a dignity about him that matched the most aloof of the island nobles.

Kaumualii was engaged in an intense conversation with his kahunas. They kept eyeing the captain and his men until the foreigners grew restive and nervous.

At last Malu was commanded to appear before King Kaumualii. What followed was a long and involved conversation. At first Malu was certain that he was not hearing correctly, but finally he turned and addressed Captain Cook.

"The priests have decided that you, Captain Cook, as the leader of the people who arrived in the floating island, must be a person rare indeed. They have reached the conclusion that you, Captain Cook, are in reality the god Lono. They now wish some sign from you that you are indeed the god Lono come at the time of the festival of *makahiki*."

Chapter XIX

"The thunder of the cannon determined it. Proved to these people that you are indeed Lono, god of thunder," Malu said to Captain Cook. "Come to share their festival with them."

"Did you try to tell them otherwise?" Cook inquired, touching at his upper lip with the back of his index finger.

"I tried, but to no avail," Malu said. "It was the thunder of the cannon, and the fact that you arrived on the great floating islands during the festival of *makahiki*."

Pleased, and telling himself he was helpless with the barriers of language and all to dissuade these people from their mistake, Captain Cook merely shrugged and smiled benignly at the kahunas, priests, chiefs, and kings. The smile cinched it. To these simple people he was professing that he was indeed the kindly god Lono. They fell to their knees before him, prostrating themselves and weeping at the wonder of the moment.

Only Kamehameha remained standing. He stood to one side, his huge arms folded across his chest, watching the pageant unfolding before him. When Malu, troubled, looked at the young king to find out what was wrong, Kamehameha only shrugged. "Tell the god Lono," he said to Malu, "that I want a cannon like the one that belched fire."

The day was spent in ceremony. The natives treated Cook with the greatest respect possible for human beings to show another. They even took him on a tour of a nearby *heiau*, an ancient temple built in honor of the god Lono. "Tell them that I feel in my bones that I have been in this holy place many times," Cook instructed Malu.

The people demonstrated for Lono-Cook their skills in making *tapa*, the Polynesian cloth fashioned from tree bark.

Everywhere the captain went, he was regaled with gifts and entertainment. Pottery, statuary, gifts of food and fruit, were pressed upon him. He thanked and blessed each person who so contributed and had the gifts carried away at once to the cutter.

By now discipline had disappeared aboard

the two British ships. Several boats were lowered and filled to capacity with anxious sailors. Seamen, disregarding their officers and duties aboard ship, had swarmed ashore in a kind of benign anarchy. When they saw that festivities were under way on shore, nothing could hold them back. These men were soon spoiled and pampered by the happy natives, fed until their bellies were stuffed full.

Cook saw the anarchy, the total breakdown of discipline, but he was feeling good from the native drink and gave himself over to celebrating. Everywhere he turned, the word *aloha* was called out to him by bashful natives whose natural curiosity would not let them run and hide from this spectacular sight of white faces, pale eyes, strange clothing, and huge floating islands and guns that spoke with fire.

Cook encouraged peaceful bartering between his crew and the islanders. Cook sent out to the *Resolution* and had brought back knives, iron nails, and cheap trinkets which he knew these people had never seen before. The people were fascinated and rushed to exchange live pigs and fresh vegetables for these baubles. The islanders were particularly impressed with the metal objects; a knife, a fork, the buckle of a belt, fascinated them. Every man stared longingly at the six-inch steel-bladed hunting knives, the desire showing in their eyes and their hands as they reached out to touch them. The only obstacle was price. As soon as the sailors found out how dearly these items were desired, their prices soared. One seaman offered his knife for four women and three live pigs.

Cutter Murphy found the islands the kind of paradise he had always dreamed he might someday discover. It seemed to him that his entire past was wiped clean. That everything that had happened to him had pointed toward this hour and this place known on no maps of the world. It was as if he were born when he stepped out of Captain Cook's cutter onto the sandy shore. The partially clothed and naked natives, as open and natural as children in their nudity, stirred something deep inside him. He knew that in a place like this the hypocrisies and pretenses of his past life could be shed.

He wandered about the village, followed by admiring, giggling young women and looking carefully and with wonder at everything. He found huts securely made, snugged down against the strong trade winds with roofs made of tautly woven fronds. He peered into the huts while the girls stood aside like a small covey of birds and giggled. These young girls were spectacular in their nudity. They appeared to be in their late teens; their breasts were fully developed and their bodies struck him as ripe for the picking.

He strode along the beach, breathing deeply, feeling as if his tightened lungs were filled with pure fresh air for the first time in his life. He felt good, as if he had just come truly alive.

When he had walked a mile along the beach to a place that was wild and deserted, he found that eight or ten of the young girls still followed him, silent and watchful. When he was not looking, they whispered to one another, giggling and pointing, but when he turned his head, they fell silent.

He felt hot and uncomfortable in his dress uniform, unnatural. He gazed longingly at the nudity of the native girls, the perfection of their bodies, the high-standing golden breasts; the purpled hint of pubic hair, the long legs and smooth calves, the narrow shapely ankles and small clean feet.

All around him hung an aura of quiet and misty stillness. The sounds of the village were behind him. He could see only the boats at anchor out in the bay. The sense of unreality spread through him. The girls came together. Some of the bolder ones met his eyes, but most of them kept their lovely heads lowered.

He felt himself responding to their beauty. His breath tightened and burned in his throat. A fire flickered in his chest, and he felt the hardness rising in his groin.

He wondered what they would do if he spoke to them, if he summoned them nearer. It was a chance he didn't want to take.

He sat down on the beach, his legs drawn up, his gaze fixed out across the sun-dappled water. He could hear birds in the jungles behind him, and waves lapping on the shore, but mostly he could hear his heart pounding in his rib cage. He was breathing with difficulty now. He knew what he wanted—to touch and explore those naked bodies—but was desperately unsure of how to make his wish a reality.

He glanced once again from the corner of his eye and found the girls edging closer, like frightened little birds to a suspect feeding tray.

He reached casually into his pocket and removed a few shiny new shilling pieces. He heard an immediate reaction as the girls glimpsed the coins.

Slowly, they approached him. He remained perfectly still, afraid of frightening them away. They held their breaths too and stared at the coins glittering on his open palm. When they were only a couple of feet away from him, he extended his arm.

It was as if this were the signal the girls had awaited. They pounced upon him, clutching at the coins, biting them and gazing at them in awe. He withdrew more coins from his pocket and handed them out. They bowed to him, thanking him, crowding around him, chattering and touching him, drawing their hands through his hair, across his cheeks, and down along his throat.

They couldn't seem to get enough of touching. First came his clothing. A girl snatched the scarf around his throat and wrapped it about her own throat, preening and posing and laughing happily. Three girls worked frantically with the buttons on his jacket and shirt.

The giggling girls passed the heavy dress jacket among themselves, but soon discarded it as too heavy and itchy. Cutter had no idea what they were saying, but their exclamations as they passed around his shirt indicated pleasure. A girl wearing the shirt pirouetted, letting it flow out behind her nude body as she danced. The others applauded and laughed.

One girl, intrigued by the shiny buckle, wanted his belt. She pulled it through the straps; Cutter shrugged, motioning to her that the belt was hers, his gift to her. She nodded as if she understood and wrapped the belt about her waist, its buckle hanging heavy over her navel.

Now that he was more certain of himself and his own attraction for these girls, he decided that the time had come for a trade.

The girl who had removed his belt still knelt directly in front of him, only inches from him, on her knees, her legs apart. Her breasts stood proud and enticing.

Need surged through him and he reached out slowly, cupping his hand and touching the girl's crotch. All the other girls cried out in delight, and the girl before him forgot his belt, opening her legs to him, encouraging him. There was no sense of guile or of pretense. She wanted him and she showed it without hesitation. Nothing else mattered, her eyes said. Her full, lovely mouth parted, and she began panting.

Thinking that he had died and gone to heaven, Cutter played with her clitoris, moving his finger slowly at first and then more quickly. With his other hand he fondled the breasts of the other girls crowding around him.

He drew the girl in front of him up to him from her knees and sat her across his lap. Two of the girls on either side of him loosened his trousers, and he felt himself released, throbbing and aching, pulsing with life. Crying out, the girl set herself upon him. She slid all the way down upon him, driving her hips in a frenzy, her eyes wide with pleasure.

Gasping for breath, Cutter drew another girl across his chest and kissed her roughly, cupping his hands over her hard nipples. He drove his tongue between her teeth.

When he released her, she cried out in delight and the others watched in wonder at the marvel of this kiss. Each of the other girls had to be touched and kissed precisely in this manner.

The girl riding him screamed out her passion and sagged, sated, upon him. She was dragged off by other girls and another quickly straddled him, working herself furiously down upon his mast.

When all the girls had tested and tasted and enjoyed him, they spent hours simply loving him with their hands, moving them over his body. His white body, his hardness, his kissing, drove them into a mindless frenzy.

He began to laugh to himself, wondering if these succubi intended for him to leave this beach alive. They were insatiable and uninhibited. Blessedly unfettered by rules or morals.

His jacket and trousers had disappeared, but he was too tired and too enthralled to care. He saw that the girls took turns wearing his shirt, and he tiredly gave himself over to watching the girls dance around in it.

He saw that it was getting late. He wondered what the chiefs would do to the ten girls who disappeared with a sailor from the ship. Even if it was the ship of the god Lono. There must be rules of some sort for these lovely little pagans. He sat up and by sign language told the girls they had to return to the beach village.

They agreed and jumped up, pulling him to his feet, but then they demanded to be kissed again and fondled. When he asked for his clothing, they merely stared at him as if they had no idea what he was talking about. So finally, wearing only his shoes, stockings, and underwear, he walked back into the village with the girls clinging delightedly to him.

One thing Cutter Murphy now knew. He had discovered that one place he had sought all his life. Here, among these simple, honest, direct, and free people, he found what he had been seeking. But how could he stay here? Desertion would mean the firing squad if he were caught. But whatever the cost, it would be worth it. He had found his people and his place on this globe.

Chapter XX

Unbridled chaos reigned on the water and on the shores of Waimea Bay. The few men left aboard the *Resolution* or the *Discovery* soon abandoned their posts, removed most of their clothing, leapt overboard, and swam to the beach. The boats, abandoned and forgotten, rocked in the shallows of the bay. Officers and men alike had rushed into the orgy.

Not in their maddest fantasy had such a situation existed: women—naked, beautiful, enchanting, and available. The men swarmed over the village, dragging naked women, laughing, giggling, and willing, into the jungle. Men who had once been shy suddenly became bold and assertive. Men who had always revered womanhood took one look at the naked, rapturous women and forgot all they'd been taught. They took the women standing, simply lifting them into place, working them frantically, adoring, kissing, caressing, deflowering.

Dr. Robert Lord strode through the village, asking by sign language and the slow, loud tones one uses with the deaf and dumb, for the whereabouts of Captain Cook. People stared at him, smiling. He was a comely young man, and all who saw him wanted to please him. They offered him food, fruit, gifts, and even sexual favors, all using the same sign language, but he smiled and shook his head.

Dr. Lord was a young man, newly out of medical training. This tour with the navy was his first real experience, but it was a practice consisting mostly of treating knife wounds, rope burns, splinters, sore throats, piles, and hangovers. He appeared tall and rigid in the dress uniform, which he still wore after the long day ashore, although one of the women had removed his scarf. His hair was thick and dark. Except for a slight cast in his right eye, he was a handsome youth with a jutting chin and straight profile.

He came to a large grass hut that belonged to one of the nobles. He pushed aside the cloth door and at last found Captain Cook. The captain sat cross-legged on a mat near the door, in a state of dishabille, and partly drunk from swilling the native drink of alcohol sweetened with pineapples, coconut milk, and papaya juice. He saw the Kauai princess Lelemahoalani lying naked and fast asleep on a mat far across the dimly lit hut. The doctor averted his gaze from the woman's nude body. It was none of his affair, and he never spoke of what he saw.

Captain Cook smiled crookedly at Dr. Lord. "What's the matter? Were you looking for me?"

He nodded, rather self-consciously. "I'm afraid we have a problem of some magnitude, Captain." He winced when he spoke.

"Oh? Problem? A problem you can't handle?"

"I'm afraid, sir, it will call for all your sagacity and influence."

"Oh?" The captain managed to straighten slightly. "What's wrong? Are the men rioting? I've decided simply to overlook that today. Tomorrow we return to a tight command. I promise you that."

"Tomorrow may be too late, sir."

"Too late? What's wrong?"

"It's a matter of life and death. And for us, a matter of morality, sir."

"Morality? Life and death? What the hell are you talking about?"

The doctor sighed and spread his hands, uncomfortable but determined. "Well, sir, as you must know by now, these people have never seen a white face before."

"Yes? Well?"

"That means they have spent hundreds of years like this, living apart from the world. They've had absolutely no contact with outsiders."

"That's fairly obvious, Doctor. We have discovered primitive islands, unknown to the white man."

"I'm afraid you miss my point, Captain. They've had *no* contact with outsiders, and this means with outsider's diseases. It occurs to me, sir, that our men could start a plague among these people—men, women, and children—which could totally wipe them out in a year or so—a few years at the most."

"What in hell are you talking about, Doctor?"

"About our morality in allowing these diseases to be transmitted freely among an unprotected, unsuspecting people."

"What disease are you talking about?"

"About syphilis, Captain. And gonorrhea."

The doctor saw the captain becoming sober. "You're talking about the diseases carried by some of our men?" he said.

The doctor nodded. "The syphilis bacteria, carried by at least a dozen men, known to me. I've treated those men with mercury ointment. But the cure is uncertain; the infectiousness may last long after a person is apparently cured."

"Jesus Christ." For a long moment Captain Cook's head sagged on his chest. "These men infect the women, they infect their own men and . . ." He let his voice trail off, the vision too painful to face.

The doctor nodded. "Exactly. And most of your men have the clap. It is highly contagious. This disease can affect women terribly and kill their babies."

The captain stood up, straightening his jacket, tying his scarf and placing his hat firmly and squarely upon his head. "The first thing to do is to find those known to be infected and force them to return to the ship and to stay here."

"I'm afraid that's easier said than done."

The captain stared at the doctor coldly. "Then you don't know me very well, Doctor. You round up the guilty men and I'll have them returned aboard ship at gunpoint. And they'll stay, the same way."

The doctor sighed. "When you left the ship this morning, sir, leaving behind those men who were on duty, something happened which I think you ought to know about, and which will alter anything you plan to do."

"What are you talking about?"

"About these young women. They are so natural and uninhibited, guileless, and so desperately eager to please us. . . . The girls swim out to the ships. The point is that removing the men to the ships may not be the end of it even if we can find the infected ones."

"Well, we'll find them. We'll round them up, line them up at the boats, and as you pick out the diseased men, they will be returned to the ships. And they will stay, quarantined, until we sail. I'll guarantee that."

The doctor had been sickhearted at the thought of the epidemic being spread among these simple-hearted, open people. But he had indeed underestimated the captain. Within half an hour every man and officer was lined up on the shore, in various stages of undress. The captain had guns pointed at the crew while he lectured them. The natives gathered, silently, troubled, to watch. Malu attempted to explain to Kaumualii and the princes but found few adequate words.

"Any of you men with the sense to understand what havoc you can wreak among these people, what horrible things you can do to a helpless race of people, and know yourselves to be infected with the clap or with syphilis, I ask you to get into the cutter at this time."

The men glanced warily, sheepishly, at each other, but none made any move toward the beached boats. Some had the grace to blush, to drop their gazes, but most continued to stare straight ahead.

The captain merely waited. His face was set and cold, and, to the doctor's amazement, stone sober. This was the Captain Cook he had known over the long voyage from England, severe, despotic, uncompromising. The very human captain he had found in that hut with the sleeping princess was wiped from his mind.

"All right," the captain said, "if you will not step forward willingly, you are ordered to drop your pants where you stand."

"In front of all these people?" one seaman protested.

"You've been dropping them all day," the captain replied sharply. "This is an order. Drop your pants and prepare for short-arm inspection."

Unwillingly, protesting aloud, the ship's company, officers and men alike, dropped their pants. The natives giggled, nudging one another and pointing at the men and at their genitals. They set up a chattering among themselves, punctuated with loud laughter. Cutter realized that while these men may have been received earlier as demigods, the natives were having second thoughts about the white men's immortality.

The captain bowed to the young doctor. "You may take over now," he said. "It's all up to you now."

The doctor nodded, stepped to the head of the first line. "As I stop before you," he said loudly, "you will skin back the foreskin of your penis and milk it down."

He checked for redness and swelling of the clap, for the chancre sore and discharge of syphilis. The first man he tested he slapped on the shoulder and told him to get dressed and to report to the nearest cutter. The man pulled up his pants and stepped out of line. The captain nodded to his yeoman, who also stood half naked, and the man's name was entered in a log.

"You men returned to the ships will be under quarantine," the captain said. "If you are caught with a woman aboard the ship, you will be confined to the brig on bread and water for thirty days. Is that clear to all of you?"

The men muttered under their breath. But the captain merely stared at them, his face uncompromising. At last they all nodded; it was understood.

Dr. Lord came to the last man. Cutter Murphy stood silently while the doctor inspected him. "What happened to your clothing, midshipman?" The captain stood forbiddingly at the doctor's shoulder.

Cutter Murphy took a deep breath. "Some of the natives, sire. They wanted my clothing enough to remove it."

He saw that the captain did not believe him. "You will return to the ship," he said.

"You will stand armed guard on the way out. You will stand armed guard for the next four hours, or until relieved on your watch. As soon as you have dressed in the uniform of the day."

"Thank you, sir," Cutter Murphy said. He tilted his head. Perhaps it was a trick of the sunlight. Standing with the nobility of the island was a girl who seemed to hold herself aloof from the spectacle before her. She had all the loveliness of the native Polynesian— thick black hair framing her lovely face and spilling about her bared shoulders and breasts. Her teeth were white, sparkling; her features were perfection. Her breasts, while not large, were high-standing, their bronzed skin touched with pearl which shone with highlights, fresh, clear, unblemished. She stood, smiling and laughing, and he had the terrible sense that she was laughing at him.

He felt his heart sink in his rib cage. This was the girl he had been looking for all his life. If the gods intended for two people to be one, it was surely them. Standing there, he knew that if he could not have her, his life would be empty, and no matter what good accrued to him, he would be all his days unfulfilled.

Malu stood at the captain's shoulder and Cutter whispered to him. "Did you meet that princess up there? The one standing between the king and the handsome young warrior?''

Malu smiled at hm. "I did," he said. "The girl is the Princess Misau. The young warrior beside her is Mihuana, her betrothed."

Cutter stood staring at the girl. He hadn't even heard the words "her betrothed." He had found the one girl the gods had meant for him since time began.

Chapter XXI

The infected men were hustled into the cutters and took their places silently. Cutter was ordered to the stern of one of the whale boats. He was given a loaded rifle, with orders to shoot to kill anyone who attempted to leave the boat before it reached the *Resolution*. He sat with the musket across his legs, feeling naked and foolish.

Cutter could not keep his eyes off the Princess Misau. Misau. Misau. What a lovely name, and what a lovely girl. In all his life he had never seen a lovelier girl, with such a graceful body and large, luminous eyes. He kept staring up at where she stood with her hand lightly upon the arm of the young native man beside her.

The boat rocked in the slight swell of waves at the shoreline. Cutter grew sleepy, exhausted after his lovemaking with the native girls. His eyes closed involuntarily. Suddenly a shout and cries awakened him. His gaze flew up the beach to the line of the jungle. Four or five men were dragging someone over the ground. He sat forward, coming fully awake when he recognized the cabin boy, Billy Hutch.

He was dragged protesting and cursing along the beach toward where the captain stood. Another boy, naked and sobbing, was staggering along in their wake.

Malu ran to meet the angry men. He listened closely to them, then walked ahead of them to where Captain Cook stood, erect and forbidding.

Malu said, "It is the cabin boy, Billy Hutch. With all the girls and women to choose from, Billy Hutch had sodomized a young boy—and terrorized him."

The squad of outraged natives reached the captain and stood, waiting to see what justice would be dispensed. Wide awake now, Cutter sat on the edge of his seat and stared up at Billy Hutch. There was something in the way the boy now stood, a swaggering sense of victory. Cutter's heart sank. He knew in that instant what was in Billy Hutch's mind.

Billy Hutch's chance had come to prove his manhood. Rather than taking one of the native girls, Billy Hutch had lived out the fantasies that drove him all these months. He had dreamed not of girls but of regaining his own manhood in the way his had been taken from him. Billy Hutch had dragged a young boy into the forest, brutalizing him as he had been brutalized that first day aboard ship.

Staring up at Billy Hutch, standing between his captors, Cutter saw a change in the youth. Gone was the hangdog look. He stood taller, his shoulders back, a smirk on his face. Billy Hutch's strange reasoning told him that now he was a man. He had brutalized a lesser male.

Captain Cook drew himself up to his full height, his indignity and his contempt obvious. "I thought I had ended this perversion business with the flogging aboard ship," he said, his mouth twisting.

"You flogged me. Not him that done it to me."

The captain stared at him as if the cabin boy had taken leave of his senses. "What are you talking about, boy? You were flogged for masturbation, for practicing perversion. Perversion is something I will not tolerate aboard my ship." He glanced around, ordered three riflemen to stand at the ready. "I will pluck out this evil where it abides," he said. He drew a deep breath and ordered Billy Hutch shot.

Billy Hutch evidently no longer expected

justice or understanding on this earth. He was expressionless as he was led away.

A lieutenant gave the order. The muskets were raised and fired. The sound of the three guns frightened the natives as the cannon explosion had terrified them earlier. Some of them went scurrying away into the forest. Others, Kamehameha among them, came forward, demanding to hold and inspect the gun.

Billy Hutch was dead by the time his body struck the beach. Cutter sat unmoving, sickness welling up in his throat. Natives ran from all directions, crowding around the body, chattering, pointing to the bloody bullet holes in the corpse.

Malu approached Captain Cook nervously. He had seen Captain Cook punish the bearer of bad tidings before. He said, "These people. They want the boy's belly."

"What?" Captain Cook's face blanched.

"The belly is the succulent part, they say. And they want it."

"My God," Captain Cook said. "What we feared is true. These people are cannibals."

"Less now than they once were, I think," Malu replied. "Now they eat only the belly and the entrails of an enemy. I think it would be wise to allow them to cut out the boy's belly."

Captain Cook stared at Malu, sickened. But the ecstatic looks on the faces of the people surrounding the dead body, the outrage in the faces of the captors of Billy Hutch, the sense of tensions mounting, made up his mind. He nodded.

Two of the natives knelt beside Billy Hutch's body and, using a small wooden instrument set with shark's teeth, cut out the fleshy part of the boy's belly. They bore it away quickly as the blood leaked between their fingers and dripped on their bodies.

Sickened, Captain Cook waited until the natives abandoned the cabin boy's body and then ordered it wrapped in canvas and buried at sea.

Kamehameha was beside himself with excitement at the spitting guns that carried death in small pellets. He imagined himself winning over all the islands, terrorizing his enemies and vanquishing the greatest of his foes. All he needed was the musket.

His flowered cape wrapped around his huge body, he approached Captain Cook and stood looking down upon him. Malu translated for him as well as he could. "King Kamehameha requests that you turn over to him a supply of the muskets and gunpowder and pellets."

Captain Cook looked up at the young king and shook his head. "Tell him it is impossible. I will make him a present of one rifle, but I will not sell him the other guns."

Painstakingly, Malu translated for Kamehameha, who already knew from the captain's attitude what his answer was.

"Tell the captain that I will pay a fortune for the guns," Kamehameha ordered Malu.

Malu relayed the message. Captain Cook remained adamant, but he read in Kamehameha's face the truth. Kamehameha was going to have the guns he wanted, at whatever price he had to pay. The captain realized that Kamehameha regarded him as a mortal, and not a very formidable mortal at that.

Captain Cook sighed heavily. "Tell the king that I might permit him to have twenty guns. At a price."

Malu drew twenty lines on the shore with a long spear borrowed from one of Kamehameha's bodyguards. Slowly, the young king counted out the number of rifles. At last, he nodded. "And pellets to go with them," he said.

Slowly Captain Cook began to recite to Malu the price for these weapons.

At first Kamehameha did not understand, but gradually his face darkened as he heard the number of mats, of pearls, of statuary the captain was demanding. His mouth was pulled into a hard line and his eyes were clouded with anger, none of which was lost on the captain. As the price mounted, so did the king's rage.

Finally, Captain Cook stopped enumerating the price for the weapons. Kamehameha knew he must have them. He nodded and the deal was closed. So, the captain noted, was the cold hatred the king felt for him.

He shrugged. He could not be concerned with the hatred of a minor native king.

Cutter returned aboard the *Resolution* and went directly to his own quarters to dress in the uniform of the day. He continued to be haunted by the face of the lovely girl Misau.

As he stood his watch, he was struck again by the desire to escape this ship even if it meant being stranded in this godless place for the rest of his life among cannibals and natives who did not speak his language.

There would be no more gaslights of London. He sighed. He had seen London and its shadows—the poverty, the cruelty, the crime. No, he would not miss the streets of London or its people.

He *had* loved gambling. If he jumped ship here, that life was forever over too. Gone as well would be civilization. But civilization had beaten him down. He could get along without it.

There remained the idea of being stranded. He could not change his mind. There had never been a European ship in this port before, and God knew when there would be another. If he stayed, it was forever.

He tried to concentrate on the sense of quiet and peace and contentment he would find here. The language would not be a barrier for long. There were a few simple words for everything; he could memorize them and then he could transact business with these people. He did not fool himself that the orgy that had been in progress since the arrival of the ships would continue. Life would settle down to routine. That, he told himself, was what he wanted, what he had always wanted.

In his mind he began to plan his escape. It was only a matter of discovering when the ships were sailing, and he could disappear into the jungles and mountains until Captain Cook and his company were gone.

He would do it. He felt his heart increase its beating at the thought of his freedom, lying there before him for his taking.

As he got into one of the cutters to return to the *Resolution*, Captain Cook was deeply troubled. He had been greeted as a god. The natives had been ecstatic at seeing him and his great floating island. But after one day that welcome was wearing thin. He admitted his men had passed the bounds of decency, that they had overrun the island, taken everything they saw, and treated the islanders as less than human. No wonder they were resented.

He decided to improve relations with the islanders. He asked that King Kamehameha be brought to him on the ship so that the guns and gunpowder could be given to him. Through the translator Malu, he asked the king to gather all his people along the shore as soon as it was dark.

Although Chinese fireworks were well known in all the civilized world, Captain Cook decided they would be a novelty here. The sun set, turning the sky a brilliant orange, then black. Firepits glowed on the island. Along the beach people gathered by the hundreds. Captain Cook gave the order and the display began. Rockets and pinwheels and great waterfalls rose noisily into the sky. Their light illuminated the shoreline. Some of the islanders had fallen on their knees in terror. Others had fled into the jungle.

His heart sank. What had been planned as a display of friendship had ended badly. He could hear moaning and screaming on the shore. Not even the most beautiful of the displays pleased them. He gave the order to end the fireworks display and the lighters were doused.

Afterward one of the braver islanders paddled out to the ship and demanded to be shown this wonder of fire bursting in all directions. When he was ordered off the ship by the translator, he refused to go.

An armed sailor fired at the man. He fell dead, toppling from the ship into the water. His friends in the canoe cried out in terror and rage. They retrieved his body and slowly paddled the canoe back to shore.

The captain stood on deck, staring at the island. How long would these people continue to worship him as a god? They were a strange tribe. They chastised and criticized their gods and had proven that they were cannibals.

The true aim of his voyage was to find a northwest passage to America. It might be prudent to take up that venture again as soon as the *Discovery* was repaired.

Chapter XXII

For Misau these were the happiest days
of her life. Mihuana had returned from the
savage wars of Molokai. In her heart she
admitted she had not expected to see him
return. She had been privy to the deceits
and dissembling of the priests, kahunas,
and the nobles. To put an unwanted person
in the forefront of a battle was an old ploy
among her people. Even when Mihuana had
assured her of Kamehameha's friendliness,
she had had doubts. She had lived in sick
suspense until the outriggers returned to
Kauai and she saw Mihuana's boat among
them.

Against her better judgment she had allowed herself to be convinced that Kame-

hameha was different, that his upbringing among the common people had altered his thinking, that the kapus did not control his life. And now that the great floating islands were out in the bay, and the people had acclaimed the white leader as the god Lono, she found Kamehameha less concerned with her and her private life, and she exulted.

She even began to plan her wedding. The thought seemed daring, and yet she heard from the priests nothing to the contrary. She and Mihuana met openly. There was much whispering and nodding, but this was understandable. For the first time in the history of Kauai, and perhaps of her people, a commoner was fraternizing openly with the *alii*.

Her body, her face, her complexion, her very hair, took on a beauty and a sheen it had never known before. She could explain it only in that she was happy and her body responded, but she saw the way people, especially one of the officers from the floating island, turned to look at her. He seemed to seek her out, walking about the island until he found her. This flattered and amused her but did not interest her. Her interest was Mihuana.

Still, the beliefs of ancestor worship and taboos were deeply ingrained in her. She knew that the breach of taboo could bring misfortune on the entire tribe, and for this

218

reason she could not believe that the rules would be set aside so easily. Although she was happy, she lived in fear that it was all a dream and would soon end.

She was singing in the large grass hut, dreaming ahead to the wedding ceremony, when the *tapa* material of the doorway was brushed aside and Kamehameha strode into the room.

Misau gazed up at her brother, her mouth parted in shock and surprise. Since he had been sold the guns from the floating island, all his time had been taken up with training his men. She thought he had forgotten her.

He seemed to fill the room. She had not seen the young king, except at a distance, since his victory at Molokai. Warfare and victory had changed him. There was an arrogance about him that she had never seen before. The paste or powder he wore in his hair made it stand on end and gave him a fierce and terrible look. His face had assumed a new savagery, and his cold and calculating eyes seemed to look everywhere at once.

Her heart sank. This man was not a compassionate being.

Misau dropped to her knees and bowed her head, as much to escape facing his fierceness as in respect. "My brother," she said, her head lowered, her voice empty. "My dear brother."

"What is this I am hearing about you?" he asked at last.

Her stomach felt empty and her heart pounded raggedly. She dared to gaze up at him. "What manner of thing is one hearing?"

"Don't pretend with me. I am hounded by some commoner who says you return his love."

She straightened slowly. Her heart felt heavy in her breast; all her fears had been at last realized. She tried to recall all the good things Mihuana had reported that Kamehameha had promised. She spoke in a tense whisper. "Mihuana."

Kamehameha nodded coldly. "That is the name. I will not withhold the news from you any longer. The man Mihuana has been arrested. If you will not honor tradition, I shall honor it for you."

"Why have you arrested Mihuana? What crime have you charged him with?"

He smiled faintly and looked about the room, trying to show her that his anger was not directed at her, that he charged her with no crime, that his entire rage was centered on Mihuana.

"I have charged the commoner with breaking taboo. Last night he stood with you in the company of nobles and touched you. But now I have come to speak with you. I would hear what you have to say before I proceed against this commoner."

She sighed heavily and her eyes filled with tears. "I love Mihuana. Is that what you want to hear?"

He took an involuntary step toward her, his huge fists clenched. "That is the last thing I want to hear from one of the nobility. A girl like you, one who was trained from birth in what is proper. I cannot believe I am hearing such from you."

She stood straighter. She had right on her side. Mihuana had told her of Kamehameha's promises. She spoke very clearly, but with her voice lowered. "He told me he had spoken to you."

Kamehameha laughed angrily. A muscle twitched in his firm jaw. "Ah, yes. So he has spoken to me. Several times. At times when I was preoccupied with important matters, too busy to pay full attention to him. As he well knew."

"He said he spoke to you when you came for his help in the battle," she said. "Help you needed badly if you were to win."

He waved her objections aside. "That too. But you may as well know I never meant the things I said to him. I needed his outriggers and his men. He should have offered them to me as his duty. But he did not; he tried to bargain with me at the wrong time."

"Whatever he did, he did for love of me. You must be able to see that," Misau pleaded.

"I closed my mind to the evil things he was saying because I thought he would be killed in battle. He should have been. I placed him in positions of great danger. I pretended no friendship with him. If he had been slain, it would have been easier for all of us."

She spoke softly. "But he did come back. He told me of the dangerous places he was sent into, the great peril he faced. And survived. This should count for something. You should honor your word to him."

He caught his breath, trembling with rage. "Do you dare to question my authority?"

She shook her head and spread her hands. "No. I say only that you tried to kill him."

"Did I? Or did I place him at his battle station because someone had to fill that place?" He sighed and strode about the room. At last he turned and faced her. "It would have been kinder to have him die a hero. If your commoner had been wise at all, he would have seen the impossibility of what he sought. The lives of the *alii* and the *muahainana* can never be one. You know this. You must have known it all along."

She drew a ragged breath and looked down at her hands. Her voice brimmed with tears. "Perhaps I counted too much on your compassion."

He made a slashing, downward gesture. "Do you, then, question my compassion? I have compassion. I am a most compassionate man. Even now, with the man tied up and under arrest, I feel compassion. These mistakes of the heart . . . they happen. But they are put aside. By the wise they are put aside. Life goes on."

She gazed into the dark and savage eyes fixed upon her. Her hands trembled and she locked them together before her. "What will become of him?"

Kamehameha scowled. "I will not be questioned."

She reached out to him, then let her hand fall to her side. "But he is the one I love. The man I love with all my heart. Am I simply to forget that he exists? Is this what you ask of me?"

He nodded emphatically. "That is what you must do," he said. "You now have reached the age when it is time you put away the childish dreams of the young girl and look forward to your marriage."

She knotted her hands together. "I shall marry Mihuana—as you promised him we might marry, as you gave your word—or I shall marry no one."

Again he made a threatening gesture with his great arm. "Stop this idle and foolish talk. Of course you shall marry. It is the place and the destiny of the daughters of the *alii* to wed and to be fruitful."

But she shook her head, staring past him at nothing, at the nothingness of her life without Mihuana.

"Listen to me," the young prince said earnestly. "Listen well to me, for I lose patience. He is not suitable for you. Mihuana is a good man, and the gods know him to be a brave one. I acknowledge all this. But he is a commoner. There is no way we can change that, but I have searched for someone suitable for you to wed."

She shook her head again. "I shall marry Mihuana or no one."

"You will listen to me. When, as sometimes happens, there is none among the *alii* suitable for the daughter of a king, kapu says she will marry within her own family."

"A brother?" She whispered the word, staring at him, shocked and dismayed, hurt and angered.

He nodded again. "Yes. The wedding will take place at once—tomorrow to avoid any possibility that anything should go wrong. You will marry our brother Taguana."

She stared at him, aghast. "But he already has two wives . . ."

"I have spoken to him and he agrees," Kamehameha insisted. "You will put aside all foolish thoughts, wipe Mihuana forever from your heart. You *shall* marry as I order."

"And Mihuana?" she whispered. "What of him?"

He scowled. "What happens to a commoner . . . to a prisoner who has broken taboo is not of your concern."

She sank lifelessly to the mat, as if all the

bones in her body had suddenly become liquid. She fell forward upon her face, sobbing.

Kamehameha stood a long time over her. At last he knelt and touched her shoulder lightly. It troubled him that she did not see the compassion in what he did.

"If you marry Taguana quietly and obediently, I might be tempted toward mercy on this . . . commoner."

She tilted her head to look up at him. "You lied to us before."

He stood up. "I told you, it was a matter of state. Lies for the sake of the state are not lies. I lied to the commoner because affairs of the state dictated it. I would do it again. I have no qualms about lying to commoners. But to you I speak the truth. I would consider leniency."

"Leniency. Does that mean you would not put him to death?"

He shrugged. *"Pu'uhonua."*

She gazed up at him. "A sanctuary where he could live unmolested?"

He smiled coldly. "I would be inclined to allow him to run ahead of my warriors. If he reached *pu'uhonua* before they beheaded him, yes, he would be allowed to live out his life in peace in the sanctuary."

Chapter XXIII

Cutter Murphy watched the repairs on the *Discovery* with great interest. Work progressed slowly, if at all. Thomas Edgar, the *Discovery*'s master, was more interested in life on the island. He spent most of his time ashore and although he did leave orders that any of his men infected with clap or syphilis were to be denied shore leave, he knew that the men used every scheme possible to smuggle women aboard. They even dressed the women up as men. When Captain Cook censured Commander Edgar for his laxity, Edgar defended himself and doubled the watches aboard his ship. Still, the lure of the island was too much for him, and he went ashore daily to enjoy its exotic delights.

Cutter, too, went ashore at every opportunity and prowled the island looking for the lovely princess Misau. He had in the past week learned more about her, that she was sixteen years old, which was mature by island standards, and that she was in trouble with her brother because of her love for a commoner. Not that this commoner was an ordinary man. His name was Mihuana and he was one of the island's heroes.

When Cutter was not hoping for a glimpse of Misau as she went about her daily affairs, he was stalking the jungles, looking for hiding places. He spent hours gazing up at the twin peaks of Kawaikini and Waialeale, which rose toward the sky from the middle of the island. It occurred to him to climb through the jungles to one of those peaks. He figured that island trackers could find him, perhaps in a few hours, but he would have a good chance of escaping the ship. If he were smart, and took nothing with him but the clothes on his back, perhaps the ship might be far out at sea before he was missed.

One thing was certain. He'd had enough of life aboard the *Resolution*. His career in His Majesty's Navy was about to end, one way or another.

Meanwhile he prowled the island, trying to ingratiate himself with the natives.

Likely, he would be among them for many years to come.

Captain Cook was troubled by the attitude of the nobles of this island toward him. He remained the god Lono. He had stopped protesting and decided to enjoy all that came with being a god. Gifts were showered upon him. He was openly worshipped. When he went ashore the natives all bowed and covered their faces with their hands until he had passed. Opulent sacred ceremonies were held in his honor. Boxing and wrestling matches were staged for his entertainment. The nobles took great pains to show Cook the white *kapa* banners held aloft on crossbars, an ancient symbol of Lono, which resembled the British ship's masts and sails. Often when he came out of his quarters onto the deck of his ship he would find Kauaian natives prostrating themselves in his presence. They would lie on the deck until he pleaded with them to rise, and only then would they get to their feet, their faces rapt with the expressions of adoration. By the masses he was loved and revered, and yet among the nobles there appeared to be a sense of impatience.

The accidental murder of the curious Kauaian youth still rankled. The natives were very alert and watchful when they came out to the ship. Whenever a man approached them carrying a gun, they fell to their knees in a signal of surrender.

Cook had decided that as soon as the *Discovery* was repaired, he would take his leave of the island. It was far preferable to depart a god than to overstay his welcome and have the natives, and there were thousands of them, armed and with an appetite for human flesh.

He determined that Thomas Edgar was not moving swiftly enough with the repairs required on the *Discovery* and ordered the work crews doubled.

Meantime, Cook used Malu to question the island nobles, the kahunas and priests, about the other Sandwich Islands, as he now called the chain of land he had discovered. He made a crude map and checked it with the most knowledgeable men on the island and was told it was very accurate. According to them there were seven inhabited islands among the hundreds comprising the long chain of seven volcanic lands.

Cook smiled, pleased with the thought of his return to England with news of this great discovery, a new land claimed in the name of George Third. He would be lionized in all the best drawing rooms of England. There was no end of the honors that would be bestowed upon him now.

Then, toward the end of the second week, illness struck the island. The people moaned aloud, crying out in horror at the strange illness. Young women were infected with all the ills the men carried. Deaths were already beginning the rapid destruction of the Hawaiian people.

Captain Cook sent Dr. Lord and his medical teams in at once to do what they could. There was little the doctor could do, of course, except advise the natives to keep the sick women apart from the others for as long as they lived. "It's your only chance of survival," he told them through Malu, but the people did not understand.

For a long time after Kamehameha had left her hut, Misau remained sprawled on the mat, inconsolable. Eventually the other women of the hut came and tried to reason with her. They knelt beside her. They spoke the truth: *Alii* and commoner are forever segregated. A woman of nobility can never marry a commoner. These were truths as old as her people, and despite what she had believed, and what Mihuana had been told, they had not altered.

Her body sagged on the mat; her dark hair was wild.

"For a little while," Misau whispered, "I dreamed. I loved him and my heart quickened at the sight of him. But I cannot dream now. I cannot go on living. To die and part, that is a sadness. But to part and to go on living, that I shall not endure."

Frightened, the younger women withdrew. Nothing they could say reached beyond the empty glaze of her black eyes. The older women spoke kindly, remembering, some of them for the first time in many years, forbidden loves in their own pasts. We survived, they said. We learned to go on living.

But Misau looked at them unseeingly, unheedingly. Their words of kindness could not penetrate the cocoon of her despair.

She sat up at last, rocking back and forth. "I have my love," she said. "If I die, I keep my love. The only way to keep my love is to die with it."

The women sent one of their elders, Kiliki, to Kamehameha. The woman put a flowered robe about her shoulders, for she was an *alii*, and sent word that she must see Kamehameha at once. The priests surrounding the young prince kept her waiting. She stood in quiet dignity.

At last she was ushered into the august presence of the young prince. Kamehameha stood tall and forbidding, his face scowling, his hair wildly sculpted. He spoke in a cold tone. "What is it, sister? Does one forget how busy I am?"

"I do not forget. I would not come except in matters of utmost importance."

The young prince smiled, shrugged, and asked her to state her business.

"It is Misau," the woman replied. "I fear she has been stricken. She has taken leave of her senses. We talk to her, but she hears us not. She speaks now of dying for her love.''

Kamehameha remained aloof. ''That is nonsense,'' he said. ''I myself was recently with her. I spoke with her.''

''I know. I know you were with her and I know what you said to her. It is when you left her that she took leave of her senses. She weeps. She stares at nothing. She speaks only of death.''

Kamehameha sighed. ''She is merely unhappy. It is a passing thing, I promise you. A young girl's infatuation.''

''That is why I have come,'' Kiliki persisted. ''She is not a woman merely unhappy. She has taken leave of her senses. I have seen it before in my life. It is a terrible thing.''

''Nonsense,'' Kamehameha said. He would not have it. He had taken a position on a kapu. It was the correct one. The girl knew it to be right. In time she would come to accept it. ''She will recover from it.''

''I have come because it is the belief of the women who are now around her that she will not,'' Kiliki said.

Kamehameha's mouth hardened. ''I have spoken to Taguana. He has agreed to marry the girl. She will soon be busy preparing for the wedding. Too busy for this carrying on. Too busy to think of unsuitable men. Taguana will go at once to talk with Misau.

She will be made to see the rightness of what we are doing."

The older woman saw that Kamehameha was adamant. To him Misau was still a child. A recalcitrant child. Give her a little time, he thought, and she would come around.

The woman bowed low, shrugging her shoulders under the flowered cape. There was none so blind as he who refused to see.

Taguana arrived at the grass cottage just as Kiliki returned. Taguana had come with an entourage worthy of his position as a prince, as one chosen to marry a princess, as a favorite of Kamehameha, the new king of Molokai. With Taguana also had come his two first wives. They were lovely girls, only a few years older than Misau, and one of them was pregnant.

Taguana was a cousin-brother of Kamehameha. His mother was named Pelei and had long been out of favor with Kaumualii. Kiliki nodded to his wives and allowed Taguana to enter the cottage ahead of her.

She paused just inside the door. The other women of the hut stood at the far side of the room. Taguana stood at the edge of the mat, looking down in consternation at Misau.

Taguana was in his late teens, a very sober and serious young man. He took his position, his responsibilities, and his privileges very seriously. He was built like his father Kaumualii, broad in the shoulders and the chest, thick in the hips and the upper legs. His hair was smoothed back from his face, and his features were regular and comely. He was a handsome young man, and few were more well aware of it than he.

He talked to Misau in low tones, but she ignored him. He spoke of his wealth, which was considerable and was growing every day from the tributes paid by the masses to the royal family. "You have always been a favorite of mine, Misau," he said, speaking to the top of the girl's head. "You are the loveliest of girls. I will do all in my power to make you happy. It is sometimes too bad when there is no one among the nobles worthy of a princess. Then, as you know, it becomes necessary that she wed inside her own family. My wives will welcome you. I will welcome you. We will find much to make us happy in the years to come. Kamehameha has sent me to marry you, but I want to tell you, I do it with pleasure. When will it please you to marry me and come to live with me in my house?"

Misau tilted her head and stared up at him. Her eyes were empty, glazed, and unseeing. He seemed unaware of her grief, and smiled, awaiting her reply.

Misau said only, "Mihuana."

Taguana frowned but continued to stare

down at the girl prostrated on the mat. Kiliki moved forward quickly. "The child is overcome," she said, smiling up at Taguana. "As who would not be? To be asked to marry a fine and handsome young prince? Surely, you can understand her confusion?"

Taguana stared down at Misau. He shrugged. "Are you sure that is it? She is confused because of my proposal?"

"What young girl would not be?" Kiliki said. She stood between the prince and his unhappy sister. "I am sure that when you return the next time you will find her happy and singing. Do not, I beg you, concern yourself over a date for the wedding. Choose such a time as will please yourself. Perhaps you might want to talk it over with your wives? When you return you will find her eager and anxious to please you."

"Do you think so?" Taguana kept trying to peer around Kiliki, to see the girl slumped upon the mat.

Kiliki smiled widely. "I know it to be true. In my heart I know it." Kiliki tried to back him toward the front door of the hut. "I well remember how it was when the man I married came to my house. I was speechless. I was numb. But numb with happiness. Oh, I was so happy. As is Misau. You have made all of us so happy here today."

Chapter XXIV

The days passed quietly. Misau remained unmoving on the woven mat. Her eyes were dry. It was as if her tears were all shed. She could feel nothing anymore. She could only stare out at an empty world.

The sun rose and went down. By night the village grew quiet. Kiliki and the other women of the hut, exhausted by the long vigil, went to bed.

Misau did not sleep. She heard the sounds of the night. Dogs barked in the distance. The waves ran up onshore. Before dawn Misau got up. It was the first time she had willingly risen since she had sunk down there under the weight of Kamehameha's ultimatum. She felt as empty as a gourd.

Empty, lifeless, and worthless. She had no reason to go on living. Life spread out like an ugly vista that she did not care to see.

She pushed aside the cloth screen in the doorway and walked slowly out of the cottage. There was a crispness in the air. The world seemed fresh and clean and untroubled. A faint breeze stirred the palm fronds and wafted the fragrances of jasmine and trumpet vines and olapa to her.

She found the sweetness poignant. She walked slowly along the beach. How many times in her childhood and young girlhood had she run along this beach, finding it lovely and inviting? Now the night world was without promise, as was the day ahead, and all empty days of her life without Mihuana.

A small fire on a far hillside caught her attention for a moment, but only for a moment. She was unable to turn her thoughts outward. She no longer cared what happened.

She walked upward, toward the distant mountain peaks. Her lithe body seemed to float in the mists, her head tilted slightly as though she heard something that no one else could hear, something calling her in the night. A strange, chilling smile curled her lips as she listened. The call in the night was for her ears only.

The land grew steep, but she continued to walk easily and slowly upward. Past the *ohi'a*, shrouded in mists, its deep green leaves and bright blossoms providing shelter for the honey creepers and other small birds. Through the great and tiny ferns growing out of the fertile volcanic earth of the hillside. The rocks increased and the steep hill in places became sheer.

The sun broke through the dense jungle. She forded the occasional small streams, her bare feet chilled in the icy water rushing downward over the rocks. The water was the color of tea, stained by the pigmentation in leaves. Sometimes she sank to her ankles in black mud. But she was barely aware of her surroundings. Her mind was still turned inward, though she did smile faintly at the sound of morning birds in the underbrush, or the whisper of waters rushing to the sea.

Mihuana. That name was repeated over and over in her mind. She recalled his face, she saw him standing before her laughing, and at the memory of his laughter, tears filled her black eyes.

The sun was well up in the eastern sky when she reached the summit of the peak and the bower that she had built so slowly and lovingly. She went inside and was lost among the branches and overhanging ferns.

"Mihuana?"

She waited, listening, for a long time. When there was no reply, she felt emptier than ever. The thought of this special place and Mihuana had kept her moving forward. Now that she realized he was not here and would never come again and that she had known it all along, everything went black.

Her hands cut and torn, she wandered mindlessly away from the bower where she and Mihuana had lain together and loved. She came at last to the brink of a huge crater. For a long time she stood on the precipice, staring toward the sea, clean and calm in the distance, sparkling under the morning sun.

Her eyes filled with tears, but it was not as if she were weeping. It was the brilliant sunlight. She drew her arm across her eyes. Then she turned slowly all the way around. One more time she whispered the name of her love. "Mihuana."

But there was no longer any hope in the way she spoke. No sense of expectancy when she said his name. Once when she had whispered his name her loneliness was comforted. Now she knew there was no comfort on this earth for her without Mihuana.

She closed her eyes and walked forward. Her body plunged over the cliff, struck a ledge, bounced, and fell far below to a protected shelf. There she lay, unmoving, her body shattered and broken.

The sun continued to climb above the rain

forests, its rays poking and probing down into the crater. Misau's love was at last safe.

Mihuana sat in the prison compound, his ankles and wrists bound. He was unaware of the other prisoners surrounding him. He saw only the hatred he felt for the man who had lied to him, betrayed him, and finally imprisoned him.

He tried to tell himself that he had known the truth all the time, that he was a commoner and Misau was the most elite of the *alii*, a princess.

He tilted his head back against the coral wall of the compound. He had fooled himself because that was what he wanted. His desire for Misau had blinded him. Deep inside he had known that Kamehameha would never alter the kapu. He had been a fool and Kamehameha had treated him like a fool, telling him what he wanted to hear, lying to him when both had to know it was all lies, laughing behind his savage eyes. And it all ended here where he awaited— what? Death?

He rolled his head back and forth, captured and enslaved. There was not room enough inside his skin for the terror and agony eating at him. In his mind he went back over Kamehameha's lies, over the dangers he had willingly faced because he was buying the right to the hand of his love. How Kamehameha must have been laugh-

241

ing the whole time, sending him out on the most dangerous tasks, from which he always returned, to face a new mission, a new peril. What a fool he had been!

One of the other inmates shuffled across to where Mihuana sprawled on a mat. His ankles were fettered and he had to move slowly. Too big a step and he would fall, sprawling on his face, to the amusement and merriment of the other prisoners, all of whom were identically shackled.

At last the man knelt beside Mihuana. He spoke, but Mihuana was too filled with his own hatreds and agonies to care what went on outside his own tormented mind.

The man whispered it again. He said, "Misau is missing."

Gradually, Mihuana became aware of the man kneeling close beside him. He stared at him. "What? What did you say?"

"Misau is missing," the man whispered.

Mihuana felt his heart lurch. It was as if it had been barely functioning and was now abruptly pumped back to life again. His mind cleared. Of course Misau was missing. She had run up to their hiding place, and she awaited him there. Why had he not seen that this was what she would do? He did not know where they could go; it was only a matter of time until the hiding place was uncovered. But for this moment, none of that mattered. All that mattered was Misau waiting for him.

Mihuana nodded at the man who crept away, afraid to be seen by his captors in the company of the doomed Mihuana.

Mihuana looked at the ropes binding his ankles and tested those securing his wrists at the small of his back. Whimpering, with the frustrations gnawing at him, Mihuana worked the ropes, moving his wrists back and forth. They chafed and cut and his wrists bled, but still he kept working at them. He was like an animal obsessed. There was no physical pain. There was only the distance separating him from Misau.

Finally, he was able to catch his thumb under the bloodied knot. He kept pulling at it, until his thumb felt ready to drop off. The knots gave at last, and the ropes parted and slipped from his wrists. He felt the blood running down his hands and between his fingers. He did not stop. He had become like a frenzied animal. At last his ankles were free as well.

The man who had spoken to Mihuana now hopped slowly across the compound to where the guard stood with long spear in his hand. Mihuana had not spoken to the man, but he knew what the fellow would do. He would have only a few seconds in which to scale the high walls.

Across the compound the man began to stumble, to fall, to pick himself up. He screamed in rage at the guard. The guard watched him for a few moments in amusement. Then the guard lost his patience as the man cursed at him as if he'd lost his mind.

The guard lifted his spear and ran at the man. He jabbed his spear within inches of the man's face. The other prisoners began chanting and yelling.

Mihuana watched no more. He sprang up and clambered up the wall, catching the top with his fingers and levering himself over. Across the compound the guard saw him and screamed, commanding him to halt.

The guard forgot the cursing man and raced across the compound. The man sighed, smiling, watching Mihuana scale the wall.

Mihuana pulled himself over the jagged edges of the top of the wall. He dropped to the ground, running toward the jungle as soon as his feet struck the ground. He had only a few moments before the guard would shout for help and the sentries would be on his trail.

Running felt good. He massaged his torn and bleeding wrists, but they did not matter. Not now. Nothing mattered except that he was free and that Misau awaited him. For the first time since his arrest, he felt alive and purposeful.

He spent almost an hour laying down a false trail. He wanted the guards to believe he was headed for the rough terrain of the north shore, inaccessible land where a man could hide for a long time. As he ran, however, he climbed, returning always to the rain forests, the high tor shining above him.

He laughed involuntarily. Soon he would hold his love in his arms again. She awaited him, and he had only to throw the stupid guards off his trail and he could run to her.

He was moving upward through the dense jungle. The birds came to life, taking flight in their bright plumage and chattering wildly as he raced past.

He could see his pursuers. They were like tiny men far below him. He watched with pleasure as they followed one of the false trails he had carefully laid down for them. He grinned coldly. By the time they found it to be a false lead, he would be at the peak, and truly lost to them.

He came out àt last to the secret place he and Misau had shared. They had lain together, discovering everything about each other. Here they had loved and dreamed together.

He stopped short, thinking he had come to the wrong place. Yet, when he looked around, every other sign was right.

Only the bower was gone. The plaited roof had been torn down, the hut destroyed.

Unmanned, he stared. At first he was certain that Kamehameha's men had followed him and Misau up here, discovered their hiding place, and destroyed it.

But there was no sign that men in any numbers had been here. The quiet and serenity still prevailed, the beauty was untouched. Only the bower was destroyed.

Gradually, he found signs of Misau. His heart sank. She had been here, and only recently. She had torn the little bower to pieces, even shredding the mat she had woven.

With his heart in his throat he followed her path upward. He found the tall ledge where she had stood overlooking the crater. His eyes filling with tears, he gazed down into the calderas.

Far down below, he saw her. She lay on a small outcropping of rocks, her body twisted at an odd angle, her head back. She lay very still.

He bit back the sobs that welled up from the pit of his stomach. He knew she was dead.

He stood for a long time, staring down at her body. He could not leave her down there. She looked lonely and abandoned. He must go to her.

Slowly he let himself over the side of the cliff. For a moment he was suspended in space. Then his foot found a limb, and he cautiously worked his way down the face of the cliff. He had to stop often, perching above nothingness, until his foot could find an outjutting rock or a stunted tree. It would be so easy to let go, to plummet downward into the crater.

The rocks cut into his hands, but he paid no attention to physical pain. It could no longer touch him. He had been hurt as badly as a human being could be hurt. His heart was broken, and he no longer noticed that his wrists were torn and his arms ached from holding on to the side of the sheer precipice. At last he reached her. The overhang was small, only a few feet of rock and vegetation jutting out of the volcanic soil. He rested a moment, his back to the wall, staring down into the cone of the crater.

He knelt beside her broken body, weeping.

He never knew how long he stayed beside her, holding her shattered body in his arms. After a long time he looked up. A small goat's pathway led toward the top.

He took her up in his arms and began the slow, arduous ascent. The sun crested, but he was unaware of anything except the slow climbing, one foot after the other, her body close in his arms.

Chapter XXV

Grief was his only reality. Rocks cut his hands, briars snagged at his legs and arms. Mihuana was unaware of physical discomfort. He tried to think what he might do now that Misau was dead. But he could not think beyond his desire to carry Misau back home. When he reached the edge of the cliff, he paused.

He laid her down upon a mat of wildflowers and vines and knelt beside her, alternately weeping and speaking her name. Taking each of her hands in his hands, he massaged them, as if willing life into her body from his own. He bent over her and kissed her, pleading with her to answer his kiss. Her lips were cold. He shuddered.

Finally he took her up in his arms and walked downhill through the jungle and the rain forest. He talked to her as he walked. Quietly. He tried to remember all the small and happy times they had shared. He foraged deep in his memory to the first time he saw her, the first time he'd kissed her lips, the first time she'd surrendered herself to him, happily, wholeheartedly, with pagan abandon.

He plodded through the jungle. His arms became numb under the dead weight of her body, but it never occurred to him to lay her aside for a moment. He kept his head up, his strangely lighted eyes fixed on something ahead in the distance.

He had been walking downward through the ferns and the trees for several hours when he heard movement in the underbrush. He stiffened, paused, and looked around.

Suddenly, Kamehameha's warriors appeared before him. They spoke to him, but he did not answer or slow his pace. He kept plodding forward.

The soldiers, startled, thrust their spears and hatchets out before him, blocking his way, but he did not blink, nor did he appear to see the weapons barring his path.

Again they ordered him to halt, but he continued to move forward with the girl's body hanging awkwardly from his arms.

The leaders shrugged and then fell into a

lock step behind Mihuana, their lances at the ready. They had heard that the princess had taken leave of her senses, and they could see she was dead. They believed that Mihuana had also lost his reason, but as long as he continued walking toward the village they would follow him. Their mission had been accomplished. Kamehameha had sent them out with orders to return with Mihuana as their prisoner or carried across a shield.

Before the strange entourage reached the village, word of their coming had preceded them. People ran out of the huts and stood shading their eyes, staring as Mihuana passed. Seeing their hero so, some bit their lips or blinked away sudden tears.

As they approached the hut where Kamehameha lived, the warriors tried again to stop Mihuana. They had heard of Mihuana's legendary exploits on the field of battle and few cared to tangle with him, even as exhausted as he was, with his mind addled by grief. They were brave but not foolish: Mihuana was a legendary warrior.

Mihuana seemed not to see or hear them. He was listening to voices inside his own mind.

As Mihuana reached the hut, the cloth flap was thrown back and Kamehameha appeared, standing tall and fierce.

He saw his sister's dead body and heard the silence of buried hopes and lost dreams.

"This is the price of her hatred, and of his rage," Kamehameha thought to himself. "The wounds of the heart. How they cry out in their pain and loss. I suppose I ought to hate her, too, for doing this terrible thing."

He realized his eyes were wet. It was not only because the dead girl was his sister. It was because she believed so little in the way of life that drove him, that pointed the true way for all people, the laws and the taboos. If only she had listened to him. He felt alone on the shoreline of an immense and empty ocean. Nothing he could do would change anything.

A few slow tears rolled down his face. The soldiers watched, uneasy.

Mihuana stared at the young prince. His mouth twisted with his hatred, his voice was hoarse with grief and despair. "I have brought her back to you," Mihuana said, his voice cracking with weariness. "Do you not see what you have done? You who would play as the gods with our lives?"

"Enough!" Kamehameha's roar was heard by the farthest person in the village. "I have committed no crime. I followed the kapus. I tried to make her listen. She would not. No more than you would. If now she lies dead, I am not at fault."

"You will stand branded forever liar, betrayer. You lied to me. You betrayed your sister. The hardness of your own heart condemns you. The lies of your own lips condemn you. The death of this innocent girl stands as a mark against you into eternity."

"Take him away," Kamehameha ordered, swinging his arm in an imperious gesture. "My sister shall be buried at sea. This man shall be returned to the stockade, where he shall be bound and watched constantly until time for his trial."

Mihuana was too exhausted to protest when the soldiers took Misau from his arms. He stared at her, then reached out to touch her one last time. When she was gone, borne away by the soldiers, he had no reason to go on standing, or living, or pretending to live, and he sank heavily to his knees. He was aware only of bone weariness. He stared up at Kamehameha, his hatred intense and livid.

Kamehameha signaled the soldiers to lift Mihuana to his feet and to hold him.

"When you are ready to apologize to me, I shall listen. But you shall stand trial, and you shall die for your crimes against the kapus of our people."

"Crimes?" Mihuana's head jerked up. He spat at the prince. "What crimes greater than yours? You cannot hurt me now. You can no longer touch me at all." He gestured in the direction the soldiers had carried Misau. "There goes my life. With her. With your dead sister. Whatever you do now is on your own head."

Kamehameha swore. It was one thing for

Mihuana to speak to him with less than worshipful respect when they were alone, but for him to rage like this, in front of the entire village, this could not be borne.

Kamehameha swung out savagely, as if to break and destroy anything near him. His voice trumpeted his anger. For a long time after he returned to the interior of the house, he went about destroying everything in his way with his fists.

Kamehameha stood silent and withdrawn at the head of the council of the elders. He remained quiet and controlled as they brought the prisoner before him.

He stared at Mihuana, shocked. After all this time in the stockade, bound hand and foot, how could Mihuana still stand unbowed and unrepentant?

Kamehameha felt the choler rise inside him. It was as if somebody had set off fireworks in his brain. His mind flared and burned with hatreds and nausea. This trial would rebound against him, no matter what he did. Mihuana was a commoner who had risen to great power and legendary status through his own wit and strengths and power. The stories told about Mihuana around the campfires at night were almost as popular as the tales of the gods. That was the trouble with allowing a commoner to rise above the masses. The masses revered him and spoke in awe of his exploits. It would be a long time before the stories of Mihuana would be wiped from the minds of the masses, but erased they would be.

Kamehameha saw that prisoner and council waited, silent and cold. All eyes were upon him. He burned with self-righteous fury. There was enough evidence for any council to lop off this criminal's head. And yet, they spoke of *pu'uhonua*, the place of refuge for lawbreakers. There was no justice when a commoner could flaunt the rules and be permitted a chance of escaping punishment.

Kamehameha spoke at last. "Criminal. I ask you one more time. Do you repent of your crimes against the kapus?"

"I have no crimes," Mihuana replied in that soft, reasonable tone that made Kamehameha's insides rage. "The only crimes are yours. You have forgotten your own beginnings. You have become law only unto yourself. The death of your sister is on your hands."

"Stop," Kamehameha commanded. "You are not here to make charges but to receive sentence. I hearby sentence you to death. By beheading."

A cry went up among the people. Kamehameha's head jerked up. His teeth chattered with savage impatience. His word was law. He would not tolerate this display against his word. He stared out at the people who so recently had hailed him as hero.

He drew himself up to his full height. The sun suddenly flooded the world with its light. Kamehameha glared at the people, trying to intimidate them by the strength of his gaze. He wanted them to know that any one of them could stand in the place of this prisoner if he ordered it.

"By beheading," Kamehameha repeated. Until this moment he had not realized the restrictions on his power.

One of the kahunas spoke, hesitantly, yet with conviction. "It is our feeling that the prisoner deserves the right to run to *pu'uhonua*."

Kamehameha turned the full fury of his gaze upon the priest who dared confront him. "And I say he has forfeited the right by his refusal to recant, to repent, to apologize for his charges against his rulers." Kamehameha spoke coldly, loudly, aware of the voices of dissent from the crowd.

The kahunas spoke in measured tones, calmly explaining to the monarch the limits of his power. The rights of the masses called for the prisoner's being allowed to run for his life, to race for a place of refuge and to remain forever removed from threat of retaliation from the state.

Kamehameha touched the knife in its sheath at his side. He could stride forward to where the insolent Mihuana stood and chop off his head as he had chopped off the head of that other criminal, Aprilhana. It sickened him that now when he was fortified with the guns from the white men that would make conquering the islands easy, he should be thwarted like this. He felt the illness stirring deep inside him. He would not endure it. Didn't these people see the destiny ahead for him? Supreme ruler of all the islands. Did they not see that his power was growing, would grow, and as he found laws like these limiting his power, he would do away with them? As he would deal with any man who dared to stand in his way.

And yet he hesitated. Inwardly, he vowed his strengths would be multiplied a thousandfold. There would be a place beyond which even the kahunas would not dare go in opposing him. But, his hands trembling, he admitted this was in the future. Though he was the king of Molokai, he was only a prince here on Kauai. At this moment it looked as if he must bow to the will of the priests and the strength of the masses.

"If you escape my runners," he said at last to Mihuana, "it is understood you are to live in this place of *pu'uhonua*, as a refugee, for all the remaining days of your life. If you ever return to this place, to any place outside the place of refuge, your life is forfeit."

To his surprise, Mihuana did not even answer him. The commoner stood, tall, invin-

257

cible, unbowed, staring up at his regent, his face cold and implacable with hatred.

"Did you not hear me?" Kamehameha raged.

Mihuana shrugged. "I hear you. But I do not believe you will allow me to reach a place of refuge. I do not trust you. Because as long as I live my life is testimony against you—your dishonesty, your lying, your murdering. . . ."

"Take him away," Kamehameha cried. He turned his back and walked. His head was lowered, his shoulders round under the flowered cape. His heart pounded raggedly.

The tattooed priest gave the signal. The ropes were removed from Mihuana's wrists and ankles.

For a moment the tall youth stood as if dazed. Then he massaged his wrists, making the blood circulate in them again.

"Go," the priest said to Mihuana. "You have the distance of the village limits as a head start. The soldiers will pursue you. The men chosen are the fastest runners of this island. They will be armed with lances, spears, knives. If they come within striking distance of you . . ."

He left his warning unfinished.

Chapter XXVI

Mihuana stared at the back of his hated monarch. He screamed once, "Murderer!"

Then he heeled about, running swiftly, lithely, naked, stripped of all protection. He ran through the crowd, which, cheering as one man, stepped back to allow him to pass. Some of the people reached out to him in affection. Others simply stood aside silently, reverently.

He was the most rare commoner of them all, a man that the priests and chiefs deferred to, until Kamehameha came along. There were those who whispered that perhaps Kamehameha was jealous of the way Mihuana was revered. He didn't want to share his glory. And then there was Mi-

huana's love for the prince's sister. It was a
taboo as old as the tribes, but it could have
been allowed in Mihuana's case.

When Mihuana reached the far limits of
the village, a cry rose up. The swift-running
guards raced out from the council seat. The
people had closed ranks after Mihuana
passed and they did not part as swiftly or
as willingly as they had for Mihuana. The
soldiers cursed them and threatened them
with their lances until they fell aside.

An obsessive idea can dominate the mind.
In the case of Mihuana, it was forceful
enough to launch him up the slope and for
the moment to rob him of all caution. He
bounded among the ferns, the briars, the
boulders. He paid no attention to the steady
rise of the incline. If he ran downslope, his
pace would be faster, but in his mind there
was room enough only for the thought that
he and Misau had become lost to the world
in the rain forests of the high peaks. Thinking of her gave him strength. Every moment he felt in greater command of his legs.
His strides were long. He knew where he
was going. His pursuers did not.

He heard the soldiers breaking through
the underbrush behind him. They were
keeping pace better than he had believed
they could in this wild terrain. He continued to climb, watching the west sun, keeping that highest peak always in sight.

The sounds of the guards made his heart

sink a little. They were chosen for their fleetness of foot, for their knowledge of the jungle. The short head start, the chance of reaching the refuge, was a delusion. Heads of state did not have to play fair. He had from the first mistrusted Kamehameha. This man was a liar and betrayer, not above setting traps ahead for him. He had proof of this perfidy.

For a moment he debated whether it wouldn't be better for him to find a place to hide; the soldiers, if they missed him, would go for a long way before they realized what had happened. But in the end, he mistrusted his instinct. He could hear the soldiers behind him. They must be listening to his breaking through the undergrowth too. If there were suddenly silence, this would alert the soldiers. They were old hands at this pursuit game. They knew all its tricks. They would simply stop and search until they found him.

And so he continued to climb. He was panting now, partly, he admitted, from fear. How he wished for a cool mouthful of water. He crossed small creeks, but the sounds behind him were too close. He dared not pause.

He came upon rocky ledges, and knew he was reaching the tree line. He raced along in the ravines. There was only silence now, silence broken by his strained effort to breathe.

His heart felt as if it would burst. He slowed, listening. There were no sounds of running feet. He must have, for the moment at least, thrown them off his trail. This meant a redoubling of effort, it meant scrambling over boulders and huge rocks to race upward and then around. Suddenly, he was descending the other side of the mountain. The view was splendid, but he had no time to enjoy it. One false step and there would be a lance in his back.

He was lost now. As lost as any of the soldiers might be; this was strange territory. He glanced up at the sun as he ran wildly downhill.

He heard a shout far above and behind. A lookout had spotted him. The soldiers gathered, racing downhill behind him. The pounding, pulsating, throbbing of his heart seemed to threaten his sanity. He grew dizzy from fatigue.

Once he burst into the forested area again. The sun burned and blinded him. His mind began to play tricks. He heard sounds ahead of him in the forest. He paused, deciding to run in a new direction. But when he stopped, the running sounds also stopped and he realized they were in his mind.

Fevered and fatigued, he ran on. Mechanically, he placed one foot ahead of the other. He became aware that the ground was flat. An overwhelming realization flashed through Mihuana's mind. He had crossed the island. The refuge was ahead.

He stumbled, falling to his knees. His legs felt weak. It was as if all his bones were broken. He stayed on all fours for a long time, breathing through his mouth, his head hanging. He tried to listen for sounds behind him, but he could hear nothing except the pounding of his own heart, the rushing of blood like waterfalls in his temples. At last he pulled himself up before a spear could flash through the forest and embed itself in his back. He stood weakly, trembling.

When he lifted his head he saw four men. They were climbing over a stone wall. They looked emaciated, old, and weak. He felt suddenly overcome by a heaviness of his legs and a palpitating of his heart that made movement impossible.

"My dear friend," a voice was saying. "You have almost made it. You are at a refuge. Come."

"Please come," another man urged. "Please hurry. You must be all the way over the wall or the spears can get you."

Mihuana nodded and stalked forward, seeing the wall ahead of him. Behind him, he heard the pound of running feet as the soldiers burst out of the forest, shouting.

They hurled their lances, but they were too far away. The four old men hurried him. They reached the wall, scrambling over it.

Mihuana pulled himself up and fell to safety beyond the high wall. The old men had stayed behind, their bodies shielding him. He felt a sense of supreme victory. He sprawled out on the ground and lay panting, aware that someone was holding a gourd of water to his lips.

He drank greedily. Some of the dizziness faded and he began to believe he might live. Life held no passion for him, no great promise. He suddenly realized that he did not care whether a soldier's lance had pierced his back beyond this wall. It was strange. To have run so desperately and then decide that life was not worth the effort. Gradually, he began to think differently. *I am alive. So long as I live I mock the callousness, the evil of Kamehameha. Perhaps that is the reason I live.* For the moment, it was enough.

Cutter learned of Misau's death from the natives. Afterward he wandered the island for hours recalling her strange, exotic beauty. He had seen her only a few times, and yet how deeply she had become embedded in his heart. He regretted what he felt might have been between them.

That night Cutter saw that Captain Cook was preparing to sail, and he made plans to desert. He knew Captain Cook wanted to sail before trouble broke out between the natives and the seamen. The day before, a cutter was turned back several yards from the beach. The native men, bearing spears and lances, had encircled the boat, the lances held at ready. They spoke loudly, though none of the seamen knew what they were saying. The cutter turned back and was accompanied all the way to the *Resolution* by the grim-faced natives in outriggers.

Later that day, word reached the ship that several young girls had died of the diseases spread by the seamen. The natives demanded to know how many more of the young and lovely girls would fall victims to this disease. Captain Cook was distraught but helpless. He could not answer the question. He foresaw the decimation of the tribe and realized that the kahunas must too. There was no longer the old warmth between the natives and the visitors. Warriors stood armed at the shoreline, the people were surly, and the flow of gifts had dried up.

When Captain Cook learned that the *Discovery* was repaired well enough to sail he declared: "Then we sail with the tide." Cutter Murphy and several men were sent ashore to fill kegs with fresh water. It took all of Malu's statesmanship to convince the priests that the men would not fraternize with the people while they were onshore. All afternoon kegs of water were ferried out to the ship and Cutter planned his desertion.

In the night, before the ships sailed, Cutter Murphy let himself over the stern and, carrying nothing of his worldly goods, he headed for the shore. His breath burning in his chest, he swam underwater as far from the *Resolution* as possible. Then, with long, easy strokes, he swam quietly to the beach.

The town was asleep when Cutter came ashore. He crept through the village, heading toward the jungle. Dogs ran out, sniffing and growling, but he stood quietly until they lost interest and returned to their resting places. He entered the jungle and followed a trail he had discovered weeks earlier, finally reaching a promontory from which he could overlook the bay, the ships, and the village. It was quiet in the darkness. Not even the birds stirred as he passed. He was damp and chilled, but this did not matter. What mattered was that he was free!

At last, exhausted, he sank against a tree and was soon asleep. He awoke with the rising sun of morning. His heart sank. He felt the tug of uncertainty as he watched the two ships move slowly out of the harbor. He was cut off, perhaps forever, from the outside world he knew. Still, it was a decision he had made calmly and rationally. The life he had lived until this moment had left much to be desired; now he could start his life anew, doing the things he wanted to do here in paradise.

He sat still until the ships had cleared the bay and were bobbing in the rough waters of the open sea. By now he would be missed. It was the hour for his watch, and a search would be made. Not that Captain cook would care very much that a junior officer had disappeared during the night.

He sagged against the tree. He had cast his die. He was not blind to the recent hostility of the natives. He had no idea if they would welcome him or behead him then cut out his belly and feast on it.

Cutter sat with his back against the tree until the ships' sails had disappeared over the horizon.

Kamehameha came out of his hut and stared at the open bay. The hated ships of the British were gone, thanks be to the gods!

Kamehameha felt that his life was taking on new meaning. He had done well in his trades. He had a supply of gunpowder and he had twenty rifles. Twenty rifles against men with axes and spears would certainly turn the tide of any battle. He imagined himself conquering the inhabited islands of this chain. He would be the king of all the islands, his power the greatest ever known by these people. He would make changes in laws, in taboos, and customs. With guns to back him up, there was nothing he could not accomplish. He spoke to the lieutenant standing beside him. "I think places of refuge are dangerous. They harbor criminals who would overthrow law and order. My first order will be the end of these places."

The lieutenant winced. He knew it still rankled Kamehameha that Mihuana had outrun the soldiers and was safe.

"It is a custom as old as our people, sir," the lieutenant said. "If a man can run to safety, then the gods themselves forgive him and he is innocent."

Kamehameha's face twisted. He stared out across the clear bay to the place where those ships had ridden at anchor for the worst two weeks of his life. "It may be a custom, but it is not a law that I view with favor," he said. "And I shall change it."

The lieutenant merely sighed and shrugged. He had learned one thing in the past months with Kamehameha. One never got anywhere by arguing with the prince.

Chapter XXVII

The *Resolution* and the *Discovery* sailed from the bay into hell in the open waters of the Straits of Kauai. Waves battered the ships. Storms bore down on them immediately without compassion. The winds howled from dawn to dusk, and increased their fury by night, screaming down upon the helpless craft from an empty heaven.

Captain Cook, looking forbidding and imperious in his oilskin, its collar turned up about his face, his hair wet and clammy and plastered against his skin, fought his way to the bridge. His mouth was set and his body strained forward against the wind as he clutched at the railing to keep from being blown away. This storm was another

269

bloody nuisance, and he was wholly sick and tired of these Pacific typhoons. No wonder the Spanish had missed this part of the Pacific in their mapmaking. It was a hellish good area to avoid. But he had made up his mind to one thing. He would not be put off by storms.

He recognized the executive officer, Lieutenant James King, fighting his way aft amidships. He liked the young officer, found him intelligent and knowledgeable about the sea. Not this sea, for hell's sake, because no man could read it, but Lieutenant King was a good seaman. Coming face-to-face, both shook their heads and hung on for dear life. They put their heads close together to be heard against the roar of the storm. "Never have known such weather in all my years at sea," the lieutenant observed.

"Nor I," the captain said, his modulated Oxford accent battered slightly by the wind. "Anyone missing?" he asked.

The lieutenant shook his head. "Only the midshipman."

"Well, he was a strange one. He had little place in the navy. The navy's a place for discipline, or it's nothing at all."

"True. We believe the midshipman went over the side in the bay. He was not at muster the next morning."

"Good riddance. We can cover his watches."

270

"That's all taken care of, sir. We're riding out the storm rather well. But the sail-maker reports the ship is taking a beating. A real battering."

The captain shook his head. "We'll be lucky if we can ride this one out."

"Very lucky," the lieutenant agreed in a sardonic tone. He gripped the railing, the wind spitting rain directly into his face no matter where he turned. His eyes smarted. His head was ready to burst.

"I truly believe," the captain said, "that once we've cleared these latitudes, we'll hit smoother sailing."

"We'd better," the lieutenant said. "We need a letup to make repairs, or we'll have to turn back."

"Turn back?" The captain shook his head. "No, mister. We won't turn back."

"We may have to, sir," the lieutenant said. "If we sustain much more damage, we'll have to run for a harbor."

They had left that island under a cloud, and the captain realized there was danger in returning. He did not bother putting his fears into words for the young lieutenant. Plenty of time for that if this weather didn't let up and they were forced into some port for repairs. They saluted smartly and moved forward slowly, bent against the wind.

The men could barely move, the decks were inclined so steeply. They walked, gripping the railings for dear life. The wind stung tears into their eyes. Narrow escapes became routine. They spoke to each other, vital, life-saving warnings, only to have their words blown apart upon the wind, unheard. And so they worked on, hour after hour. The ship labored onward; the high white crests ran past, hissing and screaming in the wind.

The word from the captain was to hold fast, they would worry through it somehow. And most of the men believed this, or wanted to believe it. After all, Captain Cook had the deserved reputation of being the world's greatest navigator. He must have seen and weathered greater storms in his long and noble career. The men nodded, agreeing with the captain's assessment. They would ride it out, and they were still saying this when the foremast crumpled and the captain surrendered, ordering a wide, one-hundred-and-eighty-degree turn and a run for the safe harbor at Waimea Bay.

Kamehemeha began to suspect that Mihuana lived a charmed life. How many times had he sent the warrior to places of greatest peril in battle, only to see that hated face, set and cold, return time and again. There had to be the power of kings that a hated commoner could be put to death quietly and finally. He made up his mind. He would send spies across the island to watch the place of refuge. If Mihuana showed his face outside it, or even lifted his head above the wall, his life was forfeit. Kamehameha admitted he was obsessed by the need for the death of Mihuana. But he felt he could never truly rule these islands as long as the hated commoner lived.

Nor was Mihuana his only problem. On Molokai, the former king was stirring up trouble. King Keoua had agreed to live quietly, but he was already growing restless, testing the winds for an uprising against the absent King Kamehameha.

Kamehameha's spy network kept him closely apprised of the moves of King Keoua. But Kamehameha, who had magnanimously allowed the monarch to go on living, gradually became convinced that only Keoua's death would bring peace and tranquility to the island. He suspected that many of Keoua's ministers and followers were fomenting trouble. His spies assured him this was true, and Kamehameha announced a list of names to be erased along with the king. The list grew longer with each name carefully memorized.

Kamehameha decided he would return to the island. Only this time he would arrive armed with muskets and firepower.

He paced the floor. How he wished for a cannon. Even the smaller swivel gun that Cook had demonstrated for him. But what he needed most of all was one of the cutters from the big ships. He had attempted to buy such a craft, but Cook kept putting him off, not refusing his generous offers, but simply delaying until the ships sailed off with all the cutters. He wished now he had been more forceful. If Cook had not been willing to give him a cutter, he should have had the courage and the strength to take one.

With a cannon, he could sail into the harbor at Molokai, where one well-placed shot would end the uprisings against him forever. He felt an almost sensual pleasure from contemplating it. He could see himself standing in the bow of the cutter, the swivel gun fixed on shore, and surrounded by a hundred of his outriggers. This would stir up terror in the hearts of the bravest monarchs, and Keoua, he already knew, was not one of these.

He would settle with Keoua once and for all. Then he would turn his attention to the other islands. He called in his ministers and boat builders. They discussed the cutter for hours but arrived always at the same discouraging conclusion: without one of the boats as a model, his builders could not hope to duplicate it. Kamehameha finally threw up his arms in defeat. They would continue to build the kind of craft they understood best. They bowed and retreated from his scowling presence.

There were so many things Kamehameha

would do differently if he had to do them over. He would have personally driven a spear into Mihuana's body. He would have sent Keoua into exile and ordered the king, and whatever followers cared to go, aboard outriggers and sent them out to sea and into the hands of the gods.

He saw one thing clearly: it was not allowed for a monarch to be kindly, or to act generously. He admitted that in every instance his instincts had told him to go for the belly, and in the future, by God, he would follow those kingly instincts.

He had women, but like most men obsessed by war or ambition, women failed to gratify him, or to tire his fretful mind. He didn't sleep well. Once he finally calmed his busy mind enough to fall asleep, he was beset with dreams. And of all the dreams he hated and feared most was the chilled sight of Misau reaching for him across a damp and forbidding morass. She said something to him. She kept calling out his name, and when he would reluctantly reply, she would say something, and though he strained with all his might, even woke sweating and straining, he could not hear what Misau was saying.

He told himself he didn't give a damn about a girl weak enough to take her own life for love of a commoner. Yet what he would not pay for a single night's untroubled rest! Still, every night he saw Misau's lovely face across this misty and bottom-less pit, calling to him, saying things that he knew he must know if he were to live and prosper, and yet the words were un-clear, lost in the night.

He shuddered.

His second or third day in the mountains, Cutter began to feel the urge for a full meal. He had been eating the inexhaustible sup-ply of fruit on the island. But he longed for a pot roast or English mutton fixed with po-tatoes and onions. God, how he longed for a meal in London.

Cutter stared down at the village, the shoreline, the empty harbor. Thank God the ships were gone. It was time for him to go down to the village and turn himself over to the natives. He could not stay up here much longer without someone finding him. It would be better by far to turn himself in, and yet he delayed.

He kept remembering the wooden knives with sharks' teeth the natives had used to remove Billy Hutch's belly and entrails. These people were cannibals, although they seemed not to feed upon one another. Per-haps they butchered and ate their enemies. He wasn't certain, any more than he was sure how he would be received in the vil-lage, as friend or foe?

If it had not been for the unfortunate spread of syphilis and gonorrhea, he would not have hesitated. But they were dying down there. He watched the burial ceremonies and he knew. And God knew how many more would die before the epidemic was brought under control, if it ever was. He, of course, would be suspect.

And so he delayed, living off coconuts and papayas and yams and berries. He came to sense that he was being watched. If one person knew him to be hidden up here, soon the whole island would know. Every rustling sound in the jungle became a watcher. He crept about, constantly looking over his shoulder, panicking at the movement of a bird in the underbrush.

One day, restless, he wandered away from the camp he had built on the hillside. He had walked less than a mile as he mulled over the wisdom of turning himself in and facing death by cannibalism, or being allowed to partake of roast suckling pig and hot yams. God, how his mouth watered.

He heard a stirring in the underbrush. Steadying himself, he kept walking slowly, as though he heard nothing. He made a complete circle, and when he heard someone break through the ferns, he lunged out, spreading his arms and dragging the watcher down.

For a few moments he lay on the ground, under a canopy of flowers, of colorful birds, and of overhanging trees. His hands told him he had captured a woman.

Slowly, cautiously, he released her and stepped back. She dragged herself away and then turned to stare at him. There was no sign of fear or trepidation on her face. Her face was expressionless. There was no trace of self-consciousness in the way she sat, her full breasts bared, a flowered sarong loosely hung about her hips. He stared at her beauty, grace, and loveliness.

A thousand questions rushed to his lips, questions he could not ask and that she could not answer. He knew one thing for certain. He had never seen her before. If he had seen her, he would have recalled. She had the beauty and charm and tranquility of Misau, and yet her beauty far surpassed that of the lost girl.

She was slender and sat with her shoulders straight, like a dancer; her neck was long and graceful. Her brown eyes, fixed on him with interest but without fear, were deep-set, soft, gentle, and trusting. He sensed a wounded look lurking in their depths, but a lovely smile hid the pain. Her face was set in tranquil composure, with that solemn dignity that was a heritage of her people. Her black hair was long, flowed smoothly past her hips. Her nose was straight, slightly upturned at the end above lips that were perfectly formed, and white, even teeth. Her smile clung to those lips, lighting those dark eyes and lingering for a moment after her face had returned to its natural repose. She was dazzlingly lovely. She watched him with more than detached interest, and he was certain that it was she who had been watching him silently for days. They looked at each other without words. They had no words. They had only the language of the eyes. Her dark eyes raked his face with pleasure.

Cutter stared at her beautifully molded face. She smiled in a faintly embarrassed way. She sprawled there, unconsciously twisting a tendril of black hair about one long, shapely finger.

When she finally did speak, her words were alien and meaningless to him, but her throaty voice entranced him so that he longed to keep her talking.

Gradually, they learned to converse in sign language, naming the word in their own language, repeating it over and over until the other understood, could repeat it and point to it, It was slow, but rewarding. At last he discovered her name: Waialua.

"Waialua," he repeated the name, tasting it upon his lips. She smiled and nodded and touched his chest with her hand.

"Cutter," he said. "Cutter Murphy."

"Cutter," she repeated. "Cutter Murphy."

They laughed together. They had come so far together in such a short time.

She asked him about hunger, and he nodded. He took her to his hideout, and she seemed to know the place as well as he.

After many hours she disappeared, and though he begged her to stay, she seemed not to understand him. She vanished in the jungle and he sat emptily, wondering when she would return.

At dawn the next morning he tossed, troubled, on his bed of branches and vines. He opened his eyes and found her kneeling, staring down at his face.

"Cutter," she said.

"Waialua," he answered, and she showed him the food she had brought. He ate ravenously, and, smiling, she watched him. But when he gestured that he should go down to the village with her, she looked blank and shook her lovely head.

Chapter XXVIII

The daily language lessons went swiftly. Her native language was easier, because it was simpler, with fewer letters. Its vowel combinations were complex and there were few consonants. One word did duty for several. *Aloha* was hello, good-bye, a festive occasion, a parting, a partying. The abstract words were toughest.

But they were happy working together, being together. This was all that seemed to matter to Waialua. She arrived early in the morning, bearing him daily gifts of food— roast pig, wild foul in sauce, poi, salads with every exotic fruit stirred into them. She loved to watch him eat, and sat contentedly with him all day. She seemed to ask nothing more than his company; she made no demands for the future. It was strange. Very strange.

He tried to talk to her about when he should go with her to her village and present himself to her people. It was a simple question and clear enough, it seemed to him. But each time he broached the subject, telling her that if he were discovered here it might well go harder upon him than if he turned himself in, she misunderstood and then said, "I do not know. I do not know."

Once she looked at him oddly, and her eyes seemed to fill with tears. "Later. Later," she said.

It troubled and perplexed him that she was frightened. But most of the time she was content. She laughed and chattered in a fractured combination of her language and English that he followed as best he could and that he found musical and lovely. He encouraged her to speak and would teach her involved English sentences because it was so lovely to hear her wonderful voice struggle with the strange words.

One day he sat looking at her. He reached out and took her hand and held it tightly against the pounding of his heart in his rib cage. He gazed into her eyes, smiled gently, and said slowly, "You—have—my heart."

She smiled, nodding, and took his hand

in her own, covering her breast with his fingers and pressing them.

"You," she said in that musical, slow, halting, and solemn way, "you have my heart."

His hand remained on the fullness of her breast. It was the first time he had touched her, and he waited for her to withdraw. But she sat motionless. His fingers closed on her hardened nipple, cupping her breast, caressing. Her eyes glazed over slightly, and she leaned toward him. With his other hand he reached out and caught her head, bringing it closer to his parted mouth. Her eyes closed like a baby's and she seemed to melt against him. It was as natural as breathing.

For a long time he held her, caressing her and kissing her, fondling her smooth body. It seemed a moment, it seemed forever. It seemed the answer to everything he had ever been seeking. He drew her so that she lay across him and he could feel her heart surging and pounding against his own.

It was late afternoon, later than she usually stayed up here; the setting sun spread a brilliant red over the island and the bay below. His head came up. Something in the bay below caught his eye, and he stared helplessly.

It was impossible. He was seeing tricks of light on the water. She felt the change in him and sat up, staring out across the jungle, to the beach and the water far below.

"The ships," she whispered.

"My God," he said. "The ships have come back."

The *Resolution* and the *Discovery* fought their way across the riptides outside the bay and sailed into it, finding it smooth and calm, as if the storms they had endured days before were figments of the ships' company's imagination. Though it was late in the afternoon, crowds of people gathered onshore. They stood, immobile, watching the ships drop anchor almost precisely where they had ridden before. Only this time was different. They didn't leap into outriggers and paddle out to welcome the ships. They stood silently, staring at the floating islands, watching as they would watch intruders advance upon them.

The captain stood aboard the *Resolution* and stared at the unfriendly people gazing back from the shoreline. Plainly, the *makahiki* festival that had been in wild and wanton progress upon their first arrival was *pau*, finished.

"As I feared," the captain said to his officers, "the people are not as friendly. I think we may well wait for morning before sending a landing party to call upon the king."

Lieutenant King agreed. "Morning will be better," he said. He glanced around. "I believe repairs on the ship might be started at once, however."

The captain nodded. "Yes. Have the workmen fall to. The sooner repairs are completed, the sooner we can leave. We have a long voyage back home."

"Will we return home from here?" one officer asked.

"Yes. It's been a long time. A long voyage. We'll go home from here."

"Secure the ships," Lieutenant King ordered. "All hands will remain on board until morning." The lieutenant held a spyglass to his eye. "Captain, I am sure you made the wisest decision to remain aboard. I see a funeral procession moving along the beach."

Cook straightened, looking ill, gray about the eyes and mouth. He had no idea how many funerals had been celebrated in the past days or how many were to come. There was nothing he could do. "Jesus Christ," he said under his breath. "Little wonder they don't send out a welcoming committee."

The ships rode at anchor. Gradually, the people ashore went about their business until no more than two or three stood in the brilliant red afterglow of the sunset, staring out at the ships. The sun dropped over the horizon, and darkness settled in across the island. Ship lights were fired up, their yellow glow shining through the portholes and lighting small paths across the water.

Onshore, people gathered around the pit fires.

The captain retired early. He spent a miserable, sleepless night dreaming of epidemics and plagues. He rolled and tossed in his bunk, got up, lit a lantern, and tried to read. It was no good. The words simply ran together. He blew out the light, got back in the bunk, and lay staring through the porthole at the tropic heaven.

At six he was wakened by a pounding on his door. He got up, threw on a robe, and opened the door to Lieutenant King, who was already fully dressed. "I am afraid I have bad news, sir. The late-watchman has been slain."

"What?" the captain felt his heart sink.

"We were attacked during the night," the officer said. "They came silently, awoke no one. They split open the head of the man on watch and left him lying on the deck."

"What did they take?"

"We are still checking, sir. So far, we know one of the cutters is missing—"

"Yes. I'm not surprised. Kamehameha wanted one of the boats. The bastard. What else is missing?"

"A swivel-gun cannon. They took it and its base. How they removed the base without arousing anyone aboard ship I'll never know. They also took kegs of nails."

"Nails?"

"They were very taken with any metal objects, sir. They were as pleased with a nail as a gift as something worthwhile. Anyhow, they've taken nails and a gun and a cutter."

The captain paced his small cabin. "Well, they won't get away with it. Dammit, if I'd meant for them to have a boat, I'd have given it to them."

"I understand sir. Those cutters are invaluable. There are just enough of them to carry the men in case the ship goes down."

"Exactly. I will have the boat back. I want the other cutters put out, the bay blockaded, and every man to carry a gun. You will call to duty nine armed marines and be prepared to go ashore within the hour. I will not tolerate this theft. They shall return the boat even if I have to take their king hostage until the missing cutter is returned."

The lieutenant saluted smartly and left. The captain, growing more infuriated by the moment, finished dressing, buckled on his sword, and armed himself with a pistol. These people were angry, and he admitted there was some reason for their rage, but there was no need to come silently in the night and attack his ship. They could easily have slain every sleeping man aboard. What a bloody carnage that would have been! And who could say that was not the plan of these pagans for the future, for tonight, tomorrow night?

Enraged, but holding himself erect and

haughty, he went up on deck. He found the men strangely quiet and uncommunicative. They all realized there could have been a massacre aboard the ship. Most of the men seemed willing to lose the cutter. When ordered to double-time the work repairing the disabled ship, they had fallen to with alacrity, wanting more than anything else to escape this island with their scalps.

The captain stared in at the beach. No one was standing on the shore. People moved around the village, going about their ordinary business. The captain scanned the beaches and coves, looking for some sign of the missing cutter. It was nowhere to be seen.

"Well," the captain said to Lieutenant King, "they won't get away with it. They've hidden the cutter, but they will be pleased to turn it over to me before I am through with them."

Nine armed marines manned one cutter, Lieutenant King and Malu awaited the captain in the other. The captain let himself over the side of the ship, and with as much dignity as possible, leapt out into the cutter. The oarsmen fell to, and the boats sliced toward the shoreline. By now a few of the more curious natives had wandered down to the beach to watch the sailors come ashore.

The cutters were run up on the beach and made fast. The armed marines stood, their muskets at the ready. The crowd had grown by now and the people were talking loudly among themselves.

Captain Cook looked to Malu for a translation. "They say you are not the god Lono. How can you be the god Lono when your ship—the floating island—is damaged by the storms. Lono's ship would never suffer damage at sea."

Cook imperiously demanded to see the king. The people spoke among themselves for a moment and then a messenger was sent running up the beach.

King Kaumualii kept them waiting for more than an hour. They stood, armed and at attention on the beach, the flies, the morning heat, and the humidity nagging at them and raising their level of frustration and anger. At last the king appeared. With him came a full complement of kahunas, priests, and three dozen armed guards looking ferocious, wearing loincloths and carrying long spears. They paraded in a lockstep down to the water and surrounded the nine armed marines.

Captain Cook grew rigid and his face flushed. The damned impudence of these people. He spoke slowly but forcefully, waiting for Malu to interpret what he had to say for the king, who stared at him imperiously.

"Your men attacked my ship last night," Cook said. "They killed a seaman. They stole nails and a cutter. The cutter must be returned at once."

The king stared at him blandly. "A cutter? A boat? Ah, but anything that washes ashore belongs to the chief."

"In the first place, the cutter did not wash ashore. It was stolen from my ship. It was brought ashore."

The king remained calm and unmoved. "That is a serious charge. This *stolen*? What means *stolen*?"

"You know damned well what it means. It means you took what did not belong to you and which belongs to me. That is the charge I make."

"That is a serious charge, really and truly."

"We want our property returned at once. Or be prepared to suffer the consequences."

"What are these consequences? You are not a god."

"I am not a god!" Captain Cook cried, infuriated. "I tried to tell you people from the first."

"You are not Lono."

"No. I never said I was Lono."

"Your men brought disease that is killing the young of my island."

Captain Cook spread his hands. "And I regret this. With all my heart I regret this."

"And yet, if you were the god Lono, you could cure this disease. You could take it away with you."

"Dammit. I am not the god Lono."

The king spread his hands, speaking slowly, reasonably. "Your ship is damaged. Damaged by a storm at sea. You cannot be the god Lono. Or your ship would withstand the storms."

"I've tried to tell you. I am not a god. Nor have I ever said I was a god. But I do represent the King of England, and I demand the return of the stolen cutter."

"Ah, the cutter. What washes ashore becomes the property of the king."

"You've said that and now I demand the return of the cutter and of the swivel gun which you also took."

One of Cook's men jerked up his gun and took aim at the chief's protuberant belly. Cook turned to order him at ease, but before he could speak he saw a lance hurled at the marine. It drove into the marine's back and he dropped his gun. One of Kamehameha's guards leapt to pick it up before a marine could claim it.

The other marines stood as if in a trance. The muskets were suddenly useless against three times as many spears in the hands of warriors who knew how to use them.

Just as Cook wheeled around to protest to the king, an unseen club caught him behind his left ear. His cocked hat was knocked off to the ground. One of the guards clutched it up and set it proudly upon his own head.

Captain Cook stumbled, landing upon his knees in the sand. His skull bled. People wheeled and skidded before his eyes. He tried to speak, but the pain was too intense. He wanted to cry out. Order his men to fire. To retreat to the boats. To set bayonets. To protect themselves. But for the first time in his life a situation was beyond his control. He sagged, grabbing at the bloody hole in his skull.

The natives crowded around him, crying, wailing. "Look. He bleeds. Like any man. He suffers pain. Like any man. It is not Lono. Not the god Lono."

From the ground the bleeding captain looked up, pleading with the people to understand. He had never claimed to be a god. He had never said he was a god. If they would stand back, he would take his men and return to the ship, and they could keep the cutter, the nails, the gun. He kept trying to speak. But Malu was busily defending himself. The king stood imperiously aside. The natives crowded around Captain Cook, beating at him with clubs and spears, driving lances into his body until he was a pulpy mass.

In the violent scuffle that followed, the warriors charged with their spears. The marines knelt, fixed muskets at their shoulders. Those who were spared in the spear attack fired at the charging natives. This was the signal for the people to attack with stones, clubs, and daggers.

Horrified, Lieutenant King yelled an order to retreat, and five of the marines made it to the boat, shoving it off from the shore and rowing to save their lives.

Lieutenant King returned safely to the *Resolution* and walked as if in a lethargic dream, giving orders automatically. He inspected the ship without really knowing what he was looking for. The master carpenter assured him the ship was seaworthy and could sail if necessary.

Lieutenant King gave orders for the ship to prepare to sail. As if drawn by some terrible sight he could not resist, he stared in at the shore; the king and the natives still crowded around where Captain Cook had fallen.

His eyes followed an outrigger rowing smoothly out to the *Resolution*. When the boat came near he saw that it bore the body of the captain. But the body was no longer whole; it lay in mutilated parts. Lieutenant King accepted the remains of the captain. His belly had been hacked out. One bundle of Cook's bones, wrapped in fine *kapa* barkcloth and a cloak made of black and white feathers, included the captain's hands. Holes had been cut in the flesh of the hands and filled with salt. The battered skull and scalp were there, but the lower jaw was missing. Thigh bones and arm bones had been stripped of flesh. The leg bones, lower jaw, and feet, according to the delegation, had been dispersed among the chiefs.

Lieutenant King, his mind swirling with rage, waited silently while the delegation withdrew. Then he called a signalman and communicated with the *Discovery*. Before the British vessels left the bay, they had one more task.

The ships were made ready to sail. With soundings being taken to alert the crews to shallows, the two ships sailed in a semi-circle before the village. Cannon were turned on the island. They bombarded the village, setting fire to temples and huts and killing scores of fleeing natives. A small contingent of British seamen made a foray up on the beach. There they found two natives whom they beheaded on the spot. Then they took their long spears and displayed the severed heads in the bows of the cutters as they returned to the ship.

BOOK FOUR

Paradise Lost

Chapter XXIX

From where he and Waialua stood, high in the mountain, Cutter Murphy looked down upon the carnage on the beach. He could not see who was attacked. He saw fighting break out and the marines firing indiscriminately into the crowd. Then, as he watched, a small party of the British managed to escape in the cutters to the ship.

Cutter's body sagged in disbelief. How could the natives have so completely turned against the white men, whom they had received as gods and demigods?

For a long time he remained unmoving. When Waialua tried to speak with him, he shook his head. He felt himself changing as he watched the terror below him. He felt unreal, like some unearthly changeling. He no longer resembled the young deserter who had swam ashore. He looked at the lovely girl beside him, wondering if she could see how he had changed before her very eyes, his arms becoming fleshless, his chest leaner, his belly hollow, his legs lank, as if his body every day shrank a little more while he watched helplessly.

The girl touched him and he withdrew, his gaze fixed on that slaughter below him. She stared at him, troubled, as if he had uncovered some treasure trove of pain deep inside her. She tried to talk with him, but he could not concentrate on what she said. He squatted, taut and tense, watching and waiting for he did not know what.

And then it came. The ships suddenly moved; their great sails unfurled and caught the wind. They sailed in a strange arc and he soon understood why: They were going to bombard the island. They were going to punish the islanders for their attack. He leapt to his feet, wanting to cry out a warning. But it was already too late. Waialua pressed against him, and together they stood and watched the cannon roar, sending fire and death into the village.

They stood together, clinging to each other until the bombardment ended and the ships sailed away, unscathed. The British had done what militarily had to be done.

When at last the ships were no longer visible, Cutter shuddered as if from the cold. Waialua pulled him down beside her, trying to comfort him, trying to warm him.

"It's all right," she whispered.

"No. It is not. Who was killed down there? Some of your family? Will you hate me for what they have done?"

"I could never hate you. How can I hate you for the acts of others?"

"Your people may be killed."

Strangely, she shook her head. "No," she said. "No one of my family is in the village. And the huts of the nobles and the kahunas were spared."

"Oh, my God." He dropped his head into his arms as if he could not take anymore.

"What's the matter?" she pleaded. "Tell me. I will help you."

He stared at her. "I want those people to accept me. I want to live among them. How can I hope they will accept me after this terrible attack?"

"We are happy up here," she said in a strange way, her voice odd.

"But I can't stay up here. I can't live like this forever. I must go down to the village. It would be better for me to go before they find me."

"Why?"

"Why?" He gazed at her, puzzled. "If I remain hidden up here, they will consider me an enemy."

"Are you not happy?"

He smiled and kissed her lightly. "You know I am happy with you. But you must also know it cannot last. You found me. How long before someone unfriendly finds me?"

She sighed and pressed close against him, making no answer at once. He gazed out across the bay, the harbor empty, as if the bombardment had never happened. The two ships had sailed out of the natural harbor and disappeared beyond a far curve of land. He drew a ragged breath, and it seemed to him that he breathed for the very first time since he had seen the ships.

God knew there would be other ships. As soon as the world found out about the treasures of these islands, they would come. But the ships of Captain Cook were gone. He owed allegiance to no other vessel, and he very much doubted that the British government would bother to track down a deserter in the midst of the Pacific Ocean.

The next morning, when Waialua arrived, she was full of news. She looked at him strangely, smiling tentatively, watching him narrowly. He thought she had never looked lovelier, or more troubled, or more distant.

She said, "Your captain. He was not the god Lono. His ships were damaged at sea. How could he then be the god Lono?"

He drew her close to him. "He never said he was the god Lono. But in his way he is a god. He is probably the world's greatest navigator. He has discovered places unknown until his ships sailed upon them. He is a very great man."

"He is dead," Waialua told him haltingly. This was her fear, he saw, that he might turn against her and her people because of the death of his captain.

"Dead?" He could not believe it.

"The people turned upon him. They thought if he were a god, then he would not bleed as human beings bleed, he would not feel pain the way the rest of us humans do. Someone struck him with a club. His hat fell off and the bloody place in his head showed. It was the sight of blood that made up their minds. He bled like a man. He cried out in pain like a man. He was a man and they hated him. They set upon him and killed him. They took out his belly and used his entrails to rope off the arena for a cockfight. They will use the palms of his hands as fly swatters." She paused. "Do you hate my people for what they have done to your captain?"

He shook his head, stunned. "I feel nothing. Nothing but shock. He was not family. I regret his death. But I do not hate you or your people for it."

She smiled as though some great weight had been lifted from her shoulders. He basked in the warmth of her delight and pleasure. But for days he carried a weight in his chest. Was the sudden death of the great captain an omen of what was ahead for him? Why had Waialua delayed in taking him with her to the village? When he tried to question her about it, she retreated from him, pretending not to understand, her lovely black eyes empty.

Finally he held her in his arms and forced her to look at him. "Why?" he asked. "Why do you want me to stay up here and not go down among your people?"

She shrugged her lovely shoulders and let her gaze fall away under his. "Are you not happy, Cutter?"

"Of course I'm happy."

"You need someone more than Waialua?"

He laughed aloud. "No. I'd be perfectly happy to stay in this mountain paradise with you forever, my lovely girl, but I simply know it cannot be. It must end, and I want it to end happily."

She nodded her head. Her eyes touched at his and then, like butterflies, flitted away. "Soon." This was all she would say.

Life was idyllic. The days passed slowly, uneventfully. They explored the twin cones of the extinct volcanoes. They went down into the Alakai Swamp, a strange and eerie morass many miles long and very narrow. Thousands of birds stirred when they passed. Ferns of every shape and size sprouted from the olive-gray valley walls. Waialua plucked a bright red *ohia* to wear in her hair. They rode the waterfalls and swam together in the pools.

One day they climbed a mountain. Following a faint trail, they came out upon a small knoll that overlooked the island and the seas in every direction. There they found the ruins of a bower, lovingly built and, it seemed, angrily destroyed. For amusement they rebuilt the place, and for two days stayed there enjoying the scenery and food from the surrounding forest. They were like days in paradise, and Cutter Murphy was sure he had finally found the life he sought.

Once in a while they dared to wander into the lowlands and to swim in hidden coves. One day they heard sounds in the bay and ran, hand in hand, to hide in the undergrowth. There they looked out on a breathtaking display. Three dozen outriggers, with soldiers arrayed in flowered robes and carrying guns and lances, swept past. But this was as nothing. In their wake, manned by four oarsmen, came a cutter. In the prow, a swivel-gun cannon had been nailed into place. Standing at the gun with both hands fixed upon it, wearing a flowered robe, his hair oiled and standing stiff and straight, they recognized Kamehameha.

They watched silently as this mirage sailed past in the open bay. Never had Cutter seen such pride, dignity, and insolent self-glorification in one man. Kamehameha was obsessed with his role as monarch. One could see he meant to conquer the world, or that part of it he knew.

He held on to the handles of the swivel gun, turning it from side to side, acting out confrontations with his enemies. One could almost see his lips peel away hungrily from his teeth as he thought of future victories.

Waialua and Cutter withdrew silently, going back up the hill to the high tor. There seemed little to say.

The next morning, when Waialua arrived, she hurried him down the mountain and into the Alakai Swamp. When he asked her what she sought, she only shook her head. She located a new swimming site at the base of a lovely waterfall, and they swam nude together. After they had swum and played together in the water, they lay together in the ferns. Later they ate of the spiced chicken and fruit salad she had brought in a pouch of plaited palm fronds.

She still seemed preoccupied and troubled, but when he asked her about it, she only shook her head and motioned for him to be silent. They got up from their bower and went cautiously and silently back toward the falls.

Suddenly she stopped and placed her hand over his mouth. Then she crept forward. Cutter, puzzled, followed her and stopped short at what he saw.

Sprawled out, facedown on the grass, so still and unmoving that at first Cutter thought him dead, was a man wearing only a loincloth.

Then he saw that the man was alive; his chest was rising and falling with each deep and regular breath.

Waialua knelt beside the man and gently touched his face. The man cried out and leapt up to his feet, ready to fight.

"Mihuana, it is me. Waialua."

The exhausted man smiled and reached for her. She ran into his arms and they embraced, holding each other close, as if they were afraid to let go.

Cutter felt jealousy burn through him and, for the first time, he realized how deeply he had come to care for Waialua. She was suddenly not only the loveliest woman he had ever seen, she was the most indispensable. He wanted her for his very own, and he stood, feeling sick in his belly as the two clung to each other and talked swiftly and confidentially.

Waialua turned, smiling, and said to Cutter, "This is Mihuana. He was betrothed to my sister Misau."

Into Cutter's mind came the memory of Misau with a man. But that man bore little resemblance to this poor devil. Mihuana must have read this in his eyes, because he said, "I have been in the refuge. It is a place of living death."

Cutter's mind was reeling with what Waialua had said. Misau was her sister. Misau had been in love with a commoner and their marriage had been forbidden by Kamehameha and Mihuana sentenced to death.

As they talked, Cutter came to understand more. Waialua was the widow of A'Kane, whose death on the island of Molokai had started this entire chain of tragic events.

Cutter stared at Waialua as she talked with Mihuana. No wonder she had not wanted him to go down to the village. It would be the end of their idyll. She was nobility. She was of the highest caste of the island, and had been all these months in mourning for the death of A'Kane, which explained why he had not seen her before. He felt his belly go empty.

He stood emptily and watched as Waialua tenderly fed Mihuana from the palm-frond pouch. Mihuana ate ravenously, as if he had not tasted real food in a very long time.

He looked at them, deeply troubled. "The place of refuge is a place of living death. You are one of the dead while you are there. I could not endure it anymore. I sneaked away in the night, though I was told by others that no one has ever left the place of refuge and lived. But I was a walking dead man, though I did not feel dead. I felt hatred. Yes, hatred for that monster Kamehameha. I was consumed with hatred. All I could think, lying awake at night in that place, was that I must escape, that somehow I would live and by living be a threat to Kamehameha every day of his life."

Waialua's eyes filled with tears as she translated Mihuana's words for Cutter. Then she caught Mihuana's lean hands in hers. "Please," she said. "Give up this unequal fight. I have heard in the councils that Kamehameha still hates you. He plans to flush you out of the refuge so that you can be killed. He wants to kill you with all his heart. I believe you can make it across the swamp to the north coast. There, you can find an outrigger and escape to another island. There are hundreds of islands in this chain, some very small, many without people. You could find peace."

Mihuana shook his head. "I can never find peace as long as Kamehameha lives."

"He is too strong. Too powerful. He plans to invade the seven large islands and to make them one kingdom. You will be safe nowhere. There are too many spies, too many people willing to betray you for profit. Please, escape. Please. Just get away."

Mihuana finished off the food and wiped

his hand across the back of his mouth. "Your food has given me vigor. I promise you, I will not be caught. You found me only because I was hungry and too tired to stay awake anymore."

Waialua kissed him again and hugged him. "I love you," she said, "because my dearest, lovely sister loved you with all her heart. I know you to be a good man and I will pray to the gods for your safety."

Mihuana clung to her for a long moment. Then he nodded his head toward Cutter and heeled around, running north through the swamp. Cutter felt ill watching him go. With Kamehameha's armies all over the island, what chance had the young commoner of staying alive?

Waialua came close to Cutter and put her arms about him. Her hands closed on his shoulders, dragging him down with her. She was sobbing and he held her for a long time, kissing her lightly, trying to talk to her. But he could not forget the truth. He belonged to another race, another caste, and he and Waialua could never be together.

At a rustling in the underbrush, Waialua grew tense in his arms. She leapt up to her feet and reached down for Cutter's hand, urging him to hurry.

But it was too late. They were suddenly surrounded by Kamehameha's soldiers, their spears held at the ready. Cutter realized at once they had come into the swamp looking for Mihuana, who was safe, at least for the moment.

"You will come with us, Princess," the leader of the soldiers said. They stepped aside, making way for Cutter and Waialua to walk out of the swamp.

Chapter XXX

The prison was a stockade set back from the beach and apart from the village. A fortification perhaps thirty feet across, it was a dugout behind an embankment of lava rock, topped by hardwood trees, honed to a fine point at the top and set into the rock about three inches apart. This was enough to allow a man to see the world outside but not to reach it. It was open to the elements.

The soldiers had marched Cutter directly to the barracoon, prodding him with their weapons and keeping him away from Waialua. He realized they believed he had kidnapped the princess. Cutter submitted passively. He had what he wanted—the islanders were aware that he was among them—even if this was not exactly the way he had wanted it to happen.

Once he was inside the prison, he was shackled with rope at the ankles and given the freedom of the yard. The heavy gate was securely tied behind him and guards stood watchful and alert at the parapets. There were a dozen other prisoners, most of whom had been incarcerated at the orders of Kamehameha.

Cutter shuffled about the place; it was filthy as a pigsty. The men relieved themselves where they squatted, and until the refuse was swept up at night, it baked in the sun, covered by flies and smelling to the heavens. Finally he removed himself as far as possible from the others and sagged against the lava rock wall. But he was not left alone for more than a few moments at a time. He was a curiosity, a white-skinned, pale-eyed man. The other prisoners came close to him, but never too close. They prodded at him and then leapt back in terror.

By nightfall the men had become accustomed to his presence. But Cutter slept very little that night. He was worried about Waialua and he missed her. He wondered where she was and what was happening to her. Trying to escape the ugliness and odors, he recalled her beauty. He sat against the wall, his mind filled with pictures of Waialua swimming like a young otter in the waterfall ponds, hurrying up the hill to him, bringing new and tasty foods for him, totally engrossed in him, and happy to be all alone with him. He saw now that she had been right. People were their enemies.

He sat, sleeping for only minutes at a time. He watched the beautiful sunrise come up over the Pacific, clean and clear and full of promise. At this hour, the odor of the island flowers hung in the air, spicy and aromatic. As the sun rose and the village came to life, Cutter dragged himself across the stockade and stared through the slits in the walls, watching the village, watching for Waialua.

He stood, watching and waiting. The sun rose higher in the sky. Breakfast of some sort of bread and sauce was served. Cutter did not eat. He was not hungry enough yet.

A little man crept toward him on all fours. Cutter watched him and saw the madness in his eyes. Fascinated, he watched the man creep closer and closer and suddenly reach out and grab his food and then lunge away, his mouth peeled back savagely from his teeth as if he dared Cutter to protest. Cutter shrugged. He would have told the man he was welcome to the food, but he saw the prisoner was beyond comprehending anything except eating, defecating, and sleeping. For a long time he watched the man. It had never occurred to him that there would be insanity in paradise. He remembered Bedlam, the London asylum, where poor devils without minds were stacked and forgotten.

He remained at the wall all day, clutching the posts and staring out watching the path that led to the jail from the village. The day inched past, but there was no sign of Waialua.

He remained there until night swallowed up the village. She did not come. There was no word of her. He had thought his stay here would be short because the princess would use her influence to free him.

In the darkness some of the prisoners approached Cutter and spoke to him. They were astonished to find he could speak the dialect of the island and he was amazed to realize what a clever and able teacher Waialua had been. He could follow a conversation. Once he got the sense of what was being said, he could converse in simple words.

"Why are you here?" they asked him. "Did they take you prisoner the day of the invasion?"

Cutter shook his head. Slowly, he told them that he had jumped the ship, intending to make Kauai his home.

"Kauai is not as fine a place as it was under King Kaumualii," one of the prisoners said.

"But I was told Kaumualii is still king of Kauai," Cutter said.

"Kamehameha is not yet king of Kauai. In name at least, he remains a prince. Yet he behaves as though he is the king, and King Kaumualii allows it."

"The old king has abdicated," another prisoner said.

"Not in name," said another. "He is still the king. But his men fight for Kamehameha. The army is controlled by the prince. And the prince arrests anyone he does not trust."

"And he trusts no one."

"Daily, it is worse, the way he mistrusts those around him. Most of the prisoners in this place were once his most trusted lieutenants," one of the prisoners said. "I myself fought beside him at Molokai. I have been with him from the first. And yet here I am without hope of ever getting out."

As the days passed, Cutter remained at the wall. He began to eat the prison food. But he felt as though he was losing weight by the hour. He looked at his flat belly, his sunken chest, and knew how weak and emaciated he was becoming. How long before the madness he had seen in the eyes of the hungry prisoner would light his own eyes?

And every day, when the heavy gate was opened and a new prisoner arrived in rope shackles, Cutter found himself looking for Mihuana. A prisoner had told him that Kamehameha had swelled with rage when he learned that Mihuana had left the refuge. He was determined to hunt Mihuana down and to take him, dead or alive.

Mihuana had become the main topic of conversation at the prison. The men relayed to each other every scrap of news from outside. The word was that Mihuana was still at large. There were those who believed he was in the Alakai Swamp, hiding and watchful. Others imagined him on the inaccessible rocky north coast, hidden among the rocks and bays. Others were sure that he had somehow stolen an outrigger and made it to Niihau, or to the island of Kahoolawe. At any rate, Mihuana remained free. He was the symbol of freedom to these former lieutenants of Kamehameha. One day the rumor circulated that Mihuana had been spotted in the swamp, run to earth, and slain. But this proved to be only a rumor, designed to take Mihuana's name off the people's lips. Mihuana remained free.

Word reached the prisoners that Kamehameha had led an armada of one hundred outriggers against the island of Maui and had taken it, defeating Chief Kahekili. A celebration lit the island. From behind the walls of the prison, Cutter and the others watched the excitement that once again turned the village into a frenzied orgy. They could even watch the new king of Maui standing tall and flower bedecked before the adoring crowds.

It was only after the celebration that the secret leaked into the prison: Kamehameha had been disappointed in his conquest of Maui. None of the guns functioned right. The men did not know how to use them. Some even threw the guns aside after firing the first round. Kamehameha was beside himself. He ranted and raved, certain that his plan to invade the islands was going to fail because of the ignorance of his men.

One morning a guard came to where Cutter stood at the wall. "You have a visitor," he said. "A royal visitor. She is too noble to come into this place. You will be led out to her."

Cutter's heart beat against his rib cage. Waialua had come. He was certain it was she. God knew it had taken long enough. But at last she had come. He hurried, tripping and sprawling forward on his face. The other prisoners laughed, but he didn't even notice them.

Waialua awaited him outside the walls. For long moments he stood looking at her, her loveliness, the pain in her eyes. She pressed herself into his arms. He felt himself respond. What a hellish thing, here in this terrible place, with the prison guards watching him. He touched her gently, as if to reassure himself it was truly Waialua.

She had brought food and they sat together while he ravenously ate the roast pork and vegetables. She watched him, pity and concern clouding her eyes. "I have been all this time trying to get you free," she said. "Kamehameha has refused. But he is not the king of Kauai. I am going to King Kaumualii. I am certain you will be freed. You have done nothing to be imprisoned."

He kissed her lightly, thanking her, but he could feel no hope. Still, he understood. The funerals continued as the syphilis and gonorrhea, spread by his shipmates, continued to rage through the population, now claiming young men as well as the young women. To the rulers, he was one with the infected seamen. They did not want him free among the people.

"I know an island where we can go once I get you free," Waialua said. "I have it all planned. I have been there once myself. It is a tiny island. It is called Kahoolawe. We could be safe there. We could be together. There are no people to trouble us at Kahoolawe."

"Kahoolawe," Cutter mused. "That's strange. I just heard of that island from the prisoners. I remember now, it was about Mihuana. They said perhaps he had gotten there alive."

"I have heard nothing of Mihuana," Waialua said. "Only that he still is free. He remains free despite all Kamehameha can do. Kamehameha is beside himself with rage."

They sat talking quietly, planning for the time when he would be freed. Again she said she was going to King Kaumualii to seek a pardon for him.

The guards came at last. The visit was over. Waialua kissed him passionately, promising to return soon with good news.

Cutter stood and watched Waialua. She turned several times to smile at him. At last the guards forced him back inside the heavy gate. He dragged his legs across the compound to his place beside the wall. He stared through the wooden stakes, but he could no longer see Waialua.

Early the next morning a guard kicked him awake. Cutter sat up against the wall, staring at him.

"Come," the guard said. "You have royal company."

It was so early in the morning that Cutter suddenly had the hope that Waialua had seen Kaumualii and that he was to be freed. He moved his shackled legs as quickly as possible across the compound and out of the great gate. There he stood, stunned, and stared at his royal visitor.

Kamehameha was an imposing man. Cutter stared, impressed by the man's size and self-confidence.

Kamehameha spoke first. "I understand you speak our language?"

Cutter smiled and nodded. "If you speak slow, I can follow what you are saying."

"Why are you here on this island? Why did you leave the great ships of Captain Cook?"

"Because these islands seemed the kind of paradise I had been seeking all my life. I jumped overboard and hid in the mountains. I meant to come in and give myself up, but before I could do this, your men arrested me in the swamp."

"With my sister Waialua," Kamehameha said coldly.

"I was fortunate enough to meet her as soon as I came upon the island," Cutter explained.

"Has anyone told you that she was married to my brother A'Kane, who was slain by the Oahuans? She has been in mourning. When her period of mourning ends, she and I will marry. I must warn you away from her."

Cutter drew a deep breath, then exhaled. He had heard about Kamehameha's stubbornness. This was no time to argue with him about Waialua. Waialua had not told him she was betrothed to Kamehameha.

"I did not know about your betrothal," Cutter said. "Is that why you came here, to tell me of it?"

Kamehameha gestured with his arm, as if dismissing the entire conversation. "I have come for one reason," he said. "I want to know if you know about guns. If you do, what do you know?"

"All one needs to know," Cutter replied.

"I will tell you truthfully. I have been having trouble with the guns I got from Captain Cook. I need someone who understands them and can train my men to use them. Show me what you know about this musket."

Cutter's heart beat with a sudden renewed hope as he took the musket from the soldier who stepped forward and presented it. Seeing that the weapon was unloaded, he requested ball and powder. When a horn was provided, he carefully loaded the weapon with the niter and lead.

Kamehameha watched closely, fascinated. Cutter placed the gun against his shoulder and searched for a target. A small bird perched on one of the far stakes. Cutter aimed and pressed the trigger. The bird was suddenly a mass of feathers in the sky.

Kamehameha cheered loudly. "Do you know about using them in battle?"

Cutter nodded. "I do."

Kamehameha was smiling broadly. He summoned a guard and ordered the ropes removed from Cutter's legs. "Come," he said, "you will start at once to train my men to use these guns."

Exultant, Cutter bit back the savage laughter that welled up inside him.

Chapter XXXI

Battle sounds raged along the beach. Off to one side, surrounded by his chiefs and body-guards, Kamehameha stood quivering with delight and pleasure. He was seeing professional warmaking, and he liked what he saw. In three days the Englishman Cutter had made a difference. He had turned a rabble into a smoothly performing troup of soldiers. Not only was the monarch pleased, but he could read the pride and self-confidence in the faces of his soldiers as well.

It had begun unpromisingly, with Cutter choosing the men to be trained. Once this group was assembled, he began to march them to the rhythm of drums, until they moved in a lockstep. Kamehameha watched every step of the operation and grew impatient. Cutter had not yet mentioned the guns. He simply marched the men up and down the beach to the beat of the drums until they moved effortlessly and as one.

Then he issued the empty muskets to the men. He trained them in handling the guns, presenting arms, and in bringing the gun to a ready position at a command. Kamehameha, who had felt perhaps he had been wrong in trusting this job to the British deserter, now smiled. It was a pleasing sight to watch his men parade along the beach, three abreast, armed and ready. They came to a halt at an order, presented arms, and then fell to, ready to use the weapons.

"Very good," Kamehameha called out to them. "Very good, men." Then he walked among his soldiers, clapping them on the shoulders, praising them.

Cutter began the slow process of teaching the soldiers the correct way to load a musket with its liter, powder, and ball. Again the progress slowed and again Kamehameha strode up and down the beach impatiently.

Finally the prince saw that his men could load and prepare the muskets to be fired without spilling the powder, dropping the ball, or even misplacing the friction stick. He nodded, pleased with the progress he was seeing. It was strange, the amount of preparation that it took to get men ready to kill.

Then the marching began again. Throwing up his arms, Kamehameha prowled the sidelines watching as the men marched with the guns. He was unsure again. The Englishman took forever on each small detail. The king watched his men marching with their guns. But now the marching was different. They moved at a faster pace. They broke into two wide lines. One line went down on its knees, guns at the ready beside them. The other line, standing just at their shoulders, lifted their muskets and fired over their heads. Then the first line rose and fired its muskets while the second line knelt and reloaded.

Suddenly Kamehameha was beside himself with ecstasy. He knew enough about warfare—though nothing yet about gunfighting—to see the advantage of this plan. While one group fired, keeping the enemy at bay, the other group reloaded. It was beautiful. Before all the men Kamehameha ran out and embraced Cutter.

But target practice was a saddening experience for the monarch. Slowly the men learned to press the stock of the gun to their shoulders, close one eye, aim along the barrel, and press off the trigger. Days and weeks passed and still the men remained poor marksmen. Finally the men began to hit the targets. They cheered lustily for themselves and the king's praise.

By now, Kamehameha thoroughly approved of Cutter Murphy. He treated him as nearly as an equal as he treated any man, kahuna or chief. He moved Cutter into the palace. The palace, actually a large cottage made of wood and laced together with palm fronds and ropes, was crowded, and Cutter would have preferred a smaller hut to himself. But Kamehameha was convinced he was paying him the greatest compliment possible. He was now a member of the royal family. He dined with them, slept with them, and sat in on their councils.

In a fiery ceremony, at which dozens of roast pigs and chickens were consumed, along with a drink that caused hallucinations, Kamehameha presented Cutter Murphy to the people of the island. "Captain of the Militia" was the title bestowed upon him.

Standing at the head of the long table, Cutter searched the crowd for one face. The one face he needed to see; the one face that could reassure him that life did have meaning. But Waialua was not present. When he asked, he was told that the princess was still in mourning for her husband, A'Kane, and would not attend any public functions. He sagged back, eating without interest, listening to the conversations around him, but seeing only Waialua's beautiful face.

The next day, as he walked through the village, he was amazed as the natives moved aside and knelt to him as he passed. He was embarrassed, but he realized this was the custom, part of the kapu. He could only go along with it.

As he walked, his eyes searched the houses, the paths, the beaches. Waialua was nowhere to be seen. Once he was stopped by a sad parade. Another young girl had died during the night, one of a hundred victims of the plague. Sick to his stomach, he stood and watched the silent procession stalk past in the silky sunlight.

As he reached the farthest edge of the village, he saw a flash of color in the forest, and his heart leapt. He edged up the beach to the ring of trees, stepped beyond them, and then ran uphill.

She swung out of a bower into his trail, her face wreathed in smiles, her arms extended. He held her for a long time. He had an empty feeling inside him when she was away from him. When he didn't find her, he felt the emptiness like laces pulled taut between his fingers. He needed her. God, how he needed her.

They walked close to each other, seeking a place where they might escape prying eyes.

"Oh, I've missed you so," he told her. "I look for you. Everywhere I go, I look for you. And you're never there."

"You are in all my thoughts," she whispered, nuzzling his throat.

He smiled, holding her close, caressing her. "Somehow that doesn't seem quite enough."

She laughed. "No more than it is for me. I close my eyes and see your face above my face, like now, and I grow all empty and hot inside, and I need you so terribly."

"There has got to be some way for us to be together," he said.

She sighed, staring across the wilderness to the sun glinting on the green leaves and the bright plumage of some exotic bird in flight. "I'm afraid it is not that easy. I have seen King Kaumualii. I have begged for permission to marry you. I even told him that if he would come to know you, he would love you as I do."

"And there is no change." He said it in a dead, level tone.

"I am afraid not. King Kaumualii says I am betrothed to my brother Kamehameha. And King Kaumualii has his problems. As Kamehameha takes over the other kingdoms, as they fall and declare themselves submissive to him, he becomes stronger on this island. No one has suggested that Kamehameha would wrench power from his own father, but everyone knows that it will happen. They are simply waiting."

"When Kamehameha is king here, we'll have no chance."

For a long time he held her close, silently staring upward in the sunlit day.

"There is one thing we can do," Waialua said. "We can run away to Kahoolawe. That is our only chance."

"I don't believe that will work now," Cutter said in a dead voice.

"Why not?" She gazed at him, troubled.

"Because I have now become indispensable to Kamehameha," Cutter said. "I am the captain of his elite troops. If I ran away now, he would trail me, bring me back. And if I were with you, whom he considers his bride . . ."

She burst into tears suddenly. He drew her close, begging her to stop crying.

She spoke through her tears. "Everything is wrong. I am a princess. I am taboo to you. As you—of another race—must be taboo to me. Even to meet like this is dangerous. If we are caught together, you will be put to death. And I cannot take that chance. I cannot be the cause of your death."

Cutter walked about the island, restless, sweating, and troubled. The days dragged slowly past and he did not see Waialua except at a distance, in a crowd, or when she was heavily chaperoned. She always kept her eyes demurely lowered, and he could not even force a glance of recognition from her. He strode around with an empty stomach that had nothing to do with lack of food.

He looked at her when he chanced upon her, and she was lovelier than ever because she was denied to him. At night sometimes he plotted it out. He and Waialua would do as she had pleaded from the first. They would escape this island, go beyond the reach of the tyrannical monarch. To Kahoolawe. Waialua said it was almost barren, but it would be a paradise for them.

But, he admitted to himself, the chance of escaping was so slim as to be almost non-existent. And then, as if it all had happened while he slept, Cutter found the island suddenly overrun with warriors. When he spoke with them, he found they were from Maui and Molokai. They had been summoned by King Kamehameha. The island had become an armed camp. Finally the word came from the councils. The huge armada was preparing to sail for the island of Hawaii.

Kamehameha called Cutter and explained. "We will converge on the island, the largest armada of ships in the history of the islands. When we are all met there, your company will go ashore first. When the Hawaiians confront you, you will attack. I do not need to tell you how this will be accomplished. When they are confused and terrified by the guns, thousands of my men will swarm ashore and secure the island."

Cutter nodded vacantly. He tried to find Waialua to tell her good-bye. The outriggers were gathered, the troops marched aboard, and the sails raised. Soon the armada was streaking out of the bay into the open sea.

Cutter sat, numb, watching Kauai disappear behind him. What fool thing was he doing taking part in a battle that had nothing to do with him? He had sickened of the British navy, now here he was, going off to war with pagans, with whom he had nothing in common, especially the desire for conquest.

Cutter set out to wipe all this agony from his mind. He began at once to drink from the casks of the native drink, *okolehao*, that had been placed aboard. The soldiers squatted along the sideboards watching him with interest. The hundred-plus miles of sea voyage was sickening, but the *okolehao* was soothing and soon he didn't give a damn. Before long he fell into a deep sleep filled with ugly dreams.

After an interminable time someone shook him awake and he became groggily aware of landfall directly ahead. Even through his drunkenness he felt the old nausea returning; the spectacle of warfare made him despise the whole human race.

As he stared ahead, he became aware of the hundreds of outriggers surrounding him. It was an imposing armada. He received a signal from Kamehameha, standing tall and straight-haired, to land his boats first with guns at the ready.

Whenever Cutter remembered that night, it was as a time of confusion and chaos. He ordered his boats ashore. On land he could see soldiers lined up with their lances at their sides. The battle began the very moment when he became aware of his hangover. The entire world was unreal and fantastic. Everything happened with such suddenness, there was no time for the body or the mind to adjust to it.

He ordered his men out of the boats. One line knelt, a few hundred yards from the Hawaiian soldiers. Still far more drunk than sober and with his head aching fiercely, Cutter lifted his sword and dropped it in a signal to fire. The first line fired and the Hawaiian soldiers panicked. They dropped their spears, lances, and clubs and turned to flee. They had never beheld gunfire, and it was like the devil's magic to them.

Then from high above the fleeing soldiers, as if from some immortal signal, a volcano erupted. Kilauea sent fire and lava spewing hundreds of feet into the air. The eruptions shook the earth, the sea, everything on the land and in the air. The soldiers, running inland, suddenly turned and ran right into Kamehameha's troops.

"It is the work of Pele," Kamehameha's

men cried. The cry was taken up and sped through the hundreds of men ashore.

The Hawaiian soldiers were dropping their lances, surrendering in terror and despair. Kamehameha strode forward, declaring this island to be his own province. In the background the spewing and rumbling of Kilauea continued.

Out of the disarranged ranks of his army marched Chief Keoua of Puna. He declared the gods had spoken against him and he would not continue to fight. He knelt before the imposing figure of Kamehameha and swore his allegiance to the new king.

Kamehameha's exultance showed. Molokai. Maui. Hawaii. Three of the islands were now his kingdoms. Destiny was playing into his hands. Cutter watched the ceremony for a few minutes, then went back to the outrigger and sprawled out asleep on its rough deck.

Cutter remained sodden drunk through the days of celebration on the big island, and during the long return trip to Kauai. He even hoped that the king, noticing his dereliction, might mention it. He sincerely hoped he would. He made up his mind to demand his right to see, to love, to wed the Princess Waialua. Kamehameha might rage, might even explode and throw him into prison, but Cutter believed the odds were with him now. Kamehameha was obsessed with the idea of consolidating the seven islands under one kingdom. He was smart. He saw the advantage one man with a small brass cannon and a small force of men with muskets had over large numbers of warriors bearing clubs and spears. Cutter believed Kamehameha needed him and his expertise. But Cutter also acknowledged Waialua's fears and decided not to mention their love until the king was most vulnerable.

Strangely enough, as time passed it was the coming of trading ships into the harbors of the islands that gave Cutter the nerve to approach the unapproachable and unyielding king. More and more ships were calling. Sandalwood was one of the treasures of the island, and Kamehameha learned he could buy almost unlimited war supplies from the Chinese by supplying this valuable wood. Other ships arrived, all seeking treasures and unknown products. The king bought guns and cannon. He even traded women to those men who wanted them.

Cutter called a halt to his military exercises one afternoon when the king was giving audiences. He walked over and bowed.

"I'm glad you have come, Cutter," the king said. "We are going to attack Oahu. We will go against them with thousands of men and a grand fleet of war canoes and English cutters. I will throw all my might against the hated Oahuans, because it is the

Oahuans who started all the wars. A prince of the Oahu nation slew my brother A'Kane—"

"It is A'Kane I wish to discuss with you," Cutter broke in forcefully. "I want to marry his widow. I deeply love Waialua and she returns my love."

At first Kamehameha swelled with rage. His face grew red as he seemed to be holding his breath. He stared at the Britisher with such loathing that it should have curled his toes. But Cutter remained firm. "You have made gifts of several women in marriage to men of my race. Why not to me?" he asked the king.

"I will not be questioned," Kamehameha said, the words exploding across his lips. "What I do is not open to question."

"Nor do I question you or your motives," Cutter said. "It is just that I wish to ask your permission to marry the princess."

"Impossible." Kamehameha straightened as tall as he could. "The women I give to white men are common women. They are as nothing. They are to be taken forever from this island."

"If that is your requirement," Cutter pleaded, "I will agree to it. If you will permit Waialua and me to marry, I will leave the island with her. On the first ship which calls."

The king suddenly quieted. The fact that his military expert might leave him had never entered his mind. He sank back, regarding the young white man. A change came over his face. He smiled, a false and almost ugly smile, and an insincere look of concern settled on his wild features.

"Ah, but I do not wish you to leave," the king said. "You are one of the few men I trust completely. You are indispensable to my militia. No. No. I tell you what. You fight with me in Oahu and when we return, we shall discuss again the matter of Waialua."

Cutter nodded, retreating. He felt ill suddenly, remembering what Waialua had told him about the sad story of Mihuana and Misau and the king's extravagant promises. When he looked at the king, he saw the same falseness. Any lie, any wrong, was acceptable as long as it was done for the good of the state.

Gathering sixteen thousand men together from all the islands under Kamehameha's control took weeks. The men arrived in their outriggers, some armed, some expecting to be armed upon arrival. All were trained by Cutter Murphy and taught the intricacies of war and killing. The women prepared food and supplies for the warriors.

Cutter was almost relieved when he did not see Waialua, because he knew that when he told her what the king had said, she would brand it a lie and live in greater fear for their safety than ever.

At last the huge armada was massed in the bay. The entire waterway was covered with outriggers and armed men. Sails were set and the frail craft set out for Oahu for a final assault.

As before, Cutter began to drink as soon as the boats put out to sea. He slept intermittently and was wakened when Diamond Head hove into sight. Shocked at the great land mass protruding into the waters, Cutter watched it as the outriggers sailed past and into the harbor beyond it.

The seas had been calm, so that the armada was able to stay close together on the way to Oahu. Long before they entered the harbor, they could hear the sounds of laughter and pleasure. The Oahuans were in the midst of a celebration.

Cutter's boats landed first. He saw the panic among the Oahuans. They searched for arms, taking up weapons of any sort and running down to the beach to repel the invasion. Cutter allowed the first wave to reach the shoreline before he gave the order to fire. Not one of his marksmen missed. The Oahuans fell in their tracks.

Panic struck. The Oahuans had heard about the magic of gunpowder, but this was their first taste of it. The men in the second wave hesitated, staring at their fallen comrades. The men retreated. Cutter marched his men forward. Kamehameha came ashore with his force. Their cries, like banshees, split the air, and at the sight and sound of this fighting force, the Oahuans hesitated.

Finally they fought valiantly in hand-to-hand combat, but Cutter's militia bearing down upon them, spilling blood and dropping men in their tracks, was too much for them. The army of Oahuans retreated. Doggedly, Kamehameha pursued them. He wanted them to surrender and pledge fidelity and submission to his rule.

For hours the fighting continued, with the Oahuans setting up a line of attack and then being forced back. They were pushed higher and higher into the hills, away from the open beach. At last, pushed up as far as Nuuanu *Pali*, a cliff with a twelve-thousand-foot drop, the army was forced to stand and fight.

Kamehameha continued to press forward. Cutter's militia never stopped firing. Suddenly a sight beyond belief unfolded before the startled eyes of the Kamehameha army. The Oahuans, rather than surrender, backed to the edge of the cliff and stepped off, plunging to their deaths in the quiet, violet softness of the valley below.

Chapter XXXII

And so the world of Kamehameha expanded. No longer confined to two or three islands, it included Maui, Molokai, the Big Island of Hawaii, Lanai, and now the loveliest island of them all, Oahu. Kamehameha spent the next weeks securing the invasion.

When he was told that the Oahuan chief Kalanikupule had escaped over the mountains the night of the battle, Kamehameha raged. Kalanikupule was the father of Aprilhana, the prince who had murdered A'Kane. Kamehameha became obsessed with tracking down the fugitive king.

He called Cutter in and gave him his orders. "You will take a force of ten musketmen and you will track down Kalanikupule.

I want him taken alive. I want him brought back here to me."

Thinking of Waialua, Cutter set out on the journey across the island. If he brought in the chief, he might be able to ingratiate himself with Kamehameha and ask for Waialua with some reasonable expectation of being accepted by the monarch. He carefully selected his men and set out to climb the mountains of Nuuanu *Pali*. Over a thousand feet below lay the rotting bodies of the men who had leapt to their death rather than surrender.

He pushed on, searching the wooded interior of the island. He walked with his head up, ever alert, inspecting everything from the noble crater called Diamond Head to the grandeur of the Koolau mountain range, which ran across the island. He tramped at the head of his armed column through rolling hills and virgin valleys, full of purpled mists and mystifying silences, and then along the magnificent and desolate coast.

Cutter and his men spent days searching. They climbed the flat-topped Kaala, which rose from the mists to over four thousand feet. Flowers abounded in wonderful wild gardens. Finally they crossed the island to windward Oahu to find a sweeping panorama of sharply edged mountains, dark red earth, fields of the most gentle green, and the sea, blue and turquoise and distant.

In one desolate region three natives approached the armed men and begged for peace. They sat down with Cutter and ate ravenously. They wanted to plead for a peaceful surrender for their king, Chief Kalanikupule, they said. His army annihilated, cut off from his people, supplies, and even food, the luckless monarch had wandered in misery through the Koolau mountains. He was now ready to surrender, to trust his future to the kindness of the conquering Kamehameha.

Pleased, Cutter agreed at once. Within the hour they started back across the island to Diamond Head with the king and what was left of his followers. Three days later they arrived in the village. Cutter marched Kalanikupule quickly through the town to the palace, which had been taken over by Kamehameha. The king was pleased. He strode back and forth before the prisoners as if he himself had gone out and single-handedly brought in the defeated chief.

Cutter knew he had to get away, find some way to get Waialua and escape this madness.

Kamehameha was ranting, blaming Kalanikupule for all the catastrophes, from the bodies rotting at the base of *Pali* to the burning of one of the native villages. He listed a hundred crimes and charged them all to the former king. One thing Cutter found strange. Kamehameha never mentioned A'Kane or Aprilhana.

Almost before Cutter realized what was happening, the huge army of Kamehameha, along with the people of the island, were marching toward an obelisk, a *heiau* built many centuries earlier by ancestors of the present king. Kamehameha stood before this huge throng and continued his ranting.

"My war god, Kukailimoku, demands a sacrifice. There are many reasons for human sacrifice—to please the gods, to obtain their divine blessing on some plan, to bring luck to the luckless, to avert evil or misfortune, or to appease the gods when they are angry. The gods are not angry with us, they pour their blessings down upon us. We have taken Maui, Molokai, the Big Island, Lanai, and now Oahu. But Kukailimoku demands to be appeased. And so we make a sacrifice to the great war god."

Cutter wanted to cry out in protest, but he did not move. Though he wept and pleaded for mercy, Kalanikupule was blindfolded. The king's hands were tied behind him and he was forced to a kneeling position before the temple. The kahunas came forward carrying knives. At a signal from Kamehameha, the knives came down across the neck of the monarch. His severed head fell off and rolled down the steps of the temple.

The head was collected in a basket and

the headless body was borne away. The Oahuans wept and Cutter stood immobile, staring at the blood sinking into the sand. He felt ill. How could a king capable of such barbarity give a damn for the fortunes of two people? Suddenly he saw that asking the king's permission to wed was fruitless. It might even rouse the monarch to such a frenzy of passion, he might demand another sacrifice.

He had to escape. Somehow he had to get back to Kauai before Kamehameha talked him into invading his father's kingdom. Cutter knew Kamehameha was merely waiting for an excuse.

But in the end he delayed for good reason. It became obvious that Kamehameha was waiting for him to make a move. Kamehameha treated him like a brother, but behind all the smiles and the kindness lurked suspicion. The king suspected everybody, Cutter realized, but he saw in the king's eyes his doubts about Cutter Murphy. As the days passed, Kamehameha succumbed to the poisons of power and he was driven to outrageous excesses. He feared every man as a rival and forced those around him to prove their loyalty daily.

However, the militiamen adored and worshipped Cutter Murphy. He had trained them into an efficient and able corps, and they respected him and loved him for his strength and fairness. Kamehameha recognized this love and realized it was a threat to his own security.

As Cutter delayed, Kamehameha reached another decision. Though Kauai was ruled by his father, he decided it was far better for the islands as a whole that they be consolidated under one rule.

"A bloodless coup," Kamehameha told Cutter. "I will take a force of three thousand men and sail upon the island. I shall use persuasion upon my father."

The militia was left behind, and with it, Cutter Murphy. Cutter wanted to go along because he missed Waialua and the thought of seeing her even for a few moments, even in a great crowd, would relieve the ache inside. But Kamehameha said the guns would not be going to Kauai. He wanted no bloody battle. His father would be given every opportunity to surrender peacefully.

"I shall be lord of Kauai," Kamehameha announced as the armada prepared to sail from Oahu.

Cutter stood on the shore, sick with despair. He watched the boats until they were specks on the northern horizon and then gone from sight. He wandered the shoreline, dreaming of what he might do, where he might go. Ships of foreign lands were putting into the islands almost daily now. He decided that he and Waialua would book passage on any one of those ships. It didn't matter where they were going, as long as it was beyond the reach of Kamehameha.

Then he heard of the tragic event off Olowalu, a village on Maui. To avenge the death of a crew member and the theft of a small boat, Captain Simon Metcalfe, master of the American trading vessel *Eleanora*, ordered the massacre of natives. Under the pretense of friendly trade, he directed scores of canoes filled with Hawaiians to gather on the starboard side of his ship. When the gullible natives had clustered about the ship in sufficient numbers, Metcalfe ordered gunwales uncovered and he and his men rained gunfire down on the surprised natives with swivel guns and cannon. Within minutes the sea churned red with blood. The *Eleanora* sailed blithely away, leaving the natives to drag for their dead with nets. More than a hundred Hawaiians died.

Later the natives were avenged when an American trading vessel, a schooner named the *Fair American*, anchored off Kona. The captain of the *Fair American* was Simon Metcalfe's son, Thomas Metcalfe. A local chief named Kameeiamoku had been struck with a rope and insulted by Simon Metcalfe during his last visit. The chief took revenge by boarding the *Fair American* and killing the younger Metcalfe and four of his five crew members.

For thousands of years these people had been unknown to the outside world. With each arrival of foreigners a new series of shock waves rolled through the islands. Social diseases continued to spread. Measles, typhoid fever, whooping cough, and influenza caused the deaths of thousands. Epidemics sent hundreds of the natives running into the sea in an attempt to cool the fever racking their bodies.

The people would trade their souls for guns, alcohol, tobacco, and much-coveted western luxuries such as silk, mirrors, and other shiny trinkets, and the foreigners took every advantage of them.

Hearing these stories, Cutter became uncertain whether he could trust the captains of these visiting ships to carry him and Waialua to some safe harbor. He wondered what would happen if Waialua were exposed to the westerners and their diseases. He prowled the shores, trying to find in heaven or earth the answer to his problem. Now that Kauai was going to fall, there was no refuge on the islands.

Hoving into sight on the northern horizon he saw a tattered group of outriggers, their sails shattered and their masts broken. Stunned, Cutter stood on the beach as others gathered around him, chattering among themselves as the boats approached the shore.

Kamehameha rode in the fifth boat. He leapt ashore and strode up the beach without saying a word and went into the palace.

The other men were more talkative. They had sailed, without incident, up to the straits outside the bay at Kauai. Here a storm struck, a storm of such intensity that sails were torn away, masts were shattered, and boats were blown away, disappearing into the storm. The riptides outside Waimea Bay were so fierce that at last Kamehameha was forced to give the order to turn back. The gods had forsaken him. The tides and the storms outside the bay conspired to do what Kaumualii could not hope to do, to defeat the huge armada.

On the return trip Kamehameha was beside himself with grief. Not only had the gods suddenly turned against him after all the good graces shown in the other invasions, he was sick with doubt and despair. He had even decided that perhaps the gods frowned upon his plan to unseat his father.

Kamehameha raged savagely around the palace. He demanded an answer from the gods, but there was no answer, only darkness and despair. His wailing took on a rhythm, rising and falling, loud enough to drown the roar of the waves striking on the shore. The fierce timbre of the monarch's voice, his authority and command, challenged the gods. Then, suddenly, he fell silent and he sat with the terrible Polynesian dignity and calm and resignation. It was as if he had raged against the gods long enough. The answers rested with them now, and he would await their reply. He sat with legs crossed, face fierce and set, staring straight ahead.

Two days later Kamehameha strode out of the palace, looking renewed and refreshed. He ordered a new *heiau* built, a temple honoring his war god Kukailimoko. He had determined that the kahunas were right: the gods must be appeased. Work was begun immediately.

During the erection of the temple, Cutter was under the surveillance of the king's men; his every move was reported. Cutter began to fear for his own life. The building of a new temple, especially to a war god, would demand a sacrifice. He began to feel uneasy and troubled.

When at last the temple was completed, it was a massive building of exceeding beauty. Kamehameha set the date for its dedication. To this ceremony he invited Chief Keoua of Molokai. Chief Keoua accepted graciously and arrived in splendor, his outriggers bedecked with flowers, with beautiful women, and gifts for the king.

As soon as Chief Keoua stepped off his boat onto the beach, he was taken prisoner. At first, outraged at this indignity, the chief protested. He demanded to be taken before Kamehameha. He was dragged before the monarch, who listened for a few moments to the chief's protests. Suddenly he gave a signal and the kahunas came forward. The

chief was beheaded on the spot. The chief's
people ran for their boats but were cut off
by Kamehameha's men. They were marched
back to the temple and forced to watch as
Keoua's body was sacrificed upon the new
heiau.

Then Kamehameha relaxed slightly and
entered into the spirit of the celebration,
applauding the naked young women who
danced and gestured with their arms and
hands in sensuous, meaningful movement.

Kamehameha had rid himself of an un-
trustworthy chief. And he had appeased the
gods. He was back in their good graces. Kamehameha laughed and drank and ate for
the first time since the debacle in the straits
at Kauai.

Cutter left the celebration and walked up
the hill to *Pali*. Sitting on a boulder, he
stared out across the misty blue valley. His
own God seemed to have deserted him, and
he did not know what to do. Melancholy and
despair enveloped him. He felt paralyzed
and incapable of action or decision, because he knew Kamehameha was outthink-
ing him at every turn. He longed for a drink
to make him care less. Drunk he could find
temporary forgetfulness, which seemed the
best he could hope for now.

Gradually, his sense of frustration lifted
and he became enraged at his own inactiv-
ity. The hell with Kamehameha. When that
day came an egotistical, half-crazed island

chief could outwit him, he had come to a low place indeed.

For all these weeks he had not seen Waialua. He longed for her and meant to see her. Kamehameha had been turned back in the straits up at Kauai. Maybe the gods had been speaking to the king, but maybe they had something to say to him too. Kaumualii was still the sovereign at Kauai. He and Waialua could be married, and there was nothing Kamehameha could do about it. The time for action was at hand.

He got up and started downhill. He walked deliberately, his mind racing. He was going to make a break for the island of Kauai tonight. He would choose the time and the place and the boat carefully. He would be far up the coast before the king became aware that he was gone. Unless, of course, the king had men watching him even while he slept.

He went to the room where he slept with two other officers. They had not yet come in. He lay on his back, staring into the smoky night. At last the two entered, talking and laughing. Cutter pretended to be asleep.

It seemed an eternity before they finally slept.

He lay awake, thinking back to his life in England. He did not miss the exciting days in London. He would not look backward. He would look ahead to reaching Kauai and finding Waialua. He tried to envision her face, but he could not focus on her beauty, her dignity, her calm, or even her bright smile. All he could think about was what lay immediately ahead.

It grew still through the village. Cutter's heart pounded. The moment had come. He remembered the way he had deserted the *Resolution* in the night, taking only the clothes on his back and nothing else. It would be the same now.

He crept out of the hut and dashed across the beach. He saw no one. Which did not mean there was no one watching in the darkness, but he felt a sense of victory.

He found an outrigger and shoved it out into the water. The coral cut his feet, but he kept pushing the boat until it was beyond the breakers.

He levered himself over the side, took up an oar, and began to paddle swiftly toward Diamond Head and out to the open sea. He was struggling, caught between panic and the sure knowledge that he had made his escape. When he made the turn around the end of the jutting volcano, he pulled up the sail and tacked to catch the wind, which would carry him swiftly north.

He laughed to himself and even wished for a jug of *okolehao*.

The hours before dawn were dark on the sea, but Cutter set his course by the north star and held it steady. He was not at all sleepy and was aware that he might not be able to sleep until he reached Waimea Bay.

The sky lightened with dawn and brightened the sea around him. He stretched and peered across his shoulder. His heart sank in his chest and seemed to stop beating for an interminable moment.

Four outriggers bore down upon him. His sail moved him smartly across the water, but the pursuing boats had four oarsmen. He could almost see the distances between them being eaten up.

Cutter sank back, defeated. He could not hope to outrun the outriggers; he could only watch them gain on him. When they came in upon him, he lowered the sail and sat, unmoving. Some of the men were from his militia and carried muskets that were fixed on him.

Chapter XXXIII

The first storm to break the long drought on the island of Oahu came violently. The rain pounded down, first in a spatter of great drops and then in a continual downpour. Floods of water caused mud slides in the hills. Then the rain ceased abruptly and the sun shone once more as if there had been no rain. But the older men and the wiser heads saw this as the worst of signs. When a tsunami began like this, fierce and then breaking off suddenly and unnaturally, it meant that the rains would be violent and unpredictable.

The island had been transformed by the storm. In the few hours of the freshet, everything blossomed green and purple. Vines climbed impudently over every veranda, every grass hut and rooftop, and swarmed up the trees. Then the skies became overcast again. The rains were not through, the storm was merely playing. The islanders stood on the beach at Oahu and watched the dark clouds swirling up from the western horizon.

A crash of thunder and a streak of lightning seemed to fire up the entire world, churning the ocean and making the mountains quiver. This violence of nature brought to every onlooker a sudden humbling sense of his own insignificance. Nature and its gods, not man, was, after all, the supreme being of this universe.

The people watched this display of temper from the gods. Pele, the goddess of fire, with a willowy figure, delicate features, and brilliant red hair. Kane, chief god of the powerful trinity. Lono, who created trees and fragrant flowers. Ku, the third god, who had added man to the wonders of the universe. Tangaroa, the god of the sea, and Tane, Tu, and Rongo, the gods of nature. The people trembled at the show the gods were putting on.

At first a rumble of disbelief and then a cry of shock and surprise greeted the sight of four outriggers fighting the high waves and heading for the shore. The people ran down into the water. Some of the more venturesome swam out in the swirling surf to aid the boats in this final and dangerous run through the breakers.

Waialua was the first one to step ashore. The people stared at her, at her delicate grace, at the extreme beauty of her face and form, and knew she was royalty. She spoke softly, telling how the four outriggers had crossed the Kauai straits. It had been desperate and difficult, then the storm had blown them out to sea, but they had held on, and in the break of the storm had made for Diamond Head.

She asked that her crew be fed and then asked to be taken to King Kamehameha. People leapt to obey her, as if each word were a command, but one they were happy to perform for the beautiful noblewoman.

The rains began again as Waialua was led up the beach to the palace. Guards posted outside the door stepped before her, their lances crossed, their faces set and determined. She merely smiled calmly and asked for the king. The two guards stepped aside, and she proceeded alone into the palace.

She had plans. She had been sent here as the representative of her father, King Kaumualii. But silently, she had prayed to see Cutter Murphy again. There were moments during the long and dangerous trip across the straits when she had prayed to her gods. "Please let me touch him again."

In her heart she longed for Cutter. In her mind she thought of her mission to Kamehameha with irritation and at times with genuine hatred. But she never allowed her feelings to show. Outwardly, she remained calm and dignified, walking straight, her back arched slightly, her head tilted. She hated her brother for what he had done to her, to her sister Misau, to the poor devil Mihuana, and to the kings of the islands he had conquered. She hated him because of his indifference to her deepest feelings for Cutter.

She heard the rain slamming against the plaited roof of the palace. She was led into a large room, where after a long wait, Kamehameha appeared at the far end. He stalked toward her and she thought how he had changed; cruelty and intolerance had hardened his face.

She knelt, keeping her head up and her gaze level until he acknowledged her presence. "Waialua, what a surprise to see you arrive in this storm."

"There was no storm when we began our trek, dearest brother," she replied. "Or we may well have postponed it, though I come on a matter of utmost importance."

He gestured for her to rise. She saw the chiefs and kahunas gathering at the rear of the room, but she ignored them. No matter what matters of state were to be discussed, he was still her brother.

She straightened, aware of the pounding of rain on the roof and the way the king watched her, narrowly, suspiciously. She forced a guileless smile to her lips and stared straight into his eyes, trying to remind him of who she was.

"I am most pleased to see you, my dearest sister," Kamehameha said. "The matter must be of greatest importance to bring you across the straits in such a fearsome storm."

"Yes." Her voice remained level. "We heard at Kauai how your armada was turned back in the channels outside the bay. The riptides are fierce, and perhaps it is only luck to cross them alive."

"No matter how it may have looked, or what you may have heard at Kauai, I came in peace. I wished to talk with my father. But, as you say, I was turned back by riptides."

"Almost the only setback since you began the conquest of the islands," Waialua suggested.

The king almost smiled. "Almost the only inconvenience. The gods have been good to me. I have prayed to them and my prayers have been answered."

"I believe I bring more good news to your majesty," Waialua said in a soft tone, smiling. "I come to offer you the best wishes of King Kaumualii of Kauai. He says he has great pride in you, as warrior, as monarch, as his son. He further says that it is against the welfare of the islands for Kauai and Li-

hue to stand against you. King Kaumualii
is abdicating his throne in your stead. He
asks to be allowed to worship you and to
obey your commands as a loyal and true
subject."

Kamehameha stared at his sister for
some seconds, speechless. He had wrestled
with the problem of Kauai for so long. And
now King Kaumualii and his sister were
solving it for him.

He smiled, nodding. "I am now the lord
of Kauai."

Waialua nodded. "You are indeed."

"All the islands of this land are now under my rule. It is as if the gods planned it
this way. It was my destiny."

Waialua sighed and nodded. "You have
fared well since the first day you began."

Kamehameha strode back and forth before his sister, recalling his campaigns.
"Yes, Pele and the gods have been good to
me."

As Kamehameha paced, his robe swung
out behind him, enhancing his size. He was
a formidable man, but Waialua knew she
had to speak to him, had to convince him
that their marriage was not a good thing,
merely an old custom hastily agreed upon
and without meaning since there was no
love. "Yes, the gods have genuinely approved of almost all you have done."

He paused, glaring at her. That word "almost" stood between them in the quiet

358

room with only the tattoo of rain beating at the roof. She pressed on. "There has been much to regret in the lands that you rule. You have not done enough to conquer the epidemics and plagues that have struck our people, killing them off by the thousands—"

"Tell me," he almost roared. "What could I do against epidemic? What could I have done that I did not do?"

"You could have isolated the ill, even if it meant shipping them off to one of the least inhabited islands. The epidemics spread by contact. And contact between the ill and the well was allowed."

He was enraged that she dared to find fault with him over something beyond his control.

Her voice continued. "And there is your trade in sandalwood. You sell it off as if the trees are without limit, when there are so few of them. What will our islands be like when the last sandalwood is cut down and gone, when the sandalwood forests are completely destroyed?"

He was on firmer ground now. Sandalwood was one of his most profitable trades. He could not hope to carry on his wars, to arm his men, and build his fleets without the money that came in from the sale of sandalwood. He merely smiled at her and waved his arm. "The sandalwood will last through my lifetime," he said. "And after me, I do not care."

"But there are those of us on these islands who do care about the future."

"How dare you speak to me in this manner!"

"I am your sister," she reminded him, "and if I cannot speak truly to you, who can? You are now a great monarch. The king of all these islands. But you must protect them as well as conquer them. Your war god Kukailimoku has been good to you, but your dealings with the merchant ships that arrive in ever greater numbers have been despicable."

He laughed. "They wish to buy, and I wish to sell. I cannot see a better arrangement." He came close and touched her shoulder. "I am sorry that my loveliest sister is unhappy with me. I would be happy if you were proud of my successes."

"I am trying to show you your blindness. That is all."

"Blindness?"

"Do you not recall Misau and Mihuana?" She saw him withdrawing. "Their lives were destroyed by your obstinacy. That is why I beg you now to release me from our unhappy marriage contract and to grant me the right to wed as I wish."

"As you wish?"

"I plead with you, in the honor of your

coming to power as lord of Kauai, that you grant me this one wish of my heart."

"I am disposed to be kindly now that you have brought me this news of the capitulation of Kauai. I am sorry you refuse to recognize our marriage as obeying the ancient kapus of our people. I regret your tone, but you are my dearest sister, and I try to remind myself that you mean well."

"I wish only to make you see. Don't destroy me as you destroyed Misau."

"Misau. Destroyed Misau? How wrong can you be? I tried to talk sense to her, but she was too weak, too weak to face the truth and the future. She took her own life. You will not put the blame on me."

His anger filled the room. The kahunas and other chiefs drew closer together, fearing for the life of Waialua. No one spoke to the king like this; they had seen people beheaded for far less.

The sound of the rain on the roof almost drowned out all the sounds within the palace. The night was closing in. Fires were lighted. The king abruptly brought the interview to a close. He summoned some women, and Waialua was led away to a small room that was to be hers for the night. "For as long as you wish to stay," the king said in a forced tone of lightness.

Once in her room, Waialua, in the desperate white flashes of lightning and crashing thunder, knelt and implored the gods to intercede with the king.

Then she lay down, staring up into the lightning-streaked darkness and rain. Her eyes filled with tears, but her jaw tightened. She would make happen what the gods feared to do. There was no other way.

The prison was open to the storm and Cutter lay under an oilskin slicker.

As rainwater seeped up under it, he squirmed, trying to find a dry place. He had spent many days in prison. He was no longer important enough for the king to bother with. He was a prisoner and likely to remain so until he died or was executed.

The lightning flared white and the rains came down with greater force than ever. So this was the climax of a wasted life.

Wet and miserable, at last Cutter fell into troubled sleep. He dreamed of Waialua, but was unable to see her face clearly. And then it happened, what he feared most of all. The nightmares. They came in spite of everything. He experienced it all in a great wave of wonder and of tenderness, and he struggled under the hands grappling with him, trying to bring him up from the depths of sleep, even in this rain and storm.

He opened his eyes—or in his dream he opened his eyes—and the face of Waialua was clear before him. A vision induced by fever and by longing. But her face was so clear. Thank God, he could see her again, as she really was, in all her radiant beauty.

She spoke his name over and over, and he struggled against waking and losing this most pleasant dream. Her voice sounded odd and tear-choked, and yet it was truly her voice, and he told himself that even if he was ill, even if he burned with fever, it was worth it to have her so close to him, clutching him against her breast and whispering his name over and over.

He forced his eyes open against the pelting rain. And it was truly she. She knelt beside him here in the prison, and beyond her, he saw the guard, and beyond the guard an apparition that stunned him. Mihuana stood there, a gun fixed on the guard's back.

He sat up, staring. He said, "Mihuana."

Waialua clasped her hand over his mouth. "Don't even speak his name in this place," she pleaded. "He lives like a shadow and a shadow he must remain."

Cutter was suddenly wide awake. He grasped Waialua to him and kissed her hungrily, greedily. She clung to him, laughing and crying at once.

Mihuana said in a soft tone, "We'd better go. We don't have much time."

Cutter tried to stand, but his legs were still bound. At an order from Mihuana, the guard knelt and cut Cutter's legs free.

"We must tie up the guard," Mihuana said.

At last Cutter believed all this was truly happening and was not just a dream. He caught Waialua's hand and they ran across the silent compound in the rain. The gate stood wide open and they ran through it into the darkness.

Armed, Mihuana ran at their heels. He was attuned to any unexpected sound. He had stayed alive all these twenty-five years by recognizing trouble. Having no idea where they were going, Cutter slowed and let Waialua lead him through the village. They came down to the beach, where the waves roared up onshore like wild beasts, and where four outriggers lay on their sides.

Mihuana shoved one of the boats out into the raging breakers. "We'll have to swim with it," he said to Cutter.

Cutter nodded, helping Waialua into one of the outriggers. They thrust the boat away from shore, only to have it torn from their grasp and hurled back by the breakers.

Cutter kept swimming and pushing long after it made any sense to him. He was aware that Mihuana was up ahead of the outrigger, pulling it.

After a long time they found themselves out where the waves were choppy but not as high. Mihuana pulled himself into the craft and then helped Cutter aboard. Cutter

shivered with cold but took up a paddle.
Waialua sat in the middle of the boat, clinging to both sides, while Mihuana and Cutter
paddled with all their strength and all their
will. Cutter smiled. It was he and Mihuana
now, against the fury of the storm.

Chapter XXXIV

They found Kamehameha in his cottage, and he received them not in the audience hall, with its masks and trophies, but in his own chamber, where he sat on a mat alone. He looked tired with great dark circles under the wild, protuberant eyes. He was bedecked with jewels, every finger had a massive ring set with a priceless stone. His face was grim after all the bad news that had settled upon him these past few months.

He looked up at them and said, "Well. What is it now?"

"It is about the Englishman Cutter, your excellency."

There was no need for the messengers to go on. As always, Kamehameha knew everything as soon as it happened. "And has he been caught?"

"Not yet, your highness, though we have men spread all across the island, and we are warning anyone who might conceal him that the punishment will be immediate death. We thought perhaps you might want to see the prison."

"Why should I want to see the prison if the prisoner is gone?" he inquired.

"Because he is not the only prisoner missing, your highness."

The king exhaled heavily and levered himself up to his feet from the sitting position without using his hands. His people stared at him in wonder when he accomplished these physical feats. Undoubtedly, he was the strongest man of any of the islands, and, they were certain, the smartest.

He strode out with his messengers immediately behind him. His eyes were black with rage. The messengers quivered. Heads were going to roll over this latest catastrophe, and they suddenly felt pains in their own necks, and doubts and anxieties left them shaken.

He walked along the hard-packed trail to the prison. As he approached he saw that the door stood wide open. He stopped and faced the messengers, his jaw slack. "The prison doors are open?"

"There seemed no reason to close them,

excellency. The prison was empty when we found it this morning."

He drew a deep breath and, without speaking, strode into the prison. At the far side of the compound, he saw a bundle under an oilskin. He jerked the oilskin up and there lay the jailer, bound hand and foot.

The king jerked his head and two men leapt forward to release the jailer. The loss of all the political prisoners. Many had made threats against Kamehameha himself. He should have beheaded them. He was too lenient for his own good.

Although he knew who had done this, he pretended he did not. His voice shaking, he said to the jailer, "And who did this to you?"

The jailer winced. He massaged his swollen wrists and bloodless ankles. He looked about the group of men, all of whom stared at him coldly and without compassion. What did they know of guarding a jail, in a rainstorm, early in the morning, when all the rest of the world slept?

"It was Cutter Murphy, sir," he said. He winced again and added, "And your sister Waialua."

This was sobering news to Kamehameha. Suddenly he knew that Cutter was not hiding on the island but had headed out in the turbulent seas last night.

"And Mihuana," the jailer said, swallowing his words, speaking almost so that he could not be heard.

Kamehameha's head jerked up. "What did you say?"

The jailer looked on the verge of tears. He was a middle-aged man, scarred by many battles and weather-roughened, but now he was reduced to his last ounce of strength. He lifted his head slowly and repeated the dreaded word. "Mihuana," he said at last. "It was the outlaw Mihuana."

"Mihuana." Kamehameha stared down at his shaking hands. "Mihuana was here? In this place? You saw him? You can swear it was he?"

"It was him, all right, your majesty. He tied me up so that the blood stopped running. He is a rough one. A dangerous one. He kept a gun fixed on me, and a knife at my throat. He seemed to fear nothing."

Kamehameha was shaken. He was angry and disappointed that Cutter Murphy had escaped the prison, but this seemed unimportant now. Mihuana! All this time, living off the land and living among the people. Mihuana was loved, revered, and respected. And more than that, he was protected by the people. This came as no surprise to the monarch. There was no way for Mihuana to have survived all these years without a conspiracy among the people. What people? Those who cheered the king the loudest, smiled the broadest, and bent lowest when he passed?

He waved his arm and turned to leave. The place was wet and stinking. "I suppose you did all you could," he said to the jailer.

"Thank you, your highness."

"Were you asleep when they attacked you?"

The jailed shook his head violently. "I heard something outside the guardhouse, your majesty. I stepped outside to check on it. It was at this instant that I felt the knife at my throat. And I looked into the eyes of Mihuana."

The king nodded and turned away. He made a half bow to the people who had accompanied him here, meaning they were not to return to his cottage with him. Mihuana lived. He must redouble his efforts to run him down. He must increase the guard around the palace. He was agitated, and he strode through the morning mists, looking neither right nor left.

He felt the fury mounting inside him. He tried to think what reward he might offer for Mihuana's head. Every man had his price. The king had seen this demonstrated often enough over the past years.

The frail outrigger climbed high and fell back into the trough of giant waves. They were making such poor time that the huge humped back of Diamond Head still stood out, looming in the darkness.

"How long until dawn?" Cutter shouted over his shoulder.

"Another hour or two," Waialua answered from the middle of the boat, where she clung. It was so loud and thunderous out in the midst of the storm that Cutter realized Mihuana in the rear of the boat had not even heard him. He was concentrating on the paddle, driving it into the water and forcing the craft forward and upward over a cresting wave.

Cutter's muscles ached all the way to the small of his back. Even Mihuana looked exhausted. Cutter stared over his shoulder, barely able to see Mihuana through the spray. Waialua rode calmly with that native dignity and the sure sense that she would weather this storm.

As the little boat shuddered under the pound of waves, rode high on a crest, and fell back into the following trough, Cutter assured himself that the craft would hold, that somehow they would leave the hump of Diamond Head behind them before daybreak.

"We'll make it," he said aloud.

He had no idea that Waialua had heard him, but she did and echoed his sentiment. "I know we shall," she called to him.

The violent battering continued. Soon Mihuana and Waialua were busy bailing the boat out. Cutter glanced back at them, wondering if they could keep the small craft afloat. He bit down on his jaw and paddled harder, pulling them forward across the waves.

The time passed in terrible slowness, counted only by the strokes of the paddle in the water. His shoulders protested, unable to lift it anymore. His hands longed to open and let the paddle fly free.

And then the horizon was suddenly pink. Rain had settled now into a savage tattooing, blinding and stinging. In panic, Cutter looked back across his shoulder. Diamond Head was back there, but a long dark passage away.

He continued to paddle. He lifted his arms when, aching, they threatened to fall from their sockets. The stiffness seemed to grow upon him. As he knelt there he was fighting the growing terror inside himself, no longer just the fear of being pursued by Kamehameha's men, but worse, that they would be defeated by their own weariness. He kept thinking, "I must keep a tight hold on myself. Mihuana continues to paddle. Waialua trusts me and I must not fail her. I am not tired. I won't give in to it." He dug the paddle deeper into the sea, feeling his burning hands aching, crying for relief.

He began to talk, wildly, whatever came into his mind. He spoke to the wind and the dying rain, but he knew that Waialua heard him. "We will go away. You and Mihuana and I. We will sail on the first outgoing vessel. We won't live like frightened rats the rest of our lives. We will go where we can live free." Inwardly, he cursed Kamehameha and his customs and kapus, his terrible caste system, and he cursed the soul of the islands.

He heard himself promising Waialua ease and contentment and beauty in some other place, any other place. "We are past the worst now. I have it all planned. When we are out of this, we shall go farther east, where nobody knows us. We will build a beautiful new life. I vow that to you. We shall find a place and we shall be free."

Gradually, he became aware that daylight was full. He supposed he should be hungry, but he was not hungry, not in the belly, at least. He looked over his shoulder. The rain had passed, and the sun was breaking through the worst of the clouds.

He turned to speak to Waialua. "We've made it now."

"No. No," Mihuana shouted from the rear of the canoe. "Do not stop paddling, we are entering the straits. The riptides."

"Please," Waialua pleaded, "hold it steady. These riptides cross up great ships trying to enter the bay. They drove Kamehameha's armada back. We must ride through them."

The canoe was pummeled sideways. It

stood up on its side and danced for a moment in the treacherous currents of the straits. Cutter stopped paddling. Quickly, he tied a rope about Waialua's waist and secured it about his own. The boat was caught up like a leaf and spun around in the water.

Mihuana fought against the tides. He paddled with all his strength and, watching him, Cutter was amazed he had any left after the long night in the storm. He dug his paddle into the water, trying to straighten out the boat. This seemed to infuriate the tides. They lifted the boat and hurled it backward. It rode up on a wave and capsized. One second they were fighting the waves and the riptides, the next the boat was standing straight and tall, and then was flung over, belly-up. The paddle flew from Cutter's hands. He screamed out, "Waialua. Waialua."

She did not answer.

The outriggings were ripped from the canoe as it went over and floated away. Cutter landed in the water. The undertow, like some giant hand, caught him by the ankles and pulled him down. Waialua's dead weight pulled against him.

He fought his way to the surface, still pulling on the rope about Waialua, crying out her name. He swam, pulling her after him in the savage waters.

Sobbing, he fought the currents and the tides and the swirling undertow, and clung to Waialua. He had no idea how long he held her.

At last, weary, he gave up. It was easier, as tired as he was, to rest and let the sea do as it would. He held Waialua's unmoving body close and rode on the riptide, carried first one way and then another.

Something struck Cutter in the head, and in a reflex action he reached out and caught it. It was part of the outrigging of the canoe. The buoyant wood floated. He grasped it and pulled it under them, feeling it lift them slightly against the furious pull of the undertow.

He and Waialua were borne along like a block in a millrace. He thought about nothing. He tried to look around but could not, because the saltwater burned his eyes and the waves engulfed him occasionally and carried him along like a leaf.

He stopped thinking, stopped living, simply floated along, clinging to Waialua's inert form. At last, after an interminable time, the waves thrust them forward into what felt like a warm and silent pool. He was too tired to raise his head, too exhausted to care that he had been carried across the straits.

He kept his head up only enough to breathe. The calm waters around him were warm and restorative, but he was too far gone to care.

After what seemed like an eternity he heard the sound of waves upon a shore. He lifted his head. It seemed to be a verdant island, even if not very big. The waves carried them up into the coral and, scratched and sore, he was forced to fight again.

He pushed down on the wooden outrigger and stood up. He took Waialua in his arms and staggered up on the shore. He looked around at the flowers, the ferns, the bright birds stirred by his arrival on the narrow beach.

He loosened the rope about his waist and Waialua's. She lay, pale and unmoving, on the sand. He held her gently in his arms and kissed her mouth. Suddenly frantic, he began to work over her, slowly and unceasingly.

After what seemed like an eternity, she opened her eyes, dazed, unsure of where she was. Then, seeing him, she took his hand and placed it upon her breast. "You have my heart," she whispered, smiling.

His eyes burning with tears, he clasped her close, thinking over and over, we've made it, we've won, we're together at last.

He looked around. His gaze struck something. Putting Waialua down, he went to Mihuana and knelt beside him. He was breathing just slightly and his heartbeat was slow and measured. Cutter shook him, spoke his name, and kept shaking him until Mihuana protested and stirred.

For a long time they stared at each other in disbelief, astonished to be alive. Finally

Mihuana laughed and put out his arms. Cutter clung to him fiercely.

Cutter led Mihuana to where Waialua lay watching them. Mihuana's eyes filled with tears. "Thank all the gods," he said.

Cutter held Waialua close, feeling he could never let her go for a moment. They had been given this second chance at last. They must not waste a minute of it.

Later he saw Mihuana walking toward them; he had caught a couple of fish. Cutter sagged in the sand and watched Mihuana build a fire from sticks and weeds in a pit. The fish were soon cooking, and then the three of them divided and ate them. "We'll make it," Mihuana said. "We have protection now. Misau. She is with the gods. Her goodness shall be our protection."

Cutter smiled at the simplicity of his idea. Misau looking down and protecting them. He spoke with an edge to his voice. "But who shall protect the king?"

"That bastard," Mihuana said. "I will kill him. Ever since he took Misau from me, I've had but one reason to live. To make him pay."

Cutter felt a rising in his own spirits. Mihuana had put it in words, a reason to live. He nodded. Mihuana was right. He had Waialua beside him and she gave him a reason to live.